DYING TO MAKE YOU MINE

David Bradwell

purefiction

D1613329

DYING TO MAKE YOU MINE

"The last thing I expected was to fall in love. And in retrospect I wish I hadn't, because maybe then, fewer people would have died."

This is not a romance. Anna Burgin is happily single, with a group of close friends, and a busy lifestyle. But then she meets someone who blows her mind, and everything changes.

But it's the match made in heaven that ends in hell, and the ensuing jealously, lies and betrayal spark a deadly series of events that prove modern dating can be murder.

ABOUT THE AUTHOR

David Bradwell grew up in the north east of England but now lives in Hitchin in Hertfordshire. He has written for publications as diverse as Smash Hits and the Sunday Times and is a former winner of the PPA British Magazine Writer of the Year Award. Aside from writing, he runs a hosiery company with web sites at www.stockingshq.com and www.tightsandmore.com.

Get in touch at:
www.davidbradwell.com

DYING TO MAKE YOU MINE

A Gripping Psychological Thriller - Anna Burgin Contemporary Series: Book 1

Dying To Make You Mine was first published in 2019 by Pure Fiction
Copyright © David Bradwell, 2019
www.davidbradwell.com

ISBN: 978-1-9993394-4-9

For Mary Cafferkey.

Part 1

Prepare for take off

Chapter 1

2019

MEN, in my experience, are not like normal people, and if you need any proof of that, try dating in 2019.

I love a hug. I'm quite outgoing. I enjoy the thought of spending time with a special friend, learning from them, exploring the world together, going on adventures and getting up to mischief. I've just never been very good at relationships.

I don't do arguments, I'm not a big fan of stress and I'm allergic to heartache. I struggle with the thought of someone seeing me, the moment they wake up, before I've even been in the shower.

Some people, I think, define themselves by their relationship status. They can't abide being alone, and adopt a panic-buy mentality, lurching from one unsatisfactory partner to the next. I like being single and I don't miss the sense that I'm always going to disappoint, and be disappointed, once the first flutterings of a crush abate.

There's great satisfaction in setting my own agenda and I

cherish my hard-won freedom to do so. But despite enjoying my own company, sometimes I find it stimulating to meet someone new. And occasionally, over the last four years, I've been on what - for want of a better word - could be described as dates.

The last thing I expected was to fall in love. And in retrospect I wish I hadn't, because maybe then, fewer people would have died.

I tried a long-term relationship once, but in every respect, the end of it was less surprising than the beginning. I met someone, he made me laugh, and within a few weeks I was pregnant. I hadn't been either planning or expecting that, but there was no going back.

Inevitably, the novelty wore off, and although, for the sake of our daughter, we soldiered on for many years, our partnership eventually succumbed to the inevitable. The split was amicable. He was an entirely decent man, but I couldn't imagine us growing old together in a nursing home. We're still in touch. In the modern age, it's difficult to lose contact with someone completely.

Starting 2015 freshly single, I set out to try new and exciting pursuits. I had singing lessons and acting lessons. I tried to learn German. I started to write books based on adventures from my younger years, in the days when I shared a house with an investigative journalist and got sucked into all sorts of dark and dangerous situations. I travelled around parts of Europe, discovering Germany, Italy, France and Luxembourg, and spent a lot of time thinking about what I wanted to do with my life, given that the first forty-five years had already passed.

In the meantime, I have, of course, become utterly dependent on my phone. We all have. It's my only constant companion, and like most people, I'd be lost without it.

It's overloaded with apps, but to try to simplify things, I've grouped them all into folders based on the seven deadly sins. Gluttony is Pizza Express, Wahaca, and anything else food- or restaurant-related. Sloth is SkyGo, YouTube, Netflix, the Kindle app, and all other entertainment. Greed is shopping, including my Nectar card, Amazon and Naked Wines. Pride is work and everything to do with my business. Envy is Facebook, Instagram and other social media, dominated by pictures of friends having fun and going on holiday. Wrath is news, and one particular bank. All the dating apps, obviously, are in Lust.

At first, meeting men was so far off the agenda, it wasn't even on the longlist of potential agenda items. But then, on a whim, just before Christmas 2015, I downloaded Tinder and set up an account, and the next thing I knew, I had a very steep learning curve ahead.

I think things change as you get older. When you're young and exploring the world with a partner, you move around together, dream together, plan the future together. Everything is new, and the possibilities are endless and exciting. It's so much harder when you reach a certain age, with your own home, career, commitments and family obligations. I was happy with my life. I wasn't looking to mess that up by embarking on a relationship, unless it was for someone spectacular. I wasn't looking for a live-in boyfriend, but I thought it would be stimulating to broaden my social circle. I was too old and too experienced to want to play games.

I didn't swipe right on many. Immediate rejections were anyone with a shirt-off gym pic, a Snapchat filter, the ubiquitous fish, obvious serial killers, anyone with a prominent car, those posting pictures of motivational quotations, and, of course, anyone who thought they were being clever and original by stating they were looking for their "last first kiss". How dull would that be?

Any mention of "banter" was an immediate left-swipe, as were those who hid their eyes behind sunglasses, any form of text speak, poor grammar generally, and excessive use of emojis. Many just posted group shots and left me to guess which they were. (Clue: probably not the good-looking one.) Some looked significantly younger than their stated age. Some significantly older. Both were a red flag. And anyone who looked like they spent their summers on a sunlounger was an immediate no, because I don't like the sun. It makes my nose peel.

My first Tinder date, in early 2016, set the tone quite admirably. He was a dancer, allegedly, and, like me, he was writing a book. We met at a bar in Hackney.

"What's your book about?" I asked.

"My eight hundred Internet dates," he said, with no hint of irony.

We didn't make it to date two.

Without fail, everyone had baggage of some description. I met one potential conquest in the bar of a hotel. After a brief discussion he said he needed to disappear for a moment, but first he had to introduce me to his "Mistress". Hello, I thought. Unusual.

The Mistress subsequently informed me that the room was ready, and once my date had locked himself into his handcuffs, she'd be delighted if I would join her in giving him a stern whipping. Had he looked anything like his profile picture, I might have been tempted, just for the fun of pushing boundaries. Again, we didn't make it to date two.

In fact, many looked nothing like their profile pictures. Some were a foot shorter than they claimed. I'm in no position to be heightist, given that I can barely reach the top shelf of the supermarket in even my highest of heels, but I find dishonesty particularly unsexy.

There were, of course, those with wives or girlfriends who apparently just didn't understand them. I felt for those. It was nonsense, clearly, but they aspired to live the grass-is-greener single life. I was the real deal. No commitments. No need to feel shame in even the most debauched of one-night stands. Not that it was like that, but they weren't to know.

I moved on from Tinder to Bumble, OK Cupid, Happn and Plenty Of Fish, and learned more about the great British public than I ever cared to.

There were those who wanted me to wear particular items of clothing or, indeed, wanted to wear particular items of my clothing themselves. In the Fifty Shades era, there were plenty of budding Christian Greys, and lots who would send a message or two and then disappear into the ether. Of course there were vast numbers who thought I'd be so turned on by a badly-lit photograph of their out-of-focus penis that I'd immediately drop both my underwear and standards, in enthusiastic abandon.

Not everyone was a disappointment. There was Carl, who worked as a journalist on The Times. He was lovely, and we kept in touch, long after the distance between us ruled out any form of commitment. In fact, I made several very good friends. Another, Stuart, had moved to England from his native South Africa at the end of a particularly traumatic marriage. He was a flight attendant. We had several dates, but again, our schedules and the geographical challenges of living outside London meant that every meeting felt like the first, such was the unfamiliarity. We parted on good terms.

So, I continued exploring, getting increasingly disillusioned with the whole shenanigans, meeting endless strangers for endless first dates that rarely led to anything other than a backlog of ironing and other domestic chores. Internet dating is like a computer game. It breeds a culture of transience, in which others are seen as disposable. In the end I deactivated most of my accounts, only occasionally looking, whenever hope triumphed over hard-won experience.

And then I came across Stef and everything changed. Looking back, he played an absolute blinder. Right up until the day he was killed, by a woman I'd never met.

Chapter 2

April 2017-November 2018

I SWIPED right on Stef in April 2017. He looked gorgeous, with mischievous eyes, a touch of stubble and luxuriant male-model hair. I didn't expect that we'd match. We matched. Then I read his profile text. The most memorable line was "in a relationship". Fair play, I thought. At least you're honest. I didn't expect to hear from him, and then he said hello.

I don't know why I replied. I suppose I was intrigued. So I asked for more.

He'd moved to the UK from Milan twenty years previously, and now worked as a member of long-haul cabin crew for a well-known airline. His full first name was Stefano. He'd spent the last few months with a polyamorous girlfriend called Molly. She had another boyfriend. He'd met him. They got on. He wasn't seeing anyone else. He was tired after a twelve-hour flight but would tell me more later.

The next day we chatted more. What did I do? I told him about the books I planned to write, and my day job running an online clothing company. Where did I live? It transpired I was in the next town, only about five miles away. Had I had any experience of poly relationships? No, not knowingly, but you can never be sure on dating apps, I said. It was meant as a joke.

The following day I got another message. He was closing his Tinder account, but here was his number in case I wanted to keep in touch. I didn't think it would do any harm. So I sent a message via WhatsApp. It got the two blue ticks to say it had been delivered and read, but he was clearly in no rush. I started to question my ability to be witty.

Two months later, in early June, he eventually sent a reply. He was in Hong Kong. I was so surprised, I couldn't resist responding.

Stef: How are things? How's the writing?

Anna: Wow... So lovely to hear from you. All good here and the writing is going well. Some of it is painful to remember, but I'm learning lots about publishing. Are you back flying? Safe travels. And keep in touch. x

Stef: Yes, it's normally the USA but I get here once or twice a year. Let me know when your book is out in paperback. xx

I noticed the double xx. I'm a sucker for a double xx. And his grammar was acceptable, which was another box ticked.

Anna: The first is already out on Amazon. It's called Cold Press. *I'm on the second now.*

Stef: Fantastic. I'll order one.

Anna: How long are you away for?

Stef: Three days and then back for a bit, depending on the roster. I'm on standby.

Anna: Let me know if you'd like to meet for coffee when you get back and I'll give you a copy.

Stef: No, don't worry. I'll order one and you can sign it.

We chatted a bit more. I got a glimpse into the exhausting demands placed on long-haul cabin crew, with relentless hours and the chaotic effect on family life. He shared childcare for two daughters, but was going through an acrimonious divorce. I tried not to make comments about sexy uniforms, and largely succeeded.

Anna: How are you getting on with your girlfriend? Are things still going well?

Stef: She's got two others, currently.

Anna: She's busy. Is that hard to cope with?

Stef: It's not a question of coping, really. It's a learning process. But when she gets someone half my age you'll find me crying into a bowl of Häagen-Dazs.

Anna: Haha. Surely not.

Stef: The way things are at the moment, I'm surprised I've not turned into a drug addict.

Anna: Wow, that sounds traumatic.

Stef: There's just a lot going on. I'll tell you later xx

And that was it. He disappeared. In late June 2017, I got a message that mentioned court cases and access arrangements for his children, but my reply went unanswered.

A further six months passed in complete silence. I'd given up hearing any more, and I often wondered what had happened to him. Then, completely unexpectedly, just before Christmas, he wrote again:

Stef: Hello xx

Anna: Hi again. Long time no speak. I hope you're well.

Stef: It's chaos. I need to be careful what I say, or I'd sound like a disaster magnet, haha.

Anna: Don't worry. Sometimes it's good to let off steam, especially to a complete stranger. The offer of a drink/coffee etc still remains if that would help amongst all the drama, but I understand if the timing is rubbish, with Christmas looming. I just hope you're okay, even though I don't really know you.

And then he disappeared again. By now I was getting used to the pattern. I tried to forget about him but occasionally my mind would wander. He'd become an enigma. The curious man who occasionally sent lovely, unexpected messages and then disappeared for months at a time. The next correspondence was about eight weeks later, on Valentine's Day 2018.

Stef: I hope you got lots of cards this morning. If the coffee offer is still open, I should have much more time in March.

Anna: Haha. No cards whatsoever. Yes that would be lovely... I've got a bit more free time than normal in March too, so very much look forward to hearing from you. Let me know when you know and I'll be there. I've got another two books I can give you! I've just started on the fourth. x

Once more, I got excited about the thought that I'd actually meet him. I still didn't expect anything to happen, and I certainly didn't long for a relationship with a self-confessed calamity magnet with a track record of patchy reliability. But I did want to see him in person, just to check that he really existed, and to assuage the fear that I'd been talking to an imposter.

But March came and went. As did April. Again he'd done the disappearing act and the imposter theory gained credence. I'd had no great hopes of romance but from our limited correspondence, I suspected we shared a similar life view. In some ways, he sounded too good to be true, despite the relationship thing, but only if he actually existed. And as spring turned into summer I decided he probably didn't. I assumed I'd never hear from him again. He was always the one that got away.

Life was hectic. Charlotte, my eighteen-year-old daughter, left for Durham University. By the autumn, I was looking to move house - ironically to the same market town in which Stef allegedly lived. I had visions of bumping into him in Waitrose, but would we even recognise each other? How old were his profile pictures? I really had no idea.

I occasionally looked at the apps to see if there was anyone else new and exciting, but it was largely the same meaningless nonsense. I had a few more dates. I met some lovely people, made a few more friends, and I reminded myself I wasn't cut out for a relationship anyway.

But then, finally, at the end of November 2018, over nine months since his last message, out of nowhere I got this:

Stef: I'm LOVING Cold Press xx

Anna: Hi stranger and lovely to hear from you. Thank you! Things have gone a bit mad on the book front. I've written the fourth and I'm now starting the fifth :-)

Stef: Great news. I look forward to reading them. I'm around from mid-December to mid-January if you'd still like to meet up.

Anna: Definitely! I've got a trip to Sofia next week, but otherwise any time.

Obviously I expected him to disappear again. But this time he didn't, and that was where it all went wrong.

Chapter 3

November-December 2018

WE didn't meet immediately but we kept in touch. I offered him a free copy of book two - *Out Of The Red* - when he finished *Cold Press*, but instead he ordered the hardback on Amazon. And to prove it, he sent me a picture of it on his bunk, on board a Boeing 777. We chatted more, making each other laugh, and this time I thought it would be different. It was.

He started to send me messages several times each day, and there was no sign of him disappearing. The messages got funnier, and friendlier. Sometimes they were sent from 30,000 feet above the Atlantic, via a plane's on-board Wi-Fi. He was full of anecdotes about flying, famous passengers and hilarious mishaps. He had a wonderful line in self-deprecation.

He was still seeing polyamorous Molly, but I sensed things weren't going particularly smoothly. She'd let him down "in a big way" but further details weren't forthcoming. I felt the first stirrings of a strong friendship between us, tinged with a considerable degree of flirtation.

He started to send me WhatsApp location maps from his travels. I mentioned that I was moving to his home town and he teased me that if I didn't know how to pronounce quinoa I'd be escorted from Waitrose back to Asda.

We continued to write daily, even when I was on my writing research trip to Sofia. The messages got more frequent, more personal and more insightful. He was a lapsed Catholic, heavily into science, and the more we chatted, the closer we became. It was strange after so many months of silence, but I was thoroughly enjoying getting to know him. He asked about my writing, telling me which bits of the books he'd enjoyed the most, and left glowing reviews on Amazon. There were, however, more problems with Molly.

Stef: It's not going well. I can't say too much because it would be an invasion of privacy, but we've been going through a rocky spell.

Anna: Because of her other partners?

Stef: In part. But we're kind of drifting away from each other.

Anna: I'm sorry to hear that. I wish I could be more supportive but I'm far from an expert. I can imagine there must be all sorts of challenges.

Stef: There are. I appreciate your willingness to discuss it, but I'm not really an expert either.

Anna: It's the least I can do if it helps. Aside from sending big virtual hugs. Don't take this the wrong way, because I'm not trying to stir things up, but if she's messing you around, I think you deserve much better.

Stef: I'm withdrawing at the moment because I feel she's been disrespecting me. We shall see.

I didn't like the sound of Molly. I did like the thought of him becoming properly single, although I had to be careful not to sound too enthusiastic. My heart went out to him, but there's a delicate balance between being supportive and prying.

Anna: In what way?

Stef: Not telling me about who she's been meeting. It's all supposed to be based on honesty and openness. There's an understanding that she'll sleep with other people, but she has to be straight with me, and tell me. Not wait until I've found out about it afterwards. I don't want to know all the details, but I have a right to know that it's happening. Before it happens.

Anna: Exactly. Oh, I don't know. It's hard for me to comment because I'm obviously biased, but to me it's not just about sex. In any form of relationship, sex means little without a connection and trust and understanding. You have to be honest with someone as a fundamental way of showing you value them.

Stef: Nailed it in one. I am relentlessly impressed by your maturity on these things. x

Anna: I don't know if it's that. It's just logic, I suppose, and being a decent person. I don't know what we'd make of each other if we actually ever meet. I don't know if we'd click or find each other attractive. But you come across as a lovely person and someone who I think would make a very good friend. And even as a friend you need openness and trust. I do feel for you xx

On the plane home from Sofia I was pulled aside by the customer services manager. Stef had written a letter to the cabin crew on my flight, explaining that he wanted to go on a date with me and requesting that I was looked after. I was immediately upgraded to Business Class, with a whole row of the plane to myself, and was extremely well looked after.

I sent him a message as soon as I landed. We simply had to

meet. But Christmas was imminent, so it wasn't a great time for me, and he'd been called up for some extra flights. In the interim, however, he phoned me, and it was wonderful to finally hear his voice. I was becoming increasingly smitten.

Chapter 4

LIFE develops in all sorts of unexpected ways. There are good days and bad, triumphs and disasters, unforeseen pleasures and occasionally considerable pain. But in amongst it all, the best of friends are a constant - always there to share successes or offer an arm round the shoulder in times of deep trauma. It's what makes being human bearable. Knowing that however hard and unforgiving the world may appear, there's someone you can turn to, and pour your heart out to, and who will always take your side, even if they don't always approve of your behaviour.

All that said, I tend to keep my dating exploits private, and I certainly never mention anything about it at work. It's not that I'm embarrassed about messing around on the apps, some of which are fairly notorious, but more that I can't face the level of interrogation that would ensue.

Meeting a stranger for a drink has become the norm. There are no expectations and no agendas. But I know that friends and colleagues would want to know every juicy detail, assuming it was the start of something more substantial. How could I explain that I'm not really looking for a relationship, but that occasionally it's enriching to go out and meet someone, chat for an evening, find out about them and their life, and occasionally want to do it again? Sometimes it might end up in the bedroom, but it's rare. More often we'll stop messaging, almost immediately after. I'm better off doing these things on my own, without the added glare of others, quizzing me over every detail, to feed their own unquenchable hunger for gossip.

And yet it felt different with Stef. We'd known each other for nearly two years. We hadn't even met, but I was long past beginning to feel a connection. I gave him his own WhatsApp notification sound, so I could immediately tell his messages apart from all the others. And every time the iPhone "popcorn" alert sounded, my heart gave a little leap.

I knew I was being ridiculous. He still had Molly. And no matter how fraught that all sounded at the moment, it could still go on for years. I'd never met her. I wasn't sure I'd like her. But I didn't really know anything about her and her feelings for him.

I didn't want to get carried away. But Stef's writing had revealed a depth that was both intriguing and admirable. He was so different to anyone else I'd spoken to from the murky world of online dating. He was courteous, fascinating, endlessly funny and deeply attractive, and yet there was a vulnerability at his core. I was becoming ever more drawn to him and it appeared to be mutual. Molly was a problem, but I'd given that situation a lot of thought. I was beginning to get my head round it. I just wasn't sure that my friends would be so understanding.

I started to drop his name into conversations with my daughter, Charlotte. She, however, showed the typical disinterest of a teenager. In some respects that was a good thing, but I had to tell someone. So I sent messages to my three best friends.

Ben Maguire, ironically, was a pilot. He'd worked for EasyJet (and once, scarily, flew me home from Nice) as well as having previous stints as an air traffic controller and air crash investigator on his CV. He now flew freight planes and had mysterious assignations in places like Timișoara, Belgrade, Liège and occasionally Dublin. He was an old school friend. He was recently married to Caryn, and apparently very happy, but he was very much my voice of reason.

Chrissy McCulloch was in her mid-forties. Buxom, loud, not afraid of bleaching her hair, and one of my closest female friends, despite, on the face of it, the two of us having very little in common. We'd met about fifteen years ago, when Scarlett, her daughter, started the same reception class as mine. Chrissy was also a single mum, and we used to go out sometimes for coffee, during the day, or spend an evening together, sorting out our lives over a bottle of wine, porn star martinis, woo-woos, and various other refreshments, as current trends dictated.

We fell out occasionally, but always patched things up, because we understood each other and the challenges each of us faced. She was a huge support when my long-term relationship fell apart, in 2014. She'd had her own share of man trouble, but hadn't given up hope of finding someone. I'd tried to explain the futility of the quest, but she was a romantic at heart, always believing that there was someone out there. And not afraid of kissing lots of frogs along the way.

Mark Lockwood was a former Tinder conquest. He was slightly older than me, at fifty-two. He had an important-sounding job in a media buying agency, and was a keen photographer on the side. That was one of many things we had in common. Our first date was dinner in London. The second was far too much wine at mine. Ultimately, though, despite having a lot of fun with the lights turned low, I wasn't the answer to whatever question he was asking.

As usual, our respective locations (he lived in Blackheath, south London, while I was in a commuter town north of the city) and our busy schedules meant that once the first wave of excitement passed, neither of us was in a position to make the kind of commitment that a successful relationship requires. The norm in those situations is to say we could still be friends, and we'd keep in touch, and then we'd go our separate ways, and eventually delete the phone contact after several months of non-use.

But Mark was different. He was good fun and made me smile. He was still active on the dating scene, but growing disillusioned with the shallow, ephemeral nature of it all. I occasionally harboured thoughts of putting him in touch with Chrissy, but then shuddered at the thought of the inevitable disaster. There'd be one explosive night, followed by endless recriminations. It wouldn't be fair on either of them, and I'd be caught in the crossfire.

Modern acquaintanceships have evolved in the age of smartphones, apps, Facebook and Twitter. While I rarely looked at my Facebook account, I was as addicted to WhatsApp as anyone. With the exception of the occasional phone call, such as to Ben at the time of his wedding, all three friendships now existed almost solely in the digital realm. Having spent a fortune on mobile phone bills over the years, I hadn't failed to spot the irony that Vodafone now gave me unlimited voice minutes at a time when I hardly ever made a call.

I sent Ben a message:

Anna: Hi Captain!

Ben: Guten Tag Ms B!

Anna: God. Where are you?

Ben: Berlin. Heading back to Dublin tonight, though. How are things?

Anna: All good. I have something to confess, however, which you might not like.

Ben: That terrifies me, given your reputation. What is it?

Anna: Haha. I'm not telling you if you're going to be like that.

Ben: Spoilsport. But go on, tell me. I'll try not to judge.

Anna: You will.

Ben: Now I definitely want to know.

Anna: Okay. Here goes. I've got a cushion ready to hide behind. I'm a bit concerned I'm falling for a flight attendant.

Ben: Oh, Jesus. Who? What? Why? Seriously not a good idea.

Anna: I thought you'd say that.

Ben: I assume not a lady one?

Anna: Haha. No.

Ben: That's good. Hosties are all nutjobs, though. Often gorgeous, kinky and pliable, but nutjobs all the same. Are you sure he isn't gay?

Anna: I imagine they speak just as highly of pilots. We've not actually met yet, but we've swapped lots of messages and I don't think he's gay, no.

Ben: There's a 90% chance he will be.

Anna: There's a 90% chance you're talking shit.

Ben: We need to have a word.

Anna: No we don't, or you'll try to talk me out of it.

Ben: Of course I'll try to talk you out of it. It'll end in tears.

Anna: Maybe, but I don't think so. I hope not.

Ben: You're already sounding delusional. Trust me, it will. Look, I'm just about to go to dinner, so I'm going to have to leave you, but don't do anything rash. I'll be back in a couple of days. We can discuss it then. Evidently this needs to be addressed. I will tell you stories about hosties that will make your hair curl. And I've seen you with a perm. It's not a good look.

Anna: Cheeky.

Ben: Somebody needs to be honest with you.

Anna: Haha. Okay. Have a lovely dinner and safe flying. Say hi to Caryn for me. x

Ben: Shall do. Auf wiedersehen :-)

· · ·

I followed up with a message to Chrissy. She'd been on a date the previous night and I was keen to hear the verdict.

Anna: Good morning. How was it? Are you walking funny?
    Chrissy: Don't ask.
    Anna: Don't ask in a good way or don't ask in a bad way?
    Chrissy: Don't ask in a "maybe I should become a lesbian" way.
    Anna: Ah. Not so good then.
    Chrissy: Honestly, they're all utter tosspots. No wonder you're getting a fast track to the nunnery. I'll meet you there.
    Anna: Hmmm. There's actually a bit of news there.
    Chrissy: What? And again, what??? You haven't!
    Anna: It's early days. We haven't actually met yet.
    Chrissy: All ears. Who is he? And what do you mean you haven't met yet?
    Anna: This is going to sound made up but he's an Italian flight attendant called Stef.
    Chrissy: You're right. You're making it up.
    Anna: I'm not, honestly. And we haven't met yet because he's flying all the time and I've been busy but we've been chatting a lot.
    Chrissy: Picture required immediately.

I sent her a picture.

Chrissy: Wow. You're definitely making it up. Where did you find him?
    Anna: Long story but online about eighteen months ago.
    Chrissy: And you still haven't met? You must do so and shag him immediately.
    Anna: Told you. Long story. We've only been chatting lots over the last few weeks. He's been reading the books.

Chrissy: Your books? And he's still interested in you? Wow.

Anna: What is it with everyone? Yes. My books.

Chrissy: Oh God. I thought all male flight attendants were gay, anyway.

Anna: And again, what is it with everyone? I think it's a common misconception.

Chrissy: Well I can't pretend I'm not jealous. When are you meeting him?

Anna: Not sure yet but he got me an upgrade on the flight back from Sofia. It is a bit complicated though.

Chrissy: Sounds ominous. Is he married?

Anna. No.

Chrissy: Thank heavens for that.

Anna: He does have a girlfriend though. She's polyamorous apparently.

I nearly closed my eyes at that point, afraid to read the response.

Chrissy: Polywhat?

Anna: Multiple partners. It's the modern way. But I think they may be splitting up anyway.

Chrissy: Oh my good god. You're a walking disaster.

Anna: I know, haha.

Chrissy: Let me know how it goes. I expect frequent updates, and obviously there will be orgies. We must meet for Christmas drinks and you can tell me all about him.

Anna: We must and I will. Take care in the meantime x

Chrissy: You too x

Third on the agenda was Mark, but that needed much more delicate handling. I knew he still carried a torch for me, which was deeply flattering, but equally, I knew that I would never be right for him. We'd tried, we'd failed, and my guiding principle was to bail out at the first sign of trouble. It was my defence mechanism. The best way to keep my sanity, and preserve freedom, without giving it up for a life of stress.

But Mark was a sensitive and romantic man, and he was growing ever more disillusioned at the thought of finding anyone. He would occasionally pour his heart out to me, mourning the day we parted, claiming the connection he'd felt with me was the strongest he'd felt with anyone since his marriage had broken down nearly a decade before.

I'd often told him I'd given up on relationships completely. It was kind of true, and I didn't want to cause him hurt by mentioning meeting anyone for a drink, no matter how platonic my intentions. The truth, though, was that my halo had slipped long ago. I spared Mark the details of any assignations because it might upset him, and he'd find it hard to understand. But he was still one of my closest friends and I knew I could talk to him if there was something serious. And the situation with Stef was beginning to feel very serious indeed.

Anna: Hi Mark, how are things?

Mark: Hey gorgeous! Just dashing for a meeting but great to hear from you. How are you?

Anna: Battling on. Shall I leave you in peace?

Mark: Sorry. Yes, running late already. I'll text you later xx

I put my phone away, grateful that the decision had been made for me. It wouldn't last, though. Nothing does, as I was destined to find out eventually, in the most deadly and horrifying of ways.

Chapter 5

December 2018-January 2019

STEF had a back-to-back Philadelphia and New York trip just after I arrived back from Sofia, but the messages were increasingly frequent in both directions. Sometimes he'd send me another location map. Sometimes just a string of kiss emojis. Sometimes a recording of his beautiful voice with just the hint of an Italian accent. In others there was an insight into the person behind the enigma.

He hadn't smoked in five years, and even then it was a one year stint after ten without. His upbringing in Italy had been very strict. Apparently, in over twenty years with the airline, he'd only slept with another member of cabin crew once, and never been tempted by a pilot. He occasionally went to an art class while in San Francisco, and revelled in the opportunities afforded to him to explore museums and other cultures while flying around the world. He loved live comedy and some of his one-liners were hysterical.

He arrived back in the UK eventually, but there was still no chance to meet up. He was due to fly to Beijing the following week.

It was time to do a bit more digging.

Anna: Have you managed to speak to Molly since you got back? I hope she's been begging you for forgiveness.

Stef: She's been sending lots of messages but I've been ignoring them. I've been too busy reading your book!

Anna: I'm honoured. I'm not sure she appreciates how lucky she is. She should treat you like royalty. Have you seen anyone else while you've been with her?

Stef: Not really. Just a couple of platonic drinks.

Anna: Would she be okay with that?

Stef: We shall see. It's complicated. x

Anna: Understood. I do feel for you xx

Stef: Thank you xx

He finished *Out Of The Red* and ordered book three - *In The Frame*. I said I felt guilty that he had to keep buying them, and promised to hand deliver book four at some stage. We discussed Brexit, politics, childcare, religion, packed lunches, traffic, lipstick (bizarrely), and more. He flew to Beijing and the intensity increased further. I spent all day either replying to messages or waiting for the distinctive ringtone to alert me to a new one. I never had long to wait.

Occasionally, in the middle of a conversation, he would drift off. WhatsApp would say he was still online, but he was clearly talking with someone else. It could have been Molly. Maybe it was his children, or colleagues or friends. I didn't worry about it unduly, except to feel a growing sense of concern that if it was her, and they were having a stressful time, then maybe he'd be suffering. I didn't like the thought of him suffering. I was beginning to really care.

Straight after Beijing he headed to Austin, Texas for one last trip before Christmas, just as Gatwick was grounded by an idiot flying a drone. Fortunately he was flying from Heathrow. It was a relentless schedule.

Anna: As ever you have my deepest admiration xx

Stef: I only do the same as everyone else.

Anna: Haha. Most people are battling the queues in Sainsbury's and getting annoyed by the price of gift wrap. You're squeezing in a bit of transatlantic travel and yet cope with it so calmly. It's amazing.

On the day before Christmas Eve, he sent a message from Molly's house. Apparently they'd been discussing me, and Molly thought I sounded great. I was happy with that, although it was unexpected. It was weird to think they'd been talking about me. Even weirder to realise that I wasn't running to the hills. But the longer we chatted without meeting, the more time I had to process all of my wild and varied opinions on the matter.

Despite wishing she was out of the picture, I didn't want to cause problems in their relationship. It sounded like there were enough already. I did have feelings of envy. They were together again and yet we still hadn't had time to meet for a drink. The time was coming close, though.

On Christmas Eve, he phoned me from his home, for our longest call so far. Christmas came and went. The messages increased even further. He flew to Milan for New Year, before heading to Tokyo immediately after. I imagined him on board, working hard, unbelievably tired, but still looking gorgeous.

When he messaged me from his hotel, I dared to ask about Molly again. I hoped he didn't think I was becoming obsessed.

Stef: Neither of us is happy with it at the moment. She gets a lot of free time. I don't. We're not meeting each other's needs. She wants us to go on a long holiday, but it can never happen.

Anna: I can see why that would be impossible. It's hard enough already with childcare but then with your schedule it would just be unfeasibly difficult. Logistics are always hard. I suppose it's a question of making the most of the time you have, however fleeting, and knowing that even when you're apart, you still care deeply for the other person, and they're always in your thoughts.

Stef: It is. But it doesn't really seem that way for either of us just now.

We frequently talked about meeting, both aware that it was increasingly ridiculous that we'd never done it. Once the Tokyo trip was out of the way, he was due to have some time at home. It began to feel like it might really happen.

He suggested Friday, January 18th. Typically, I was scheduled to be in Paris that weekend, on a work trip. It was so frustrating.

The next suggestion was Thursday, January 24th or Friday 25th. I said I'd keep both free. On Wednesday 23rd, he sent me a message, asking if we were still meeting on Friday. I was beyond excited. But on the Friday morning he had a "domestic emergency" and we had to postpone again. I may have screamed.

It had to happen eventually, though. On Saturday 26th he said he would be free to meet for a late nightcap the following night. And this time nothing would go wrong. After nearly two years of intrigue, we were actually going to meet.

Chapter 6

Sunday, January 26th, 2019

I TEXTED Chrissy.

Anna: It's actually happening! I'm finally meeting him tonight.

Chrissy: Do you want me to come with you? If you don't like him I'd be willing to take him off your hands, as a friend.

Anna: Haha. I'm definitely not telling you where we're meeting, then.

Chrissy: You have to. What if he's an axe-wielding maniac?

Anna: I'd happily let him behead me.

Chrissy: You're weird.

Anna: To be fair I think I'd let him do anything he wanted.

Chrissy: Oh, God. And to think you used to have morals. He's already got a girlfriend, remember.

Anna: I've got morals. And, yes, let's not worry about the girlfriend.

Chrissy: But she exists.

Anna: Told you, it's complicated. But apparently she thinks I'm great, so that's a result, even though I suspect she's bonkers.

Chrissy: You're heading for a world of trouble. Seriously, let me take him off you. Least I can do. You can thank me later.

Knowing Chrissy, it was a genuine offer.

Anna: It's the weirdest thing. It's the first time we'll have met, but it's not like a normal first date. I exported the WhatsApp chat. Do you know how many messages he's sent me?

Chrissy: You exported WhatsApp? Can you even do that?

Anna: Yes. Go on guess.

Chrissy: God knows. Two hundred?

Anna: 1,340

Chrissy: What?! And you've never even met him? How many have you sent him?

Anna: 1,295

Chrissy: Fuck's sake, and excuse my French. Do you ever get any work done? Either of you?

Anna: It's been nearly two years.

Chrissy: Even so.

Anna: I've got to go. I need to get ready. I want to make a good impression. ;-)

Chrissy: That's going to take a lot of work, no offence. Take care and have fun. Call me immediately with news. I'll order a hat.

I'm all for chatting to someone for a while before agreeing to meet them, as it can be instructive and prevent the almost-certain waste of an evening. But even for me, a two-and-a-half-thousand message conversation over nearly two years was significantly out of the ordinary.

But despite this, and the growing intensity of my feelings, I still wasn't confident it would lead to anything. He still had Molly and I wasn't completely comfortable with the thought of sharing. We still hadn't met. We could conceivably have the proposed nightcap, then find neither was as the other expected, go our separate ways, and never speak to each other again. It would leave a big void in my life, but there were no guarantees, and in some ways the sense of anticipation was so strong, it only served to dramatically increase the potential for disappointment.

And so I didn't deactivate my accounts on Tinder and Bumble. Every so often, usually in moments of boredom, late at night, lying in bed on my own, I'd flick through both just to keep an eye on things. It never does any harm to keep up to date with your market research.

Occasionally I'd get a match with someone who looked interesting, but that was as far as it went. My heart wasn't in it.

I was asked out on several dates on both Tinder and Bumble, but I managed to delay things without ruling them out entirely. Work was hectic. I had a looming deadline for book five - *Court Me Kill Me*. And, of course, I was starting to pack up my flat ahead of an imminent move. The truth, though, was that I didn't want to see anyone before finally discovering the enigma. Nobody else could compare.

We arranged to meet at 9.30pm. It would only be a quick drink, but at last I would know for certain that he existed. I spent all day counting down the hours, choosing my outfit, changing my outfit, changing my outfit again, and then planning just how late I could leave having a shower and still arrive on time. I know it's not the done thing to turn up promptly, but I also knew that we wouldn't have long. He had to get home for the children, so I wanted to be there at exactly the appointed time, to savour every moment.

The location was an upstairs bar in his home town, which was soon to be my home town too. I arrived early. The street was quiet. I managed to park right outside. Upstairs, however, it was music night, and conversation wasn't going to be easy. I went back down to wait for him by the door. I couldn't have been any more nervous.

And then, he appeared. He was late, but frankly I didn't care. I was waiting in the cold, just inside the doorway, when I heard footsteps on the street. And the next moment, he was there. I almost couldn't believe it. He smiled at me and we hugged, and my heart flipped because the man I'd thought about and written to for so long was finally standing in front of me.

He looked just like his pictures. Slightly larger, maybe, and definitely more tired, but he was real. And he'd turned up, to see me. I felt so incredibly privileged to be in his company, but I couldn't read his expression at all. He looked bemused. Was I a disappointment? Was he regretting putting so much time and effort into getting to know me? I really had no idea.

We went upstairs, but both agreed it wasn't going to work. We needed somewhere quieter. So I offered to drive to another bar, called the Old Corn Exchange, on the Market Place, about three minutes away, very close to my prospective new flat. I had no idea what Chrissy would have said if she'd known I was getting into a car with him, within seconds of meeting, but it felt like the most natural thing in the world.

We parked up. I quickly showed him my new place, and then we went into the bar. It was quiet. I gave him a copy of book four - *Fade To Silence*. I'd written an inscription inside: "For Stef. It's an absolute pleasure to meet you at last. I hope you think it's been worth the wait. Let's not leave it so long next time. Anna xxx".

He reached across and hugged me.

"I can't believe you're actually real," he said, smiling at me, and then lightly squeezing my arm. He looked adorable in a white shirt and dark navy pea coat. The way his deep brown eyes looked into mine was mesmerising.

"I was thinking exactly the same," I said, feeling the happiest I could remember in a long time. It was one of those moments you want to bottle and keep forever. If only that were possible to do.

Chapter 7

Sunday, January 26th - Tuesday, February 12th, 2019

OUR time elapsed quickly. There were so many questions I wanted to ask, but we found ourselves talking over each other, both with so much to say. I knew it was only ever going to be a brief one, and sadly, after one drink, it was time to leave. I drove him back to where he'd parked his ageing VW Golf. We said farewell, and then I unbuckled my seat belt and gave him a parting hug.

Maybe if we'd left it there, he'd still be alive now.

By the time I arrived home, I had a message on WhatsApp.

Stef: Safely home xxx

Anna: Me too. Thank you so much for coming out on such a cold evening xxx

Stef: I met a flasher on the way home, but it was so cold he just described himself, haha. I loved every minute. You're even more beautiful than you look in the pictures.

Anna: Ooh, that's exciting to hear. I thought you were absolutely lovely. The trouble is, now I've met you once I've got an even bigger urge to do it again. And even though I didn't think you could possibly go any higher in my estimation, you nevertheless did.

Stef: I look forward to that. I'm in bed now so I'm going to start reading Fade To Silence.

Anna: I hope it lives up to expectations. x

An hour later I got another. I was still awake.

Stef: I've still got a warm glow. I didn't really meet a flasher, by the way. That was a joke. Sorry... I'll try to come up with some better ones. I've packed the book to take with me to San Francisco tomorrow. I'll read it in my bunk. Molly was asking about you but I gave a very positive report.

Anna: Eek. I hope she was okay. I won't ask what was said as it's obviously private, but just so you know, I'm very respectful of that relationship (and I think she's a very lucky woman!) At the same time, I'd absolutely love to see you again when time permits. xx

Over the next couple of days he sent me dozens more messages, and each one filled me with joy. We'd crossed the first hurdle and we were still talking to each other, only now with an even greater intensity and ever more flirting. And, true to his word, the jokes did improve. And then he started talking about Molly again.

Stef: I know you probably feel you can't ask questions about my relationship, but please feel free. Anything you like.

Anna: Okay, shall do... There's lots I'm curious about, but you're right - it's a question of not wanting to overstep the mark. I do worry about you though because I get the sense she takes you for granted, although that may be unfair.

Stef: Understood. Oh, I'm free on the 13th if you would like to meet again.

Anna: I'd love to. In fact, if you're prepared to share your local knowledge of the best restaurants, I'd be willing to treat you to dinner.

Stef: It's a deal. But I'll treat you. xx

The 13th was nearly two weeks away, and that seemed like an eternity, but my heart gave a surge at the thought of a second meeting. Especially as we'd have a whole evening together this time. He arrived home from San Francisco on February 1st and immediately called me. We spent about an hour on the phone, catching up, talking nonsense, and making each other laugh.

The next day he went to stay with Molly, but still sent me dozens more messages. She lived in an ancient farmhouse in the woods that hadn't been touched in decades. She sounded like a mad-haired hippy, and was known to host the occasional yoga retreat. I found it hard to picture her with Stef. He was so sophisticated, educated, and cosmopolitan. I had to ask.

Anna: How did you meet?
Stef: On a dating app.
Anna: Ah, she beat me to it then :-(
Stef: Only by a few months actually.
Anna: I'm not sure, but I think that makes it worse! How are things?
Stef: With her?
Anna: Yes, if it's okay to ask.
Stef: It's okay to ask. There's not much to say though. It's a bit like Andy Carroll's leg muscles.
Anna: What?

Stef: Permanently strained.

Anna: Oh. Who's Andy Carroll?

Stef: Footballer, sorry.

Anna: I was beginning to wonder. Hopefully not because of us?

Stef: In truth, I don't think that's helping.

Anna: That's not good. But you said she thought I was great?

Stef: I'm not sure that's still the case now I've met you, sadly. I think the fact that we live close together is making her nervous. Maybe not nervous, actually. But unsettled.

Anna: And yet she's the one into polyamory.

Stef: Quite.

Their situation did bother me, on so many levels. It wasn't jealousy. I just hated to think of him being in a stressful environment. And more than that, I hated the thought of her putting pressure on him not to see me.

Anna: It's strange, the unconventional relationship thing. I've decided I'm not squeamish about being with someone who is also intimate with someone else. I think by our age it's inevitable people will have had quite a few partners, so it's just a matter of semantics, if that's the right word.

Stef: How do you mean?

Anna: Just that if you meet someone, there's a significant chance they've been sleeping with somebody else. Whether they did it last week, yesterday, or they're still doing it now, it doesn't make any real practical difference, as long as there's respect and nobody is lying or betraying anyone's emotions. It's just an act, at the end of the day.

Stef: Although we haven't actually slept together yet. ;-)

Anna: Not yet, haha, but if you play your cards right, you never know. But on top of that, I think if you care for someone then you should want them to be happy and have fun and explore themselves, rather than place restrictions on them because of your own insecurities. That's my current opinion, anyway, although I admit it has been influenced a lot by thinking about you and your situation. I'm very open-minded and respectful of other people and relationships. I just hope you're happy and don't feel like you're being taken for granted.

Stef: Sometimes I do. She doesn't try to control me but she has let me down several times now.

Anna: Obviously you must have some sort of connection and care for each other, though? I hope she always uses protection. There's obviously that to consider, on a practical level.

Stef: That depends on what she's doing.

Anna: I won't ask, but I can imagine.

Stef: Indeed.

Anna: Are you having a good evening? I'm imagining all sorts of cuddles with a large degree of envy.

Stef: I'm sorry. I don't want to make you envious.

Anna: Don't worry about it. It's okay. Envy is different to jealousy. I just think about how lovely it would be to have a cuddle with you, and I wish I could be doing it right now.

There was a lot more of the same over the next few days. He was supposed to be flying to Mumbai, but managed to swap the roster as he was just so tired. I understood that completely. I was in the final stages of planning the house move, working hard, and had a book to finish. I was shattered and I wasn't even suffering from extreme jet lag.

But even when we weren't swapping messages, I couldn't help thinking about him. Chrissy kept pummelling me for information. Mark wanted to meet me, to pour out his heart over his latest failed relationship. He was giving up on women for good this time. Which is what he always says, until the next one.

They'd been out on four dates and then she'd ghosted him. Eventually he got a reply saying she thought he was wonderful, and definitely her type in so many ways, but she couldn't see the relationship developing in the way she was seeking. He was devastated. I felt sorry for him, but it was definitely not the time to mention that I'd met somebody I was beginning to fall for.

Instead, I sent a message to Ben.

Anna: Hi Captain.

Ben: Don't tell me. You're still with your hostie?

Anna: Okay I won't tell you.

Ben: Oh Christ. Have you shagged him?

Anna: Nooo! We've been for one drink. Literally one. We're meeting again though. I'm taking him to dinner.

Ben: To be fair to him, he's not exactly rushing it. They normally have to act quickly, before the flight back home.

Anna: Is this the "one in every port" theory? Implying they're at it the moment they land, until the moment they take off again?

Ben: It's an occupational hazard.

Anna: Which is presumably the same for pilots, in that case. Does Mrs Ben know about this?

Ben: Pilots are different. We tend to be a bit more sophisticated. Less animalistic.

Anna: More full of shit?

Ben: I'm just saying. Heed the warnings. I've told you, it'll end in tears. It always does. Did I mention they were all nutjobs?

Anna: You did, but I chose to ignore it. Anyway, he's lovely.

Ben: Of course he's lovely. They all look lovely. That's their job.

Anna: It's more than looks. He's a really nice person. He's funny and intelligent. We seem to understand each other.

Ben: Oh God. Have you heard yourself? Tell him to bring a sick bag home with him, and post it to me, will you?

Anna: Haha. It is a bit complicated though.

This was high risk, but it needed to be said. I wanted it out in the open.

Ben: Because he's mental?

Anna: No, because he's got a girlfriend.

Ben: Christ. Now he tells you?

Anna: I knew from the start. It's okay though. She's polyamorous. She's seeing other men.

It took him a moment to respond to that one.

Ben: Either you fancy a threesome, or that sounds very high risk.

Anna: You've got a one-track mind. And anyway, I don't think she'd be my type. But it's not about that. It's the modern way. He's away a lot. She wants companionship. They stay together because they have a connection, but she's free to see others in the interim.

Ben: "Companionship" LOL. For someone who's not your type, you're doing a good job of defending her.

Anna: I'm not defending her. I think she's quite possibly a pain in the arse. I'm just telling you the way it is. But as it happens, I don't think they're happy together, so it may not last long anyway.

Ben: You hope.

Anna: I do, although I'm conflicted. I worry about him, mainly. I hate to think he's having a horrible time but they've been together a couple of years so there's definitely something of substance. But I can't pretend I'd be upset if she wasn't in the picture.

Ben: Is he seeing other women?

Anna: No.

Ben: Not that he's told you.

Anna: I genuinely believe him. He's been very open.

Ben: Do you want my advice?

Anna: I think I already know your advice.

Ben: Well there you go then. Forget him. Move on. Plenty of fish, and all of that.

Anna: I know but it's not that easy. I've never met anyone like him.

Ben: There'll be others.

Anna: There are lots of others. I've met a few. And in all but a few cases, I've usually ended up horrified. He's unique. He's ticking every single box.

Ben: But he's got a girlfriend.

Anna: I know. But I can deal with that. I don't want a full-on relationship. I don't have time. In some ways that's one of the boxes.

Ben: You're losing the plot.

Anna: I think I lost it a long time ago.

Ben: Well listen, being serious, just be careful, okay?

Anna: I will.

I should have listened. Really I should. But it's a bit late to be thinking that now.

Chapter 8

THERE was a lot playing on my mind. The more I thought about Stef over the next few days, the more I thought about the mysterious Molly. But, as ever, he was happy to answer my questions, and indeed encouraged me to ask them. She wasn't the only thing we talked about, but every time I was given encouragement, I seized the opportunity.

I was in the midst of a late-night mountain of ironing when my phone made its distinctive noise.

Stef: Hi gorgeous xx
    Anna: Hi. How are you? I'm ironing...
    Stef: Ooh, I like to think of you all hot and steamy.
    Anna: Don't encourage me!
    Stef: I like encouraging you :-)
    Anna: Haha. Okay. I'll bear that in mind! Lovely to hear from you.
    Stef: I couldn't resist x
    Anna: I've been thinking of a few things.
    Stef: Like what?

Anna: I'm not sure I should say.

Stef: Of course you should. You should always be open with me.

Deep breath time. In some ways it was easier to ask these questions by text. There was less chance of embarrassment. But equally, far more chance of him taking offence because of not understanding my tone of voice. It was worth the risk, though, and I was confident enough now that I wasn't going to mess things up irreparably.

Anna: Okay. Is Molly your first experience with polyamory?

Stef: She is.

Anna: Does it seem strange or is it intriguing?

Stef: Maybe strange, but there's a lot of hypocrisy in relationships, and this is the opposite of that. I had to do lots of reading to get my head round it all. It's an exciting lifestyle choice.

Anna: I can imagine it's been a learning process.

Stef: It has, although I still don't know if it's for me.

Anna: Do you find it hard to think of her with others?

Stef: No.

Anna: I think that's amazing really. I don't have any jealousy at all (envy yes, as you know - I have some of that) but I think it's rare. I do think you are brilliant.

Stef: I'm always impressed that you can see the distinction between envy and jealousy. It only bothers me if they're younger, or rich and successful, haha.

Anna: Do you worry that they'll take her away from you?

Stef: No. Just that I'll be judged in comparison!

Anna: How old is she?

Stef: Nearly 48.

Anna: Wow. I don't know why, but I thought she'd be in her mid-thirties. What does she do for a job then? I have this image of some woman living in the woods running mystical retreats with a constant supply of handsome men, servicing her wild and varied womanly needs. It's all very intriguing. It's like she's some sort of guru.

Stef: She runs a web design company.

Anna: Can you send me a picture? I'd love to see what she looks like. It's hard to imagine her.

He sent me a picture. She did indeed look a bit like a mad-haired hippy. I was struggling more than ever to picture the two of them together, but maybe I was just biased. But who was I to judge? I'd had mad hair in the 1980s, although in fairness to myself, at least it was in fashion back then. Oh, I can be so bitchy in my old age. Perhaps they had a strong meeting of minds.

Stef: This is the first time I've done this. Talking to another woman about her.

Anna: I thought it might be. I know you said you hadn't had any other partners. I don't know really where you are in that journey, but just so you know, there are no pressures or expectations from here. I understand it must be a lot to think about. There's no rush but equally you just have to click your fingers and I'm there... I think it's refreshing that you can talk about it by the way. I'm worried that I'll say the wrong thing and offend you because I only know what I think. I've only met you once and obviously don't really know how much you mean to each other or where you see things going.

Stef: Just to be clear. I'm never offended by anything.

Anna: Okay. Good to know. I go through such phases now of imagining you doing normal couple things like going to the cinema and out to restaurants and just spending time together, to the opposite extreme of wild woodland orgies.

Stef: Well, no to orgies, but I like the woodland. Do you like orgies?

Anna: Haha. I can't tell you that or you'll know all my secrets ;-)

Stef: I'll assume yes then.

Anna: I feel we're in tricky territory here.

Stef: In what way?

Anna: You know that I am interested in you and I wouldn't want you to think it was just sex. Sex is obviously important and lovely and fun, but I am drawn to you on lots of levels, not just that.

Stef: Wow. That's a wonderful thing to say.

Anna: But it's also why I'm not jealous of the thought of you having sex with Molly. The thought of you having fun, even if I'm not there, is sexy. There's envy because I think it would be wonderful to be that close to you, but it's not just the physical act. It's having that connection. I'm not sure if that makes sense.

Stef: It does. Absolutely.

Anna: My bigger and really only concern about Molly is that you are happy and feel valued.

Stef: Let's say that that's a separate discussion. Not always. It's wonderful in some ways, but in others I don't feel particularly fulfilled.

Anna: Which are the wonderful bits?

Stef: The honesty, the sex, things we both agree and disagree about, so our world view. I like the fact that it's unconventional too.

Anna: I just need to come to terms with the image of you having wonderful sex for a moment.

Stef: Are you currently seeing anyone else?

Anna: I have had a few dalliances but nothing that constitutes anything like a proper relationship. I've made some very good friends over the last four years, but I haven't been looking for the "being in someone's pocket" thing. I'm not needy, though, and I never feel lonely so there's no rush for anything. Quality over quantity etc.

Stef: I know exactly what you mean.

Anna: But while I'm on, I know we hardly know each other really, but I do find you mentally intriguing as well as just physically sexy. Early days...

Stef: And very much likewise.

It was nearly 2am. We finished talking and wished each other a good night. The following morning I awoke to a self-portrait in which he looked particularly sexy. We chatted more, and discussed our upcoming date on the 13th. He said he would make a reservation at a tapas restaurant in his town, about a three-minute walk from where I'd soon be moving. But something had been preying on my mind.

Anna: Last night, you said there were some wonderful bits with Molly, but in others you weren't fulfilled. I'm very curious about what you're looking for... In relationships, in life, in all sorts of ways.

Stef: Just normal daily stuff couples do together, I suppose. Meeting up with friends. She never wants to do that. Shopping together. Going to the theatre. Going away together. Some aspects of sex as well. She only wants to do the things she's interested in, and I'd like to do more. A bit more variety, if you know what I mean?

Anna: I do.

That was food for thought.

The following day I was due to fly to Bratislava on a book research trip. Sadly it was with Wizz Air, so he couldn't work his upgrade magic, but I had a wonderful vision of him coming with me, making disparaging comments about low-cost airlines. And even though I was flying alone, it felt like he was right by my side, all the time I was away.

The Bratislava trip filled most of my time for the next few days. I revisited some locations I was writing about in *Court Me Kill Me*, to check that they were there as I remembered them. My only previous experience of Slovakia had involved a gun-toting madman, but they were very different days, with very different friends.

Stef was booked on a trip to Las Vegas while I was away, so the distance between us was becoming extreme. But despite our respective time zones being nine hours apart, we still managed to swap many more messages. Occasionally he just sent a "thinking of you xxx" and each time my heart nearly melted. He phoned me from the plane home, and despite the shaky connection, it was wonderful to hear his voice.

Once we were both back in the UK, conversation turned to our second date.

Anna: What time should we meet?

Stef: Would 7 be good? I don't have the girls that night so I can stay out longer. I look forward to spending more than just an hour with you.

Anna: Would you like me to pick you up so you can have a drink without worrying about driving? I've got to drive anyway.

Stef: Don't worry. I'll only have a single glass. I'll be fine.

Anna: Ah, but you might want several. I get far funnier if you've had a few. It's up to you...

I was curious to see where he lived. He'd mentioned it was close to a pub, but if he'd told me the street I'd forgotten it. But despite my offer, he was adamant he would meet me at a bar in town before heading to the restaurant.

The messages continued. He was reading *Fade To Silence* and kept pointing out the bits that had kept him awake at night. I was deeply flattered. Apparently I was bad for his blood pressure but once he'd finished it, he told me his verdict, and I was even more flattered. That was the day before the second date, and it set the mood up perfectly.

Chapter 9

ON the morning of the 13th I received a WhatsApp message from Chrissy. We'd never got round to meeting for Christmas drinks. I don't think either of us was surprised.

Chrissy: It's the big day then.
  Anna: You make it sound like it's a wedding!
  Chrissy: It won't be long, I assure you.
  Anna: It's only the second date.
  Chrissy: What's the message count now?
  Anna: God knows. I'll check. One moment.

I exported the WhatsApp chat and opened it into a spreadsheet. It took a few minutes to work it out. Even I was shocked at the result.

. . .

Anna: He's sent 1,970. I've sent 1,877.

Chrissy: That's madness. Although clearly you need to up your game or he'll think you're not interested. That's nearly a hundred times you've ignored him. What on earth do you find to talk about?

Anna: Oh, all sorts. Just stuff really. Seeing how we are, discussing life and thoughts. Lots of book stuff.

Chrissy: He's not still reading your books, is he? Has he never heard of libraries? Could he not get something decent in Duty Free?

Anna: Very funny. He says he's enjoying them. You should try one.

Chrissy: I will, one day, but I think it would be weird reading about you when I already know you. At least he's doing it the other way round and reading about you first. Do you paint yourself as some sort of kinky sex vixen?

Anna: In the books? Quite the opposite actually. They're mainly me being resolutely single and eternally frustrated.

Chrissy: No change there then.

Anna: Cheers. Anyway, that's kind of how it started really. We'd only ever chatted intermittently, months apart, until he read Cold Press, *but ever since then it's been constant. It's made all those candlelit nights at home with the laptop eminently worthwhile.*

Chrissy: Haha! You've got a groupie!

Anna: It's way beyond that, my dear.

Chrissy: So how come you've only met once then? Hold on, I'm just getting a fag.

I rarely smoke but just at that moment I fancied one.

Chrissy: Back.

Anna: He's away a lot. I'm busy. And obviously there's his girlfriend.

Chrissy: I'd forgotten about her. Have you not done away with her yet?

Anna: I'm working on it.

Chrissy: Thinking about it, though, if you're embracing poly-whatnot, does that mean I can have a turn as well? As a friend?

Anna: I don't know that I am embracing polyamory. I'm just taking each day as it comes. No pressure, no expectations.

Chrissy: But in the meantime, he's fucking another woman?

Anna: Delicately put.

Chrissy: Sorry, I apologise. But he is, though.

My phone started ringing. It was Chrissy.

"Sorry about that," she said. "I was getting thumb ache so I thought I might as well ring you."

"It's lovely to hear your voice," I said. It genuinely was. We very rarely spoke via anything other than text messages.

"So you were saying? About his girlfriend? I'm all ears."

"I wasn't saying anything. You were being rude and I was trying to ignore you."

"I'm never rude. But you must want to meet her?"

"I'm not sure I do and I don't know that I ever will. I try not to think about it. But there's nothing I can do about it anyway. It's not ideal but that was the situation from the outset. He's not sleeping with lots of women or having relentless casual sex behind my back. It's one long-term relationship."

"But she does know about you?"

"Apparently. She used to think I was great, but I'm not so sure now."

"She'll be fine. She'll be wanting you to join in."

That wasn't an image I was trying to picture.

"She's not my type," I said.

"But I bet you would though, just for the experience. What's she like?"

"Based on the one picture I've seen, I'd say hairy."

"Wow. Does she not know it's 2019 and that grooming is a thing?"

"I was meaning head hair." I laughed.

"Oh, but you can imagine," said Chrissy. "She'll be into lentils and alternative healing and won't shave her legs or armpits and when she gets undressed she'll look like a hirsute 1970s porn star."

"We seriously need to change the subject."

"Okay. But going back to the central issue, can I have a turn? Please. I'm getting desperate."

"With him or her?"

"Him, obviously."

"No."

"God, you're no fun."

Being "fun" for Chrissy was not top of my agenda.

It was good to talk, though. We ended the call, making promises to meet for drinks soon, although we both knew it wouldn't happen. She wished me well. I promised to send her an update. She told me to take condoms just in case. But date two was never going to end in the bedroom. It was my first real opportunity to spend a whole evening with him. There was so much I needed to discover.

At 7pm I was standing outside the Old Corn Exchange, holding an umbrella, feeling the same nervous anticipation as I had at the first bar on the original Sunday evening. He was late, again, but it gave me one last chance to check my appearance for any traces of lipstick in places they shouldn't be. I'd worked hard to make my hair look nice, in contrast to Molly, although if he went for the mad-hippy-cat-woman look, it was probably self-defeating.

Preparation hadn't gone completely smoothly elsewhere. I'd struggled to zip up my dress completely, so it was stuck about four inches below the neckline. Asking for his help to do it up could be the perfect icebreaker, if he didn't look horrified at my evident incompetence and suddenly remember he'd left a tap running at home.

I saw him approaching across the Market Place. He looked very chic with just a hint of stubble to accentuate his jawline. He was wearing a striking white leather biker jacket with black shoulders, dark jeans and a white shirt. Had I ever mentioned to him I have a major fetish for white shirts? I couldn't remember. I stepped forward, feeling very small despite the heels on my black suede boots, and he hugged me and it was electrifying.

He fixed my dress for me, and his hands lingered, for a couple of seconds, on the back of my neck. We each ordered a porn star martini. He led me to a table and then pulled out two chairs, so we were side by side rather than opposite. He asked me to squeeze the passionfruit into his glass for him, and then described watching it as "intensely erotic". Our knees touched. I pulled away, nervously, but he didn't move. They touched again, and this time I let mine stay there.

"So," I said, with a smile, "we seem to be making a habit of this."

He laughed. The music in the bar was from the 1980s, but low enough that it didn't impede conversation. The light was seductively low. There weren't many other customers.

"You're even more beautiful the second time," he said. From anyone else it could have been creepy or insincere, but from him it seemed genuine. My heart rate reacted dangerously.

"Likewise," I said. "I love the jacket." It was a Belstaff. They're not cheap. But looking back now, knowing what happened, my abiding memory is seeing it covered in blood.

He held my hand for a moment, to compliment me on my

ring. I'd been given a Ceylon sapphire by an old friend, many years before, and I brought it out for special occasions. I say given, but I kind of stole it, and she never asked for it back. Long story. We made small talk. It felt like we'd known each other forever, although I didn't think the novelty of being in the same room as him would ever wear off.

After the first drink he suggested making our way to the restaurant. It was only a couple of minutes walk away. I thought about holding his hand on the way, but didn't want to look too forward. I still wasn't sure if he saw me as purely a friend. It was still raining so I raised my umbrella.

"Short person with an umbrella. That's very eye-catching," he said, with a wink. I punched him in the arm.

He knew the waiting staff, and we were shown to a table in the window. The restaurant was small and Mediterranean-style. We ordered a selection of tapas dishes to share. I loved the thought of sharing with him.

"I think this is amazing, really," I said, once the drinks arrived. "I can't help but think about the probability of us ever meeting."

"In what way?"

"You're from Milan, and yet you ended up here. How did that even happen, from all the towns in all the countries in the world? I grew up near Manchester then moved to London and ended up here as well. Any tiny change in any of that and we'd have never even known the other existed. And then if I hadn't seen you that day and swiped on you, we'd still never have met. I could have walked past you in the supermarket, but not had any idea about who you are, or how much I'd enjoy getting to know you. So when you think about the chances of us actually ever meeting, it's in the billions to one. I think it's remarkable."

"It is," he said, reaching for my hand. "But maybe some things are meant to be. Tell me all about you. Everything you've missed out so far."

"I'm not sure there's much more to tell." I paused for a moment, trying to recall all of our previous text messages. I'm not sure even Einstein could have remembered all of them. "I used to be a photographer, and I had a few adventures, but you know all about those because you've read the books. It's actually quite scary how well you already know me."

"Are you still in touch with Danny and Clare?"

"Danny and Clare?"

"From the books."

I knew exactly who he was referring to. But some of those memories were painful, and I was still working through them.

"I can't give spoilers," I said, with a half-hearted wink, hoping that would suffice. I wanted to keep the mood light. Now was not the time to be sidetracked.

"Okay. But there's still so much I don't know about you now," he continued, thankfully changing the subject, perhaps sensing my discomfort.

"Such as?"

"What you like doing in your spare time. Your best friends. Your favourite TV shows. Do you have any pets?"

"No, no pets." I paused to think for a moment. "I've got a few house plants because apparently they purify the air. Does that count? I don't get much free time. I try to stay active. I run an online clothing company and I love a good TV drama. Line of Duty, Luther, Sherlock, Killing Eve."

"Have you seen the new series of Luther?"

"Not yet. I'm saving it till things calm down. It's all recorded on the planner, though. The move is taking every spare minute at the moment. There are endless boxes to pack."

"I'd love to watch it with you."

"And as for friends," I said, while trying to process an image of us curled up together on the sofa, "I've got a few. Chrissy who's great fun, and one of the mums from school. Ben who's a pilot. A few others."

He smiled.

"Watch out for pilots."

"He's warned me to watch out for flight attendants."

"I'm sure he has. Don't believe a word of it."

The first dishes arrived. We both took a selection.

"Any more news on the moving date?" he asked.

"No, it's so frustrating. Hopefully by the end of the month."

"Not long then?"

"Fingers crossed."

"And how's book five coming along?"

I gave a rueful smile.

"Not well. I've not had a chance to do any writing for the last couple of weeks, so there'll be lots of late nights coming up."

"When's the deadline?"

"Officially the end of March, but I may get a week of leeway if I ask the editor nicely."

We chatted for about two hours. He told me more about his children and the challenges of arranging childcare at short notice. He had a nanny who would come to stay when needed. He wished he had more time to go to the gym. I said I was surprised he had any energy for anything.

Inevitably the conversation turned to Molly. Again, I got the sense that there were challenges.

"I've told you, you can ask any question," he said. "However personal."

"I know."

"I promise to answer truthfully."

But I didn't want to spoil the mood by being too invasive. He was, he said, essentially monogamous but he'd read books like The Ethical Slut in order to try to come to terms with polyamory. It was exciting to make such an unusual choice, and yes, there were challenges, but everything was going as well as could be hoped - or at least it seemed to be, until the last couple of months. He accepted it because it was the deal from the outset. I understood what he meant. It was one more thing we had in common.

Then, as the plates were finally cleared away and I'd settled the bill, albeit against significant protest, he produced a card out of nowhere and handed it to me. It was, after all, the day before Valentine's Day. I opened it. There was a picture of a typewriter. Inside: "For a beautiful writer. You are just my type. S xxx"

I was nearly overcome. It was so incredibly thoughtful and well chosen I didn't know quite what to say. My heart nearly melted. And in that moment I knew beyond any doubt, whatever else happened, he'd hooked me.

We left the restaurant, but neither of us wanted the night to end. Stef suggested going to another bar for coffee. He led the way. Then, after more conversation, and just as it was time to leave, he took me in his arms. And he kissed me.

Chapter 10

THERE were messages from Chrissy, Ben and Mark on my WhatsApp when I finally arrived home, but I ignored them all because there was another that was much more enticing.

Stef: What an absolutely wonderful evening. Thank you for every moment xxx

Anna: Ooh I've got such a tingle all over. And a fantastic card. I'm speechless.

Stef: Is speechless not a bad thing for a writer?

Anna: I don't think I'll be doing much writing tonight now. I want to savour the touch and taste of you. I hope you have a long and peaceful sleep and a wonderful day tomorrow. And if you're free for lunch any day just let me know.

Stef: I will. Maybe brunch one day? I very much look forward to it.

There were long gaps between his messages, but his status was still showing online. I had to ask.

.   .   .

Anna: Are you chatting to Molly? I hope she's okay with what happened. I hope you're okay with it too...

Stef: I am very much okay with what happened. I loved every moment. Molly not so much, but she will have to learn to live with it.

Anna: I understand. I don't want you to feel any pressure or concern. We can take things at any pace and there's never any rush. You should always feel comfortable. But just so you know, I feel immensely lucky to have spent time with you. xxx

Stef: I have an overwhelming urge to give you one last kiss.

Anna: Likewise. x

———

It was late but I sent a message to Chrissy.

Anna: Date two good. Very good actually. He looked so sexy in a white leather jacket, which was a lot less tacky than it sounds. We kissed. Eek. Falling for him... Proper update soon. x

It got the two grey ticks to say it had been delivered, but I didn't expect her to still be awake to read it. So I sent one to Ben.

Anna: Not sure I agree with you on hosties. Mine seems rather lovely! Just back from dinner and pretty sure he's not a nutjob. We shall see... Take care and safe travels wherever you are. x

That one got a single tick, so his phone was off. He was probably in the sky somewhere. He'd get it in the morning. That left Mark. I probably wouldn't have sent anything if the other two had responded, but I wanted to talk to him. He was such a good friend, but I had to be sensitive.

Anna: Hi and I hope you're okay. Thinking of you. I hope you're happy. xx

It got two blue ticks almost immediately. He was up late, as usual.

Mark: Hi my darling. I'm okay. How are you? x

Anna: I'm fine. Just tired. I've been out for dinner and it was a late finish so I'm heading to bed soon.

Mark: Dinner sounds ominous. Hot date?

Anna: Haha. Just a good friend.

Mark: ???

Anna: What do you mean ??? ?

Mark: My Anna radar is up. It's a bit late to be getting back from dinner if it was just a good friend, haha.

Anna: We went for a drink after.

Mark: That's worse! Who was he?

Anna: Why do you think he was a he?

Mark: You've just given it away there. I knew it. :-(

Anna: You're too clever.

Mark: So?

Anna: A needle pulling thread.

Mark: What?

Anna: It was a joke. Works better spoken.

Mark: Are you drunk?

Anna: No, far from it. You know me.

Mark: You're drunk then!

Anna: Cheeky. I was driving so no not drunk. So there.

Mark: So, back to the question. Who was he?

Anna: Stef.

Mark: Who the hell is Stef?

Anna: Told you, a friend. Just a very good one.

Mark: Oh God. It was a hot date.

Anna: Kind of.

Mark: :-(:-(

Anna: Don't worry. I'm not sure it'll lead to anything.

Mark: Hmmm.

Anna: I'm not looking for a relationship. I've told you. It's just nice to go out with people occasionally. Friends.

Mark: Where did you meet him?

Anna: Online a couple of years ago.

Mark: On an app?

Anna: Yes.

Mark: Gets worse again.

Anna: Seriously, don't worry.

Mark: Okay.

I waited for him to send a longer message but there was nothing forthcoming.

Anna: Are you sure you're okay?

Mark: Yes. I better get to bed though. I'm out tomorrow taking pictures and it's late. Take care and sleep well.

Anna: You too xx

. . .

He disappeared offline almost immediately after. That hadn't gone spectacularly well, but at least it was out in the open now. But the lack of an x at the end of his final message was so out of character, it bothered me far more than it should have.

Chapter 11

Thursday, February 14th, 2019

I FOUND it hard to concentrate on work the following morning. It was Valentine's Day. The postman didn't come, but I didn't care. Stef, however, was driving to meet Molly that afternoon, and then taking her to a comedy show in Watford, before spending the night with her.

I had a few messages during the day. Apparently he was tingling for me too. But it didn't alter the fact that he was with her, and it was the first big test of my resolve.

Stef: Just arrived. She's still in bed.
    Anna: It's 3.20pm!
    Stef: I know. I'm going to make coffee.
    Anna: Is she not at work?
    Stef: She works from home.
    Anna: I work from home but I don't lie around in bed till 3.20pm!
    Stef: I like the thought of you lying in bed though. We should arrange a

proper night out together and go to the theatre or something. That would be fun.

Anna: I'd love to, but I need to learn about your availability and roster and childcare and other commitments. It does sound very complicated but I will do my best to understand. Dear oh dear I'm missing you. I do seem to have developed quite a powerful crush.

Stef: xxx

I was brought up to think that monogamy was the norm, and here I was, facing up to the thought that if things progressed, I'd have to accept that he would be still spending time with his other girlfriend. Could I do that without feeling jealous? Could I explain that to my friends and family? Would they think I'd gone mad? Did I even want that?

But then, when I thought about what I really wanted, I began to view things in a completely different way.

My dream had become a mantra: the desire to meet someone that I was desperate to see again, the moment I said goodbye. That I was aching to speak to again, the moment I put down the phone. But I'd shied away from relationships because, in my experience, they're always doomed to failure. And the reason they're doomed to failure is largely down to me, and my constantly busy life.

I couldn't ever expect someone to put his life on hold for me. To wait around, missing out on opportunities for fun and companionship, when I was unable to have more than one or two free evenings per month.

All of that had been passing through my mind, and I'd begun to realise that maybe this was exactly what I'd been looking for. Somebody who would want to see me, but wouldn't be relying on me. And yes, he might also be sleeping with someone else, but that was within the context of a committed relationship. It wasn't like he was having endless one-night stands. Crucially, he wasn't lying to me or cheating on me.

Later that evening I got another message.

Stef: The show was good, but the evening has been difficult. Very stressful. I just want to go to bed.

Anna: Sorry to hear that. I'm always here for you if you need me. Sleep well xxx

Stef: Please don't worry. I'll be home tomorrow. Good night xx

---

I finally exchanged contracts on my new flat on February 15th. Completion was scheduled for the 26th. There was so much to do, but the excitement was overwhelming. I'd been renting for the last four years, so I was desperately keen to get back on the property ladder. I sent a message to Stef. Late that evening my phone did its special popcorn noise.

Stef: Congratulations! I can't wait for you to be near. We must celebrate soon. I have the Champagne already xx

Anna: Sounds perfect. I'd love to see you. How are you?

Stef: Tired after yesterday. I've been thinking: would you let me give you a massage one day?

Anna: I'd love that. :-) Are you safely home? Was everything okay in the end? I know you say not to worry and I really try not to, but I just love to think of you happy xx

Stef: I'm okay. It was important to talk.

Anna: Did you at least have amazing sex? Just for the avoidance of doubt, the thought of that is good from the point of view of you having a wonderful time. But equally I'd quite like to be an enthusiastic participant at some stage. Just putting it out there. I can't forget how wonderful it was to kiss you.

Stef: Yes, it felt fantastic. As did your body. I look forward to doing it again soon xx

I wasn't sure if he was referring to the kiss or the amazing sex with Molly. I'm my own worst enemy at times.

Anna: If I go quiet it's not because I've lost interest, but because I'm trying to give you time and space to work things out without any added pressure. You are the most important part of this equation.

Stef: That's very kind. Thank you. I don't know why I'm the most important, though.

Anna: Because you are. I love the thought of making you happy but I can only ever do that if you're free to live your life on your own terms, at your own pace, with your own freedoms. I'm a very laid-back person. I don't do drama or intense displays of emotion. I love every time I hear from you. I loved every time (both times) I've met you. But while I am in awe of your strength and character, I get a strong sense of a vulnerability that makes me just want to give you a great big hug. You are completely in control. You can decide to let me know when you're free if you want to, and you know I'll drop everything to come running. But equally I'm aware and respectful of your workload and children, your other relationship and your need to have time alone. So I don't expect to be able to see you very often, even though I'd love to. And I'm desperately keen to see you very soon. All I can do is try to make sure I can drop everything else in a heartbeat should the opportunity arise. x

Stef: Wow. That's so lovely and so articulate. I don't know how to reply without it paling into insignificance by comparison!

Anna: Don't worry. Always the writer. :-)
Stef: I'm going to bed now. I'm so tired. Sleep well Ms Gorgeous xx
Anna: You too xx

As it transpired, I didn't have long to wait.

Chapter 12

Saturday, February 16th, 2019

AS mentioned, I'm not an angel, and I'd matched with a few other people on the dating apps over the previous few weeks. It wasn't that I went looking, as such, just that I'd upgraded my accounts to let me know if someone swiped right on me. If they looked sane and interesting, I'd occasionally swipe back. I was so conflicted over Stef. It was going well, but I still didn't know where it could lead, or if Molly would call a halt at any moment, and break my heart.

With work, the move, and all thoughts dominated by my favourite Italian, I'd had no desire to meet anyone else, but there are only so many excuses you can give before the pressure to meet becomes unbearable. And so, on the evening of Saturday, February 16th I was finally destined to meet with one of my recent matches - Andy - for a platonic introductory drink. I'd already rearranged twice, and felt sorry for him. He seemed like a good person who could become a friend, and his messages were always entertaining. I'd explained I wasn't looking for a full-on relationship, but that hadn't deterred him. So we arranged to meet at a pub about halfway between us. He texted that morning to say how much he was looking forward to it. In some ways I was looking forward to it too. Being selfish, I thought it would do me good to have something else to focus on. Something to clarify my thoughts and feelings about my Italian friend.

But just after 1pm I got a message from Stef.

Stef: I may be free this evening. x

Well, that was a conundrum. I reread it, then read it again. *"May be free."* Not a guarantee. But just the chance was enough. I sent a reply.

Anna: That would be divine. If you are, what sort of time would work for you?
  Stef: About 8pm?
  Anna: Perfect. Let me know and I'll keep everything crossed.

I felt terrible cancelling Andy for a third time, and even worse for blaming a short-notice work crisis that didn't exist, but what else could I do? He was lovely about it, and said he understood. I promised to make it up to him.

Shortly after 6pm my phone played popcorn.

· · ·

Stef: Really sorry, but I think I'm going to be too tired tonight. I've been given the runaround by the girls. So sorry :-(

I couldn't have felt more deflated.

Anna: That's a shame, but it's one of those things. Most importantly, are you okay?
    Stef: Yes, just another hectic day.
    Anna: I understand. I hope I'm not adding to your pressures.
    Stef: Only my blood pressure, haha.
    Anna: Hopefully that's a good thing.
    Stef: It is. It's hard though. I feel intense desire and lust for you but I do feel guilt because Molly isn't happy.
    Anna: But she's the polyamorous one! She can't have it both ways.
    Stef: I know. But she's still finding it difficult.
    Anna: Well, don't let her talk you out of seeing me.
    Stef: Don't worry. I won't. She doesn't control me.

But I did worry. I set about packing boxes, and working on my day job web site, trying not to think too much about the mad-haired hippy and her potential to ruin things, or how I now felt even worse about letting down Andy, for no reason at all.
    But then, just past 8pm, I got another message:

Stef: Do you want to meet for a quick cup of coffee?

And I was back to floating again. Just under an hour later we met in a car park, walked up to a bar, drank coffee, arranged the next date for Thursday as he had a rare week off from flying, held hands, and then, as I walked him back to his car, he kissed me again. And everything was well with the world.

I was getting in deeper and deeper, and beginning to lose control of my emotions. Hindsight is a wonderful thing.

Chapter 13

Saturday, February 16th - Wednesday, February 20th, 2019

C *HRISSY: I just saw you in town! Was that him?*

Ben: Back in England. Tell me you've come to your senses? Please?

Andy: Don't worry about today. These things can't be helped. I think it does bode badly for the future though. I suppose I'm looking to meet someone who is more available. It's been a pleasure to talk to you. Take care and good luck with the search.

My WhatsApp was alive when I got home. There was still nothing from Mark. I was worried about him. I sent Stef a message, thanking him for another lovely evening, then set about the others. Chrissy was online.

. . .

Anna: God. Where were you?

Chrissy: Did you not see me? I was in the far corner.

Anna: You should have said hello.

Chrissy: I was waiting for you to go to the toilet, then I was going to pounce.

Anna: Just as well I didn't then.

Chrissy: He looked gorgeous. He's very tall. You made a lovely couple.

Anna: Haha. I don't know about that but I'm glad you approve. What were you doing there anyway?

Chrissy: What's the opposite of a hot date, while still a date? A cold date? Or a shit date? One of those anyway.

Anna: That doesn't sound good. But I thought you were seeing someone?

Chrissy: Try to keep up! I was, but I messed it up by also seeing someone else.

Anna: There you go then. Try polyamory. You're a natural.

Chrissy: If this is you offering to share, then count me in. I knew you'd see sense eventually.

Anna: On second thoughts...

Chrissy: You're such a tease. How's it going, anyway? I noticed the handholding.

Anna: That's embarrassing.

Chrissy: I thought it was sweet. Where was his other hand?

Anna: You're relentless.

Chrissy: When are you seeing him again?

Anna: Thursday daytime apparently. He's coming round here. Obviously that could all change but it's the plan at the moment.

Chrissy: He's coming to yours??? Outstanding. I hope you use protection, you don't know where he's been. Second thoughts, you do.

Anna: You're funny.

Chrissy: Let me know how it goes.

DAVID BRADWELL

Anna: I will. Sleep well in the meantime. xx

Stef replied with a location map which I took to be his home address. He still hadn't told me exactly where he lived, but I was touched by the gesture.

Anna: That is such a lovely thing to send. Thank you. x
Stef: Until Thursday... xxx

The messages got steadily more flirtatious over the next couple of days. He said where he would like to kiss me, various other things he would like to do with me, how desperate he was to give me a massage, and how he was worried about ripping my clothes. But they were always seductive and cheeky rather than creepy and I encouraged him with much the same in return. There were dozens of other messages too, checking how things were, just telling me he was thinking of me, and catching up on how our days were progressing - even, at one point, offering to cook me lasagne.

Thursday was still firmly in the diary, but on Tuesday morning he sent a message saying he couldn't wait another two days. Could I meet him for coffee in an hour?

I dropped everything. We met. We held hands again. We kissed again. And still had Thursday to look forward to.

Wednesday brought more stress with Molly, leaving him feeling emotionally drained. They were having increasingly lengthy late-night conversations. I didn't ask for the details, but I hated the thought of the stress. He continually reassured me, but more than ever I just wanted to provide him with moments of calm amid the turmoil elsewhere in his life.

74

Nothing, though, could dampen my enthusiasm for the following day. I stacked all of the cardboard boxes in the spare room, to give the illusion of being relatively tidy. I changed the bedding because, well, you never know. It's always best to be prepared, and my 1200 thread count Genuisa cotton sheet from John Lewis always creates a lasting impression. A girl has to do what a girl has to do.

I was, however, getting worried about Mark. Mid-way through the evening, when he would usually be at home, I tried to phone him. We never speak on the phone. It didn't get answered. So I sent a message instead:

Anna: Hi Mark. How did the photography go? Are you okay? I'm worried about you. Message me please when you can.

Two and a half hours later I got a reply.

Mark: Why are you worried about me?
  Anna: Because you seem very quiet.
  Mark: I'm fine.
  Anna: You don't sound fine.

He didn't reply, and went offline. But about half an hour later another message arrived.

. . .

Mark: I suppose I'm just disappointed, that's all. I thought we had something very special and you know I adore you. But you were the one who always said you were incapable of relationships. So I just find it hard to think of you with someone else.

Anna: Oh, Mark. You mustn't worry. I'm allowed to go out for drinks with people. Nothing has changed.

Mark: Are you sleeping with him?

Anna: No! I've told you. It's very early days.

Mark: But you will?

Anna: Oh, come on. I'm not a nun. I don't know what will happen, but whatever happens doesn't change anything between you and me. You're still one of my very best friends.

Mark: That's not very reassuring.

Anna: What do you mean not very reassuring?

Mark: Just you. In bed with somebody. I find that hard. I'd want it to be me, but you said you couldn't commit, so now I feel like you were either fobbing me off, or something has changed and he can do something for you that I can't, when I know that's impossible because I would do anything for you in the world. So that makes me feel pretty shit, if you really want to know.

Anna: Heaven's sake. It's not a reflection on you. You're brilliant but you live miles away. Maybe if we were closer it could have been different but nothing has changed. I still don't get much free time, so I could never pop round to see you if I had an hour free because it's a three-hour round trip minimum. But you shouldn't worry. Occasionally I meet up with friends and go for a drink. It'd be a fairly miserable life otherwise.

Mark: But this is more than just a friend.

Anna: Maybe, who knows? But it's still no reflection on you either way. I'm sorry you feel like that. :-(

Mark: I should leave you to it. I hope you're happy. I just wish it was me who did that for you.

Anna: You do make me happy. But we agreed to be really good friends. I won't mention it again.

Mark: No, you must. I'll only think the worst otherwise. I'd rather know than be left to imagine things.

Anna: Okay. Whatever. You know best. But seriously don't worry.

Mark: Easier said than done.

Anna: I'm heading to bed now. On my own. Take care and talk to me if you're unhappy, okay? I don't want to do anything to hurt you but I have to live my life as well. xx

He didn't reply. I went to bed. I struggled to sleep. Mark was bothering me. The imminent move was bothering me. But more than anything I was too excited about the morning. Just past midnight, Stef texted me. He was up late to bid on next month's rota so he could try to arrange flights around his childcare. We agreed to meet at 9am. I set my alarm for seven to give myself two hours to look my best. Chrissy would have suggested I should double that. We said goodnight and finally, some time in the early hours, I passed into a broken sleep.

Chapter 14

Thursday, February 21st, 2019

JUST before 9am, Stef sent a message. He was running late, as usual, and had to head home briefly before coming to me. I was used to that by now, so it didn't overly concern me. I was standing by my kitchen window, looking out across the car park, holding the fob to open the electric gate as soon as I saw him approach. The delay gave me a final chance to check my appearance, make sure everything was tidy, warm up the coffee machine, and make sure the distinctive aroma given off by dozens of cardboard packing boxes was suitably masked by scented candles.

But even having done all of that, I was back, standing at the window, long before he turned up. I pulled out my phone and opened my heart rate app. My normal resting heart rate is in the low fifties. By 10.43am it was up to 92bpm. And shortly after that, it probably went even higher as I saw his Golf turning into the street and heading towards the gate. I pressed the fob, and then went across to the car park to meet him.

We hugged. He apologised for being late, but I didn't care. It was so good to see him. I led him across to my flat, grateful that I lived on the ground floor, so didn't have to contend with stairs, as I'd literally gone weak at the knees.

Once the door was closed behind us, we had our first private kiss, unencumbered by the risk of being discovered by a passing member of the public. I showed him through to the front room and then disappeared back to the kitchen to make two cappuccinos.

"I find it hard to leave you alone," he said a moment later as he reappeared in the kitchen.

I smiled and we hugged again.

"I can't believe you're here."

I held his hand as the Nespresso machine did its magic.

"You're looking beautiful," he said. I may have blushed. I returned the compliment. The white shirt was sending me wild. It took every ounce of self-control not to start undoing the buttons.

My self-control evaporated when we returned to the sofa. We made small talk for about two minutes, but then couldn't resist any longer. The kisses became more passionate, the hands became more daring. I suggested moving to the bedroom so we would be more comfortable. The coffees were forgotten.

He followed me, and kissed my neck as I lit a candle. And then said something so unexpected, I wasn't sure if he was joking or not.

"I don't want to have sex."

I must have looked momentarily confused.

"It's quite a big step for me, and wouldn't feel right," he continued.

"Because of Molly?" I asked. He nodded. I tried to suppress my irritation, but equally part of me respected his values, albeit even if I didn't fully understand them. "That's okay. There's no rush, and no pressure."

"Thank you."

Nonetheless, I held his hand and pulled him down onto the bed. And over the next two hours, for someone who didn't want to have sex, he came spectacularly close. Buttons started to loosen. I reached for his belt. Within a few minutes we were naked, my most seductive lingerie largely discarded. Our mouths explored each other's bodies, leaving very little unkissed. He spent a fabulous amount of time between my legs, making me squirm with pleasure, his tongue and fingers working a magic that was only intensified by the thought that this was in some way forbidden. And then it was my turn to tease him, arouse him, and take him to the point of no return. I thought his resolve might weaken, and offered a condom, but he showed impressive and hugely frustrating resolve. He didn't object to being inside my mouth, though, and the effect was truly explosive.

As we began to relax, and our breathing returned to normal, I pulled the duvet over us, and snuggled into his naked body, feeling a closeness and intimacy that was beyond compare to any partner I could remember.

"That," I said, "was amazing."

He kissed me.

"I'm sorry about..." he began.

"Shhh." I ran my fingers through his hair, and down over his jawline. "You have to be ready. If it's not today, then hopefully some time soon. I just love being here with you. It's very early days. It has to be the right time."

After a while, I got up and made fresh cappuccinos. This time we drank them together, in bed, with his hands caressing my skin, making me tingle all over again.

"If you get your phone I'll show you something," he said as I snuggled into him. I reached out to my bedside table, hoping it would be there, but inevitably it wasn't.

"Are you going to make me get out of bed?" I asked.

He grinned.

"Second thoughts, I'll show you later." And then he kissed me again. But sadly there wasn't enough time to get any more intimate. Three hours had already passed and he would be leaving me soon. After one last giant hug, he announced reluctantly that it was time to get dressed.

I wrapped myself in my bathrobe and then headed to the bathroom to make sure my make-up wasn't in too bad a state. When I came back he was nearly ready. He took the cups out to the kitchen while I got dressed, then I handed him my phone.

"What did you want to show me?"

"Go to the App Store."

I did as requested, then he told me to type Flight Radar into the search box.

"The free version will do the trick."

I was prompted for my password, then the app downloaded, and a new icon appeared on my screen.

"I'll give you the flight numbers when I'm travelling and then you can track them, if you like. You can see where I am, and know when I'm landing."

He showed me how to do it. I was amazed by the terrifyingly large number of planes that were in the air at any one time.

"That'd be excellent," I said. But better than anything was the thought that he wanted me to follow him. I resolved to add the app to the Lust folder.

Stef reached for his jacket and scarf, and I walked him back to his car. He blew me a kiss as he drove away, and I thought of my mantra. *Someone that I was desperate to see again, the moment I said goodbye.*

Chapter 15

I RETURNED to the bedroom, convinced I could still detect his scent in the linen. I propped myself up on the pillows and sent him a message, thanking him for a wonderful morning. He replied, fifteen minutes later, with three kisses.

Chrissy, meanwhile, had been busy. There were multiple messages: asking me how it was going, telling me she could imagine me getting up to all sorts, and then letting me know that her offer to take him off my hands was still on the table, should it all prove too much.

I sent a quick reply saying all was good, but didn't go into the details.

The plan for the afternoon was to start packing boxes with the clothes I wouldn't need before the move, but my heart wasn't in it. So instead, I made a cup of Twinings Strong English Breakfast tea (which had recently eclipsed Yorkshire Gold as my favourite) and took it to my desk.

Normally, my business takes up so much of my time, there's barely enough for anything else, aside from a bit of writing, when I'm feeling creative. Shortly after the turn of the millennium, I took maternity leave from my old job, and never went back. Staying at home with a young daughter was truly enriching, but it also gave me time to evaluate my career, and I became overcome with the urge to stretch myself. With a background in fashion photography, and with contacts throughout the industry, I started an online clothes shop. Sales grew, and soon I was the managing director of my own company, employing staff, and discovering it wasn't all fast cars and expensive holidays.

Business has been tough in recent years, but we're just about hanging on in there. There's always too much to do. So, instead of packing, I spent the rest of the afternoon paying suppliers, writing emails, and working in Photoshop to produce graphics for a front page promotion.

My concentration was broken by the sound of my phone springing to life. I connected the call without any hesitation.

"Hi mum, how are things?" asked Charlotte. It was so lovely to hear from her.

"They're good, just all a bit hectic," I said.

"Are you all boxed up?"

"I'm getting there. There's still the kitchen and the front room to do. I can't wait to get sorted. It's chaotic."

"Do you need me to pop down next week to give you a hand?"

That made me instantly wary. She was up to something. I have a wonderful relationship with Charlotte. We've been through a lot together, and we're now best of friends as well as mother and daughter. But even so, the thought that she'd be willing to come to help me hadn't entered my head.

"No, I'm fine," I said. "There's not much anyone can do. But thank you, that's a lovely offer."

"If you're sure?"

"Yes, it'll be fine." I was waiting for the pay-off. "I can't wait for you to come to see me, though. I'm going to get you a new bed and make it like a little haven for the holidays."

"Ah." She paused. "That's what I've been meaning to discuss with you."

I sighed.

"Go on."

"I was thinking about Easter. I was planning on coming to stay but I don't know that I'll be able to. Not for more than a couple of days. I've been offered extra hours in the bar and I could do with the money."

"You mean you don't want to leave your boyfriend?"

She laughed.

"I can't believe you'd be so cynical."

"You can bring him with you if you like."

"Mum..."

"We're all grown-ups."

"I'll ask him. But we were also talking about going away for a week."

"While simultaneously working in the bar?"

"See? Now you're deliberately trying to confuse me. Trying to catch me out."

"Listen, my darling, you do what you want. I do understand the attractions of young love. Just be careful, okay?"

"Is this the condom chat?"

"I suspect we're way beyond that. I mean if you go away. Keep your wits about you. I know you will."

"I will. I'll let you know nearer the time. Okay?"

"Of course."

We chatted for a few more minutes, about her course, people I'd probably never get to meet, and then she said she had to go because some friends were coming to take her to a party. I didn't get the chance to tell her about Stef. But equally, I wasn't sure quite what I'd say.

He was never far from my thoughts. Later that evening we were back sending each other as many messages as normal.

Anna: I hope you're okay... I know we crossed a boundary today but it felt so good.

Stef: Yes, we did. It took a lot of restraint not to cross it further...

Anna: Indeed. But there's no rush despite the enthusiasm. Did you tell Molly?

Stef: I did, but not all of the details. Some of the things are yours to share rather than mine, so I didn't want to break any confidence. She wasn't pleased but there was a good discussion.

Anna: I understand. But I am happy for you to say anything about me, or anything we do, if it helps the situation. I'm quite a private person but I understand the importance of openness and honesty.

Stef: She wasn't happy because I hadn't mentioned I was coming beforehand. My fault.

Anna: It's good that you confessed. It's not a secret then. I'm sure it's easy to do the wrong thing with the best of intentions.

Stef: It is. xx

Chapter 16

Friday, February 22nd - Wednesday, February 27th, 2019

I KNEW I wouldn't get to see him over the weekend. He was scheduled for a transatlantic double-header the following week, starting with a flight to Philadelphia on the Monday. Understandably, he wanted to spend time with his children, and of course they always had to be the priority - especially as he was going to be away from them all week.

I was desperate to see him again, though, not least for the reassurance that he had no regrets about what had happened. The more I thought about it, the more it concerned me. I could only imagine the pressure from Molly intensifying, and the thought of losing him now was heartbreaking.

But, as ever, his messages served to reassure me, telling me I was lovely, how he wanted to undress me, that he would like to get back under my duvet, the naughty things he'd had to do when he woke up thinking of me in the middle of the night, and how he'd continued to have seriously non-platonic thoughts about what he wanted to do when we met again.

He mentioned that he was supposed to be taking the children

to see Molly on the Sunday, but there was a change of plan, and instead she was coming to visit him at home. Aside from one message to say I was thinking of him, and hoped he had a lovely time, I left him alone, giving them time together. At least I had the reassurance that she wasn't whisking him off to the bedroom if the children were there.

Once she'd finally left, he sent me a message.

Stef: It wasn't good. She needs to go through the learning and adjustment phase that I've been through, and practise what she preaches. But I definitely want to see you. I'd like us to arrange some dates. I don't want you to feel like you're the reserve.

We wished each other good night. He had an early start and a demanding week ahead.

The back-to-back trips are particularly exhausting. This time he was flying to Philadelphia on Monday, back on Tuesday to arrive in the early hours of Wednesday. Then, after one night in the UK, it was out to New York on Thursday before a late flight home on the Friday.

He told me he'd arranged to stay with Molly on the night back home, even though he was officially supposed to stay at a hotel. She lived within easy driving distance of Heathrow. But no matter how much that unsettled me, I had too many other things to think about.

I was due to pick up the keys to my new flat on Tuesday, then spend the day there on Wednesday, cleaning and waiting for the BT engineer to install the broadband. The removal company was booked for Thursday. The thought of moving was daunting, but the prospect of being a ten-minute walk away from where I was fairly sure Stef lived, made all of the efforts worthwhile.

———

Despite our respective workloads and the time differences, the messages continued to flow, and we even managed a phone call from Philadelphia. He confessed that he'd had a conversation with Molly in which she appeared to be breaking up with him, although it still wasn't confirmed. As ever, I was conflicted. I asked more questions about their relationship and how much they meant to each other, because there was still so much I didn't understand. But he just said they were boyfriend and girlfriend, and it would have been intrusive to press the point further.

But on the Wednesday night he still went to stay with her. More worrying than the thought of them sleeping together was the thought that I would be the subject of their conversation, and that Molly would try her damnedest to talk him out of seeing me. I had to be up early for the removal company, but I struggled to sleep through. Just past 3am I sent a message.

Anna: And so, I woke up about an hour ago and ever since, I've been lying here, thinking of you, picturing you, wondering how you are, wondering how things went last night, wishing you were here instead of there, but nevertheless, hoping you had a good time together and that you went to bed with peace within your heart.

And although the alarm is set for 6.30, and I really should go back to sleep, I'm thinking of you waking up at 4.30 with a demanding day ahead, wondering how you'll feel, whether you'll be happy, hoping above all else that you will be. And although I'm going to regret lying awake in the middle of the night when the alarm goes off, right at this moment I can't think of anything more special or feel any greater privilege than knowing that I can lie here thinking of you and just how incredibly lucky I am to know you.

So please take care today, fly safely and know that wherever you are, whichever bed, whichever country, whatever your mood, you have a very special place right here, in my heart, and that while of course I would love nothing more than to be waking with you at 4.30, to give you a lingering kiss farewell, I'm there with you in spirit. Holding you, supporting you, admiring you, and dreaming of the time when we can be together again. Big hugs. I'm missing you. xx

He replied at just past 4.30am with dozens of kisses. I had a proper reply from the plane's on-board Wi-Fi when he was somewhere mid-Atlantic.

Stef: Sorry for the delay. Your beautiful words have been on my mind all morning, but I had to wait till now to have time for a proper reply. How come you struggled to sleep? Because I was with Molly?

Anna: A combination of things really. Definitely that but also knowing I had to be up early for the move. More just thinking about you and Molly and hoping you were okay. It's what I said in the message really.

Stef: I worry that I cause you emotional trauma.

Anna: You don't. It's okay. Hopefully, once she's through this phase and things settle down, it'll be much smoother. I'll know that if you're there, you're happy. The concern at the moment is that if she's unhappy or stressing you or threatening to finish things then I worry about the effect on you.

Stef: You are so sweet. xxx

Normally being called sweet has a similar effect on me to being called cute, but coming from Stef, it sounded like a compliment.

Chapter 17

Thursday, February 21st, 2019

I SPENT all day with the removal company. My old flat was on the ground floor, but the new one was on the second, and while the whole process should have been simple, a stuck lift caused all sorts of delays in the unloading. They were due to finish by 5pm but it was closer to nine when they finally left me on my own, in the midst of chaos, with no idea where anything was, apart from their invoice, showing a hefty extra charge for the overtime.

I'd labelled every box, explaining which room it belonged in, but that had been largely ignored. There was barely an inch of uncluttered floor space. My L-shaped sofa was in four separate parts, none of which were actually in a position to sit on. And, to make matters worse, I'd spent two hours on the phone to the bank, trying to get them to make a payment to a supplier in the USA that should have gone out two days previously, but which had yet to leave the company account.

I had no idea where my bed linen was, so I was a long way off being able to go to sleep. On the back of a restless night, I was exhausted, stressed and hungry. I looked up the address of the nearest Domino's. I very rarely have a Domino's pizza, but there's a time and a place, and this was both. And while I waited for it to be prepared, I popped into the nearest newsagent. I very rarely smoke, either, but sometimes a cigarette is entirely justified.

There was an elderly man on the stairs as I made my way back.

"Are you just moving in?" he said.

The pizza was getting cold. I was tired. I wanted to be polite and friendly, but now wasn't the time.

"I am. Pleased to meet you. I'm Anna." I reached out my spare hand to shake his. "It's been a bit chaotic. I'll be glad when I get to bed." I carried on walking.

"You must come and say hello when you get properly settled," he said. "I'm upstairs at the back. I can tell you all you need to know."

He winked, and then told me his name, but I wasn't really listening. I was desperate to get my key in the door.

The only bright spot of the whole day was a call from Stef in New York, although he didn't have long because he was going out for a meal with colleagues. I finally got to bed just past 4am, but still didn't sleep well in the alien surroundings of the new bedroom. There was so much to do, but all I really wanted was a hug.

His next message came while he was en route to JFK for the return flight home.

Stef: How are things? Are you settled yet?
   Anna: Don't even ask. It's chaos.

Stef: That bad?

Anna: It's going to take ages. The stress of yesterday was horrendous. Don't tell me off, but I even resorted to cigarettes by the end!

Stef: Why would I tell you off? That's sexy.

Anna: Haha, it didn't feel sexy last night.

Stef: Well, if you have one anywhere near me, I'll be forced to kiss you.

Anna: Ooh, I'll bear that in mind. :-)

Stef: Are you busy today?

Anna: Yes, ridiculously. There are so many boxes. I don't really know where to start.

Stef: I wish I was there to help you.

Anna: Ah, that would be lovely. I can't wait to show you. It'll all feel a bit more real then. I'd love to think you'll become a frequent visitor and we could have happy times together, here and out and about. I dare to dream, and I know that's a risk, and I will probably end up with a broken heart, but just now it seems like a risk that is worth taking. xx

Stef: Thank you, that sounds wonderful. I can't wait to see it. I'm sure everything will be okay. I want to avoid broken hearts for any of us. xx

Sometimes we don't always get what we want.

I knuckled down to relentless unpacking, and gradually the flat started to take shape. Once I started to collapse empty cardboard boxes and load them into my car, clear floor space emerged, and I started to be able to arrange things. There was still a lot to do, but I was getting there.

I texted Mark to tell him about the move, and to check he was okay. He seemed much better. He'd been on a date, although apparently it wasn't going to lead to anything. He said he still missed me, and asked when he could come to visit. We didn't set

a date, but agreed to arrange one, once things calmed do
I'd made the book deadline. He was in a much happier mood.

Fundamentally, though, I was still desperate to see Stef. And yet, over a week since that wonderful morning in bed together, I was no closer. Molly had visited on the Sunday, he'd stayed with her midweek, and now the weekend was upon us, he was going to stay with her again.

I found it hard to picture them together. The mad-haired hippy woman and my beautiful, sophisticated, international jet-setter, together in a remote farmhouse. What did they even find to talk about?

No matter how I tried to rationalise it, I was starting to feel short-changed. I knew that those arrangements had been made long before I'd arrived on the scene. I knew that his time was precious, and in short supply. I knew it was important that they had time to sort out their problems. And I understood that by its very nature, a polyamorous relationship would always bring challenges, and that I had so much still to learn. But equally, it just didn't seem fair. I'd have given anything in the world to see him, if for only ten minutes, just to hold his hand. But I couldn't have that, and instead he was spending his fourth day and second night with her since I'd last felt the touch of his body.

I began to question whether I was really cut out for this. Yes, he'd had a huge impact on me. My feelings for him were stronger than I'd had for anyone I could remember. And when we were together it was wonderful. But at the same time, I wanted him to want me as much as I wanted him, because otherwise I was only ever going to be deluding myself. And despite the wonderful messages I couldn't shake the doubts that perhaps I was nothing more than a diversion. Someone filling a need to reset the balance in his already complicated love life, but no bigger a priority than that.

Maybe he sensed my discomfort. He told me to feel free to

send messages all weekend, and then asked if he could come to see me at my new flat on the Sunday evening, and bring Champagne as a toast.

I was perhaps less enthusiastic than I should have been. Yes, I was looking forward to seeing him, and excited by the thought of showing him round, but there were things I would have to say, to clear the air, and put my mind at rest. I spent the next three days arranging the flat, while simultaneously running that conversation through my mind. It wasn't a question of giving him an ultimatum. I just wanted to know where I stood.

In a fit of pique, fed up with the relentless unpacking, and in the hope of taking my mind off Stef, I agreed to go on a platonic date with another of my long-term Tinder matches. It was a last-minute decision, but Craig lived within a twenty minute drive and he was another who might become a good friend. I'd been putting him off, through no fault of his own, but even without Stef, I'd hardly had any free time for weeks.

His surname was Almond. I'd always wondered if he was related to Marc Almond from Soft Cell, but decided it would be too unoriginal to ask. Didn't stop me hoping though.

I sent him a message on Saturday morning. I explained I was still super-busy, and it would only get worse with the imminent book deadline, but I could be free for a couple of hours that evening. If nothing else, I was curious to see him in person. To check for a family resemblance.

We agreed a time, and a location in a car park, and then would walk to a pub from there.

"We meet at last," he said, once I'd parked up.

"Indeed." First impressions were good, but inconclusive. We did the cheek-kissing thing and I gave him a hug. I'd expected him to be about six foot four, but he was slightly shorter than that, which meant I had to stretch less than I'd feared. Perhaps I was getting him confused with someone else. I've read so many profiles, they tend to all blur after a while. He was a similar height to Stef, in fact, and that wasn't his only resemblance. His hair was a bit lighter, but cut to much the same length, and he had a similar amount of stubble. I'm nothing if not consistent.

He returned from the bar with two glasses of wine.

"So, do you have any brothers or sisters?" I asked, reaching a new low in dating chat, but nevertheless with an ulterior motive. Which he saw through immediately.

"Sadly not. Is this where you wave goodbye, so soon after saying hello, and I go back to bedsit land, my only home?" he asked with a smirk. "How about you? Much success on the love front or always tainted?"

"You're good," I said, raising my glass. The teenagers on the next table would have missed the song references, unless they had really cool parents. "But if you call me a sex dwarf I may take umbrage."

He put his hand up for a high five, but I avoided it on the grounds of not being American. It was about the only thing he did wrong, though. He was charming and chivalrous, good to talk to, and in many ways just my type: in reasonable shape, with lovely eyes, a good dress sense and no discernible weirdness. Normally I'd have been more enthusiastic. But all the time, I felt a strange, unsettling sensation, knowing that however attractive and entertaining he was, I didn't feel the same immediate and overpowering spark. I followed the wine with a Diet Coke and then drove home.

By the time I arrived, he'd sent me an articulate message, saying it had been a pleasure to meet me, and asking if he could do it again. My reply was equally courteous. I would love to, I said, at some stage, although I couldn't promise a date just yet, given the imminent deadline. In the interim, though, we should definitely keep in touch. He was a lovely man, which is a rarity in Tinderland. But despite some physical similarities, he wasn't Stef.

I sent Chrissy a message, more out of a sense of fun than anything:

Anna: I think I'm developing a "type". Stubble, nice arms. Long story, but Stef substitute alert. Let me know when you're free and I'll bring you up to speed.

She replied ten minutes later.

Chrissy: Sounds deliciously sordid. You've always liked arms. Details required xx

———

The man himself, meanwhile, appeared to be missing me, and had sent several messages while I was out. I didn't think it would do him any harm to wait for a reply. But once I was in bed I succumbed. He replied almost immediately.

Stef: Hey, Ms Gorgeous. How is your weekend?

Anna: Busy but I'm getting there. I've just been out for a drink with a friend.

Stef: That's nice. You deserve a break. How was it?

Anna: It was okay. Just weird really. I didn't feel very enthusiastic. She was good company but all the time I kept thinking how much I'd rather it was you.

Stef: Ah, that's lovely. I'm touched. Did you tell her you wished she was somebody else?

Anna: Haha no, but I think she thought I looked distracted. I blamed it on a lack of sleep.

Stef: I'm definitely with you there. I feel exhausted.

Anna: I'm not surprised. I don't know how you do it.

Stef: Years of practice I suppose. I'm looking forward to having a few days off after next week.

Anna: I can imagine. I do worry about you. I didn't know it was possible to have so many thoughts about someone.

Stef: Care to share?

Anna: There's a lot I'd like to share with you...

Stef: Interesting xxx

I left it at that. But then, perhaps unwisely, sent a much longer sequence of messages in the early hours of Sunday morning.

Anna: So... Things I want to share with you: thoughts, dreams, fantasies, days, evenings, nights, hopes, frustrations, life, good times, bad times, wine, my bed, coffee, your bed, evenings out, evenings in, laughter, ideas, theories, 2019, mornings, travel, friends, books, adventures, this flat, chocolate, cocktails, trust, truth, sex, more than 2019, aspirations, the sofa, excitement, love, cuddles, giggles, more cuddles, history, orgasms, experiences, memories, successes, fears, failures, and ultimately the understanding that when I'm with you, I'm with the one person in the world who's completely blown my mind.

I wasn't going to write an essay but I spend all day thinking about you, wondering where you are, what you're doing, if you're happy, having sex, being respected, being cared for, enjoying life, staying safe, what you're thinking, and what, exactly, I mean to you.

And therein lies the potential for the broken heart. Time away from you makes me realise just how much I miss you, how much I yearn for you, and how much respect and admiration I have for you. But equally, when your time is so precious, I never want to burden you with expectation.

I don't know what you will think when you read this. I don't want you to worry about me. I just want you to know how I feel. To know that I have that almighty sense of elation whenever I hear from you, and that I'm happy with the thought that you are part of my life, in whatever limited form. But I also want you to know that while I will never disrespect you, question your relationship with Molly, or take you for granted, I simply would love to see you more.

So yes, there are lots of things I want to share with you. But the biggest and most important of all is time. xx

I went to bed, wondering if I'd done the right thing. Knowing that I'd exposed my emotions. Knowing that I'd made myself vulnerable. But equally knowing that if it scared him off and caused him to finish things, then perhaps it would be better for all of us, however difficult that could be in the short term.

I woke up on Sunday and immediately looked for a reply, but the message still had two grey ticks. He hadn't read it. What was he doing? Having a lie in? Having sex? Maybe just mundane "couple" things like going to the shop and tidying the house?

Eventually, at nearly 1pm, he responded.

Stef: I am extremely touched by the things you said. We should definitely talk about them this evening xx

Anna: Just a thought... Would you like me to pick you up? That could be nice xx

Stef: Actually I've not had a drink for a while and I'll be bringing Champagne. But don't worry - I'll get a taxi. I'm very excited at the thought of seeing you. xxx

. . .

Admittedly, part of my motivation in offering was to finally see where he lived. That still a source of mystery. But we arranged to meet at the Old Corn Exchange at 9.30pm, and then walk back to mine from there.

By 9pm the flat was almost presentable - with the exception of the chaos in the spare bedroom. I was freshly out of the shower and ready with time to spare.

Chapter 18

Sunday, March 3rd, 2019

ANY doubts I'd had evaporated the moment I saw him approach me across the Market Place. He looked like a rock star. He was carrying a bag. He smiled and we hugged, and it was like we'd never been apart.

I led him on the short walk to my flat, then up to the second floor. I gave him the brief guided tour, then he presented me with two mini-bottles of airline Champagne. I took glasses from the cupboard, which he suggested putting in the freezer for a moment to enhance their aesthetic appeal. We kissed while we waited, then he poured the drinks, watched while the glasses frosted beautifully, and took them through to the front room. I joined him on the sofa, but deliberately kept a small distance between us.

"So," I said. "I can't believe you're actually here."

"I can't believe how lovely it looks already. I love the mirror."

My eyes followed his to the back of the room.

"Do you think a room gets brighter when there's a mirror?" he asked.

"I don't know. I've never really thought about it. I suppose so, if it reflects the light."

"But does it though? You've got a lightbulb. It gives off light. Then in the mirror, you've got another lightbulb, giving off the same amount of light, so in theory it should be twice as bright. But I don't think it is. I can't get my head round it."

I gave him my "are you slightly bonkers" look.

"Any plans for a house-warming?" he continued.

"God no. You haven't met my friends yet. They'd trash it. I'm going to invite them one at a time, for private viewings, starting with the sexy male ones." I winked.

"Your pilot?"

"What? No! I meant you."

"But you have lots of sexy male friends?"

I shrugged and winked.

"I've got a few." I hoped it sounded mysterious and flirty, rather than challenging, but I think it was lost in translation. It was time to change the subject. "How are the girls? It must be tough being away from them so long."

It has his turn to shrug.

"It's not ideal, but it's the job."

"Are you on good terms with their mum?"

"Not really."

That was the end of that. We both took a sip of the Champagne, to deflect the awkwardness.

"There are a few things I need to say," I said at last.

He nodded, waiting for me to continue.

"I know I sent you those messages last night, but I don't want to worry you. I just wanted you to know how I feel."

"The messages were lovely. I like that you're open and honest with me."

"But I don't want you to think that I'm pressuring you."

"You're not."

"And I don't want you to think that I'm jealous of Molly. I do find it hard, though, to think of her seeing you so often, when I can't even meet you for half an hour for coffee."

"I know." He reached out a hand to touch my knee. It felt good, but part of me was worried he'd snag my best tights. "And I apologise. It's not always like this, but she's got more demanding since I met you. It's changing, though. We will have lots more time together soon."

I covered his hand with mine, and squeezed it.

"I'm not asking for exclusivity. I'm not giving you an ultimatum," I said. "I know I won't see you very often, but I would like to plan things with you. I know it may be only once or twice a month, and I'm happy with that, as long as I know that you want it too."

"I do. But we should be able to see each other every week, if you'd like to," he said.

"Really?"

"Yes, now you're closer."

"Wow. I'd love that. I wasn't expecting it."

He leaned towards me and put his arm around my shoulder, drawing me in. Then he kissed me, and part of me melted.

"Okay, so should we set some ground rules?" I asked when we parted.

"Such as?"

"Such as: you can assume I'm okay if I don't say anything. If I ever have a problem with you and Molly I will let you know."

"That seems good."

"But likewise, you must always be honest with me. If I am a burden to you, you need to tell me."

"You're not a burden to me."

"That's good to know. But if I ever am."

"Okay."

The smile returned.

"I've got you a couple of housewarming presents," he said, thankfully changing the subject. From his bag he pulled two packages, both of which were beautifully gift-wrapped. "They're from New York."

An even bigger part of me melted. The knowledge that he'd been thinking of me while on his travels was intoxicating. I unwrapped the gifts. There was a desk organiser, which would prove extremely useful. Less useful, but fun, was a novelty kitten bag clip that made a miaow noise when I squeezed it. His expression seemed to be seeking approval.

"That's so kind," I said. And I smiled. And right then he could have made me do anything he wanted.

"And I got you a card."

The card was beautiful too. It spoke of building happy memories together in my new home. My heart was won. We drank more Champagne. He topped up our glasses.

"Do you still have the cigarettes?" he asked.

"I do. I only had a couple."

"Do you want one now?"

"Now?"

"You should get them. I'll join you."

"You don't smoke."

"You could lead me astray."

"Haha. I could think of better ways to lead you astray."

A few minutes later, we were standing on my balcony. He asked me to blow smoke into his mouth. It was one of the most erotic things I'd ever done. A few minutes after that we were in the bedroom. And almost immediately we were naked and he was back to kissing every inch of me.

But we still didn't have sex, despite coming even closer than before, much to my frustration.

"Next time," he said. "I promise."

I didn't want to push it. Every inch of me desired him, but it could only be when he was ready. Instead I ran my fingers over his body, kissed him, and felt safe and happy in his arms. We chatted in an open and intimate way, about the things we enjoyed, the things we'd like to do with each other.

Then, we discussed his childhood in Italy, and his ex-wife and their painful divorce. In turn, I told him about my daughter, Charlotte, and then Chrissy, Mark, Ben, and other friends I'd made on dating apps. I revealed how Chrissy was single, and teased him that she was keen for us to fail so she could take over. How Mark hadn't taken things well, and still thought we should be together. And how Ben had mentioned his pilot theory that all hosties were nutjobs. Stef laughed. I felt so incredibly relaxed. Eventually I drifted off.

I don't know how long I was asleep, but I was suddenly aware he was no longer beside me. I reached out, panicking, but as my eyes fully opened, I saw him sitting on the end of the bed, sadly fully clothed, but smiling at me.

"You look beautiful when you're sleeping," he said.

I seriously doubted that, and was extremely nervous about the state of my make-up, but he hadn't made a run for it, so that was reassuring.

"You look like you're ready to leave," I said.

"Sadly, but it's already gone one o'clock. I've got an early start tomorrow."

"Really? Time flies." That explained falling asleep. "Dare I ask when I can see you again?"

He frowned in thought.

"I'm flying to Washington on Tuesday till Friday, which is a lot longer than normal. Then, I hardly dare say it, but at the weekend I've promised I'll help Molly decorate the farmhouse. But then

I'm back for a couple of days, then New York again, and a childcare weekend. But after that I've got a week of leave and then nearly two weeks on standby. There's nothing booked for any of it."

"Not even with Molly?"

"No, definitely nothing with Molly. I want to spend time with you. I think I need to make it up to you."

"So which week's that?" I was finding it all too hard to follow.

"The one starting the 18th."

"Of March?"

He nodded. It sounded perfect.

"Do you need a hand with the decorating?" I didn't expect him to say yes, but I had to offer - primarily because it would cut short the wait, and also because I was ever more curious to meet Molly, to try to discover her secret powers of attraction.

"Actually she'd be okay with that. I'm sure she'd love to meet you. But... I think I'd find it awkward."

"We'd be competing to kiss you." That sounded weird as soon as I said it. Luckily he laughed.

"So hopefully the start of next week, before New York, and then any time you like, the week after, if you're free?" he said.

"I'm sure I will be. Let me know. And very safe travels in the meantime."

I asked him to pass me my bathrobe and then I showed him to the door. I glanced in the mirror in the hallway on the way through. It could have been worse. I kissed him goodbye. I didn't think the warm glow would ever leave me.

About an hour later, I got a message. I was still awake, trying to write the new book.

Stef: I'm finally heading to bed, inspired by happy thoughts. If any further evidence was needed (it isn't), tonight was proof that you have amazing powers. I loved seeing you. Every single minute.

Anna: And likewise. I'm sure that there will be challenges ahead but once Molly realises that I'm not a threat and I'm not trying to steal you, then we could have wonderful times together without any anxiety or feelings of conflict. For as long as you want me, I'm yours. xxx

Chapter 19

Monday, March 4th - Tuesday, March 5th, 2019

I WOKE on Monday with a renewed sense of purpose. After spending the last two weeks consumed by the move, I was way behind on work. There were still boxes to unpack, but I had to prioritise the day job. And I was miles behind on the book deadline. But knowing I was going to have a week on my own, and that Stef and I were in such a happy place, gave me a sense of well-being that served as the ideal motivation.

But as the day wore on, and the to-do list was gradually whittled down, Stef took me by surprise.

Stef: Can I see you tonight? Just for a quick drink? I won't have long, but I would love to see you before I go.

    Anna: Of course! Do you want me to come there? Are you happy to come here? Or meet in a pub?

    Stef: I'll come to you, if that's okay. It'll just be for half an hour or so. Would 8 be okay?

    Anna: Perfect. That's a lovely bonus! See you then xxx

. . .

I had a couple of hours to prepare, so dashed to Waitrose. I put together a giftbag for him, with chocolates and a magazine, to give him something to read while he was waiting for the new book.

By the time he arrived, I was freshly showered. We kissed and I gave him the presents. He looked taken aback.

"Thank you. That is so lovely, and so thoughtful," he said. "You make me feel very special."

I secretly wondered when Molly had last done something so romantic. I couldn't help a certain smugness, but I think I managed to hide it.

True to his word, it was only a flying visit, but it meant all the more for that. It was as though he'd listened to my comment about having half an hour free for coffee, and he was making the effort.

Better still, we arranged a date to see *The Comedy About A Bank Robbery* at a theatre in London, at the start of his week of leave. He had his arm round my shoulder while I ordered the tickets on my laptop. I'm forty-nine but I felt like a lovestruck teenager again. It was tremendously exciting to have something confirmed in the diary. It felt like the dawning of something tangible. I couldn't have been happier.

Then, our time was up. I walked him back to his car, and gave him a final kiss farewell.

The next morning I woke up to the popcorn sound on my phone.

Stef: Good morning Ms Gorgeous.

Anna: Buongiorno! xx

Stef: Oh, you speak Italian now?

Anna: Haha, far from it, but I may start on Duolingo to try to impress you. What time are you flying?

Stef: I report at half three.

Anna: Do you need a hand lifting your heavy suitcase into the car? (I know you won't but I have to try.)

Stef: You're okay, but thank you! Molly has decided to come with me because it's an extended trip. I'm picking her up at one.

That rocked my world. I waited a minute before replying.

Anna: Wow... I hope you have a wonderful time. Can't deny I'm envious.... Don't let her talk you out of wanting to see me.

Stef: I won't. Sorry that you're envious.

Anna: Can I call you?

Stef: Give me five minutes.

Those five minutes were interminable. My mind was on overdrive. The thought of them together for four full days, followed by the weekend, was almost unbearable. But far worse was the obvious implication. She was staking her claim. Of course she'd be doing everything in her power to get him to end things with me. Well, I wasn't going to give up without a fight.

He rang me before I had the chance to dial his number.

"So, are you okay with that?" I asked.

"About Molly coming? Not really," he said.

"So why is she?"

"Because it's an extended trip. It doesn't make sense when it's only one night."

"But is everything okay now?"

"Between us?"

"Between you and Molly."

"It's... I don't know how to explain really. It's been very emotional. There have been lots of tears."

"But it's such a bloody injustice. She's the one with other men." I was fighting hard to keep my cool, but struggling.

"I know."

The struggle was getting harder.

"She's bound to put the pressure on."

"But I have my own mind. I told you. I want to see you, whatever she says."

I don't know if that made it better or worse.

"That's lovely," I said, "but then it's going to be so stressful for you, having somebody having a go at you for six days solid."

"Hopefully it won't be like that."

"I hope so, for your sake. Can I still send you messages while you're away?"

"Of course."

"It won't be awkward?"

"No, she knows I message you."

"Okay. I just don't know what to do, though. I don't want to inflame the situation by writing to you when you're in a hotel together. Every time I do that it's going to start her off."

"All I can say is, just be you, and send messages like normal. If she gets angry then I'll have to deal with it."

"But then you'll have a horrible time."

"I think that's inevitable."

"So why is she going then?"

"I couldn't stop her."

"Oh, that's so frustrating."

"I know. But what could I do?"

I could think of lots of things he could do, but none of them would fit the strict definition of not wanting to cause problems between them. The next six days were going to be torture.

"I wish it was you coming instead," he continued. "I'd so much prefer that."

"Hopefully one day."

"We will, I'm sure."

It felt like we were co-conspirators, united against a common foe. I changed the subject, but ended the call soon after. And as I pressed the red button to disconnect, I wondered if I'd ever speak to him again.

Chapter 20

Tuesday, March 5th - Wednesday, March 6th, 2019

THAT evening, the torture began. I knew he was flying. I knew she was on board the plane. I suspected he'd even have given her an upgrade. That wound me up more than it ever should have done.

On Wednesday I sent a couple of messages, but far fewer than normal. And his replies were equally intermittent. The time difference didn't help, of course. He apologised, saying he knew it must be hard for me, but he had very little phone battery, and was constantly on the go or in her company.

I tried to leave him alone, but I felt dreadful. I just wanted to know that he was okay. That he wasn't having a horrible time. That she wasn't tightening the screw of emotional blackmail. I couldn't face food. I felt physically sick at the thought that she'd be working so hard to break my heart, in such a blatantly hypocritical way.

I battled with it all day. Barely a minute passed without worrying, thinking the worst. Picturing them arguing. Imagining the venom in her words, directed at me. By early evening I felt even worse. I sent a message:

Anna: How's it going? I hope you're okay. I'm worried about you xx

He didn't reply. I opened a bottle of wine, instead of eating, and tried to immerse myself in my writing. But the words wouldn't flow. My mind was elsewhere, thousands of miles away, being tortured by proxy.

Eventually, I texted Chrissy. She replied almost immediately

Anna: Are you around? I think I need a shoulder to cry on.
Chrissy: Just heading out. What's up? Man trouble?
Anna: How did you guess? But it's complicated.
Chrissy: You haven't ditched him?
Anna: No, not as such.
Chrissy: That's a shame, I'm still waiting for a go.
Anna: You don't give up, do you? I should have known better than to turn to you.
Chrissy: I'm sorry, I was joking.
Anna: That's okay. Sorry I'm not really in a jokey mood.
Chrissy: What then?
Anna: It's a long story but his other girlfriend is causing problems. They're away together.
Chrissy: Not good. You know what you should do? Call up one of your fuckbuddies and try to shag him out of your system. And if that doesn't work, at least you've had sex. Good plan?
Anna: It's a plan but I'm not sure it's a good one. But listen, if you're going out, have fun and I'll catch you later.
Chrissy: Okay. Chin up. I'll message you tomorrow. x

. . .

I texted Ben, but it got the single grey tick that meant his phone was turned off. Of my three closest friends, that left Mark. And that wasn't a conversation to take lightly. An hour later I took the plunge. At least he'd give me an honest opinion. And he'd been much happier last time I'd spoken to him.

Anna: Hi and how are things? Any news on the date?

Mark: Hi. Which one?

Anne: Has there been more than one? The one you were telling me about last week.

Mark: Oh, that one. Confession time. She didn't exist. I made her up to try to make you jealous.

Anna: What???

Mark: Did it work?

Anna: I don't know whether to laugh or call the police. :-)

Mark: I'll take that as a "no" then.

I refilled my wine glass. It was flattering, in a way, that he was trying to make me jealous, but I was sad that he hadn't met someone.

Anna: I wouldn't be jealous. I'd be very happy for you. You know deep down I'm not right for you. I'm pretty sure I'm not right for anyone.

Mark: Apart from Stef, who I'm already suspicious of, because he's got a girl's name.

Anna: It's short for Stefano. He's Italian.

Mark: Oh my God. This gets worse.

Anna: Why is that worse?

Mark: I'm not one to generalise, but he'll be all smooth Latin charm and sexy accents, and then the rest of us will never get a look in.

Anna: Yeah, well I'm not sure you've got much to worry about there. It's a very, very complicated situation.

Mark: Don't tell me: he's married? He's got you pregnant?

Anna: No, he's not married and we've not done anything that could get me pregnant, even if that was still physically possible.

Mark: Right.

Anna: It's true!

Mark: So why is it complicated? Tell your Uncle Mark.

Anna: Are you sure you want to know? You're not going to go all weird and jealous?

Mark: Me? As if. Fire away. I can be your voice of reason.

And so I took a metaphorical deep breath and told him all about Stef. About Molly. About my flirtation with the mysterious world of polyamory. But then about the deep hypocrisy coming from the other side of the equation, and the fact they were currently in Washington together. About how I, of all people, normally shied away from relationships and any form of commitment, precisely because I didn't have much time, and never wanted to experience heartbreak, but how I had unwittingly made myself vulnerable, and risked losing everything for some great injustice.

It felt good to get it off my chest, but I knew, as I was saying it, that it would be hard for anyone else to understand. Especially Mark. Eventually I wound it up.

Anna: So there you go. Complicated. It's fantastic when we're together, but it's harder than I thought. And the thing that makes it hardest is that I'm willing to accept the situation, but the mad hippy who started the whole polyamory thing is the one who now seems to have the biggest problem with it.

Mark: Wow.

Anna: Are you shocked?

Mark: I don't know if shocked is the word. I think he sounds like a dick.

Anna: I knew you were going to say something like that.

Mark: But he's pissing you about, and that makes me really angry.

Anna: I know. But it's not like that when we're together. When we're together it's lovely.

Mark: But he doesn't want to have sex with you, out of some loyalty to her?

Anna: It's just about boundaries, isn't it? It's a giant leap. I've told him there's no rush.

Mark: Oh come on! He's behaving like a bastard.

Anna: You can't say that. You don't know him.

Mark: Okay, answer me this then. When did this Molly book the ticket to fly to Washington?

Anna: I don't know. He didn't say. I didn't think to ask.

Mark: But he told you when? Nine o'clock yesterday morning, four hours before he was due to pick her up?

Anna: Yes.

Mark: Well there you go then. It's not the sort of thing you can do at the last minute. That was planned. They've known about it, but he didn't think to tell you. I hate to say it but they're laughing behind your back.

Anna: I can see why you think that. But really, it's not like that when we're together.

But his remark hit home. Of course it was pre-planned, and that made everything ten times worse.

Mark: You said it yourself. He's always there. I don't want to be the bad guy here, because I care about you more than you'd ever know, but he's playing with you. Messing with your emotions. It's cruel.

Anna: But that's because all those things were already arranged. When it all calms down, I'm sure it'll change. We've already booked a night at the theatre. We're going to have lots more opportunities to spend time together after the next New York trip. But I'm the first person to say I don't want to see someone four or five nights a week anyway.

Mark: I think you're deluding yourself.

Anna: But you don't know what it's like when we're together. We've sent each other over 3,000 messages. Probably nearly 7,000 between us. That's an entire book's worth. It's not as though I've just met him. It's nearly two years in total, and we've been chatting non-stop for the last four months.

I didn't know who I was trying to persuade more.

Mark: Do you want to know what I think?

Anna: Go on.

Mark: I think you've fallen in love. But not with a real person. You've fallen in love with the person you think he is. But that person doesn't exist. He's just an illusion, created by some narcissistic bastard, fuelled by a desire to control and manipulate. And I don't know whether it was deliberately callous and cruel or just insensitive, but the real person has no regard for your feelings. Stop me if I go too far.

Anna: No, go on.

Mark: He's treating you as a plaything to use and abuse while it serves his purpose. To get back at somebody else. But the tragedy is that he's fucked with your emotions and that makes me apoplectic. You should tell me where he lives and I'll go and have a word for you.

Anna: I don't know where he lives.

Mark: What?

Anna: I know the street, I think. But he's never actually told me his address. I've never been invited round. I've offered to pick him up a few times but he always drives or gets a taxi.

Mark: This gets worse and worse. And yet he's been to yours?

Anna: Yes, several times. Both here and before I moved.

Mark: I didn't think I could get more angry. He's taking the piss.

Anna: I know that's what it looks like, and believe me, I've thought that too. But when we see each other, and we're together, it's like there's a chemistry. I'm sure everything's going to change.

Mark: Seriously, though, it isn't.

Anna: You can't say that. You're only looking at the bad points.

Mark: And you're giving him the benefit of the doubt all the time. You're making excuses for him. Look, I'm sorry if I've said too much, but trust me, speaking as a man, I know what men are like.

Anna: But if he just wanted to have sex with me, he could have done.

Mark: That's my point. He doesn't. He wants to control you and own you, and treat you like a toy because he wants to shag the hippy, and seeing you is putting pressure on her to conform. Trust me, you're only seeing what he's telling you. You're thinking that all the time they're in Washington she's going to be threatening him, telling him to end it with you. But I think - and you're not going to like this - but I think it's probably the absolute opposite. He's threatening to leave her unless she stops seeing other men. He's using you as a pawn in those negotiations, and as soon as she's agreed, he'll drop you without a second thought.

Anna: He won't.

But maybe he had a point. I didn't want to think about it.

Mark: He will. And that's what makes me the most apoplectic of all, because there are good people in the world who would give anything to be with someone like you. And you've fallen for a monumental - emphasis on the mental - bastard. I'm sorry to say it. And please don't think I'm saying this just because I'm some kind of rival, because you've made it very clear that I'm not in the running.

Anna: It's not like that. It's not that I don't want you, just that we both know it could never work.

Mark: Whatever. However you want to phrase it. But all I'm saying is that I'm talking to you as a friend, with no other agenda. If I was you I'd meet someone else, sharp style. Have a one-night stand, get him out of your system.

Anna: That's what Chrissy said.

Mark: There you go then. In the very worst case it'll redress the balance. And I'm not suggesting with me, before you think that's my ulterior motive. Seriously, go out, get pissed with someone. I'm sure you've got an address book full of people you can call at short notice for a night of abandon.

Anna: There are a few I've met over the years, but that would be meaningless.

Mark: Which is exactly what you need. Listen, I'm going to have to get to bed because I've got an early start tomorrow, out taking pictures again, but can I just say two last things?

Anna: Go on.

Mark: Number one, I really appreciate you telling me all of this. It's painful, obviously, and I wish it was me you'd fallen in love with rather than some tosspot, but it's good to know you trust me. And number two, I'm sorry if you think I've stepped out of line. You may lie in bed tonight and think about what I've said, and be angry with me because I know you'll see things differently. But believe me, I've only said what I believe to be true. And I'm sorry if I'm wrong. But if you ever do find out where he lives, it's probably best not to tell me.

Anna: Okay. Message received and understood. Food for thought. And thank you. And don't worry I'm not angry with you. I think that's part of my problem. I don't get angry. I try to look for the best in people. Sleep well and I'll let you know how it goes.

Mark: I hope it works out for you. I really do. But just think about things, please? Because if you end it now it's going to hurt like hell, but things will only ever get worse, because they're not based on reality. And I may be wrong, and if he's still with you a year from now, I'll hold my hands up and apologise to his face, if necessary. But seriously, get out now before you get really hurt.

Anna: Okay. I'll think about it.

Mark: You won't. But don't say I didn't warn you. All right?

Anna: You know me too well. Sleep well. And thank you again. xxx

Mark: xxx

Chapter 21

Thursday, March 7th, 2019

I HARDLY slept. I hadn't eaten. The constant feelings of sickness and dread only accentuated the thoughts torturing my brain. I couldn't get comfortable. Every time I tried to switch off and go to sleep, the whole process started again.

I couldn't stop thinking about all the things Mark had said. Viewed dispassionately, his warnings made sense. I couldn't argue with the evidence, and any neutral person, assessing the situation, would view it in the same way. But I wasn't neutral. I'd had the benefit of Stef's company. I'd seen the way he looked at me and the way he treated me, how he made me laugh, how he confided in me, and all of the wonderful messages he'd sent me. And in all of those respects his behaviour was exemplary. How could I ever make anyone understand that, unless they were looking through the prism of everything I'd been through over the last two years?

The sensation was much like the grief of the loss of a loved one, and yet, keeping things in perspective, I hadn't even lost him. As far as I knew, things hadn't changed. We had a night at the theatre to look forward to. He'd told me he'd have a lot more time after New York. In one sense, things were better than they'd ever been. So why was my internal radar warning of imminent catastrophe?

Maybe I just wasn't cut out for polyamory. I'd tried, I'd failed. Or maybe I should do what both Chrissy and Mark had suggested, and redress the balance with a night of debauchery. But in truth, I didn't want to be with anyone else. That would be an acknowledgement of my own shortcomings, while simultaneously punishing Stef for a crime I wasn't even sure he'd committed. The problem wasn't him. It was Molly. I was sure of it.

But was I sure of it? Because everything Mark had said made it sound like I was deluding myself, and in fairness, I'd have said exactly the same if the roles had been reversed.

So, I needed a plan. I was supposed to be working. I was supposed to be writing. But I wasn't going to be productive at either of those after a sleepless night. So, first thing in the morning, I'd start the process of trying to sort my head out. Analysing the facts. Determining the scale of the problem. And deciding if it was a battle I was willing to fight, or whether I should just move on, stronger and wiser for the experience.

Part of the problem was that my phone was silent. It was the early hours in England, but that meant it was late in the evening in Washington. They'd be back at the hotel now. What were they doing? I didn't like to think. But why didn't he message me? Sneak his phone to the bathroom, if necessary. Just a tiny message. *"I'm okay. Thinking of you."* But instead there was nothing, and on top of the exhaustion, that made everything infinitely worse.

I must have drifted off eventually, because when I looked at the clock it was just past eight. I looked at my phone. There was still nothing. And now he'd be sleeping, so there was no point even checking for the next few hours, or sending him a message myself. I resolved to leave my phone on the bedside table, untouched and unchecked, until at least after lunch. But then sent a good morning message anyway.

Anna: Buongiorno. I hope you're sleeping well. I know I keep asking but I just hope everything is okay. Let me know. xx

The message received a single tick. His phone was off. That was something. As long as it stayed single I'd know he was asleep, but as soon as it went double it would mean he was up, and then, surely, he would find time to say hello. *"All I can say is, just be you, and send messages like normal."* That's what he'd said. So why wasn't he doing the same in return? Either things were going disastrously, and they were fighting all the time, or else she'd worked her poison and he no longer wanted anything to do with me. Either way, I just wanted to know. As I've always said, the only thing worse than knowing for definite is not knowing at all.

I dragged myself out of bed, my head hurting after too much wine and too little food. A cup of tea would help to fix that. Maybe toast would help with the nausea. But I couldn't face toast. I wasn't sure I'd eat anything ever again.

An hour later, I was out of the shower and dressed, staring at my computer screen, trying to work out where to start, wondering if I should make a list or just distract myself with pointless videos on YouTube. Then the phone rang. I leapt at it, instinctively, but it was a call from work, reminding me of a supplier meeting at 11am. Of course I hadn't forgotten, I said. Of course I'd be there on time. The truth, however, was that I hadn't given it a thought for weeks, and without the reminder I'd have missed it completely. I hadn't done any preparation. We were supposed to be looking at new products for autumn-winter but I had no idea what was likely to sell. Everything was turning to dust.

I looked great, according to the agent, who was trying to sell me things. Three of my staff said I looked tired and stressed, and one asked if I was coming down with something. Yes, perhaps I was, if a broken heart could be classified as an illness.

New products were spread on the conference table. Our buyer, Lucy, and the agent discussed fabrics, delivery times and minimum orders and occasionally asked for my opinion, but my contribution was negligible. My brain was thousands of miles away, in the American capital. My phone was on silent, but within my eyeline in case a message should arrive. It didn't, but the second tick materialised on the one I'd sent. He was awake. As soon as I could get away with it, without looking rude, I called the meeting to a close and headed home.

There comes a time when the brain's self-defence mechanism kicks in, when all of the positive thoughts and euphoria start to be replaced with doubts and anger, and feelings of negativity. The risk, of course, is that once those take over, there's no way back, and I was determined to fight them as long as possible. But I was beginning to lose the struggle.

I didn't want to have negative feelings about Stef. I wanted to give him the benefit of the doubt. I didn't want to give up on him yet, but by God it was coming close. Part of me could think of any number of reasons to excuse his lack of communication, but the rational part of my brain wasn't having any of it. Logic said it was rude, and uncaring. I hated myself for thinking it, but maybe Mark was right. Maybe Stef was merely a narcissist, playing with my emotions, using me to get back at Molly. Maybe he wasn't even giving me a minute's thought. And yet it hadn't seemed like that when we were together. What had happened to the person I was so close to just three days before?

Just before 2.30pm, my phone lit up. I grabbed it.

Stef: Buongiorno x

That was it. One word. How much use was that? Okay, so he was still alive. That was a start. But why wouldn't he tell me how things were? Why didn't he ask about me? Yes there was an x, but was that used as punctuation rather than with any sense of feeling?

My determination to play him at his own game and not reply lasted less than a minute.

Anna: Good morning. How are you? I wish you could tell me. I'm thinking of you all the time. Safe travels today xxx
   Stef: Hi
   Anna: Ooh, you're there! Are you looking forward to getting home or having a wonderful time? Or both?

But that was it again. Nothing. Two grey ticks to say it was delivered, but no blue ticks to say it had been read. He'd gone again. I nearly screamed in frustration. These were the longest, most unsettling days of my recent life. I had to face facts. Whatever had happened over there, all of the evidence suggested it was over between us, for reasons I neither knew nor understood, and it was truly heartbreaking.

I texted Ben. Thankfully, he was there.

Anna: I hate to say it but I think you're right about hosties.

Ben: Why what's up? Which bit? Kinky and pliable?

Anna: No, that they're nutjobs.

Ben: That sounds ominous. How come?

Anna: Don't even start me.

Ben: Did you at least get kinky and pliable first?

Anna: Don't even start me on that either.

Ben: Wow, that sounds exciting.

Anna: Believe me, it isn't. How are you?

Ben: I'm about to fly to Berlin. I'll be home soon though. I'll come and see you in your new place, take you out for dinner, and you can tell me all about it. Deal?

Anna: Deal. I'll look forward to it. Take care and happy flying xx

That's what I liked. Simple, uncomplicated friendship. No agendas. No secrets. A genuine understanding between two people with nothing to prove, no scheming, no ulterior motive and no second-guessing. Someone who valued me as a person.

I battled with work throughout the afternoon, but it was hard to concentrate. Every minute was dominated by my growing sense of frustration, which in turn was morphing into anger. I hardly ever lose my temper, but I felt like I wanted to scream.

My phone pinged again. I thought it would be Ben replying but instead it was Simon T. Who the hell was Simon T?

Obviously I knew him, if I had his name stored on my phone, but I couldn't picture him.

Simon T: Hi. Long time no speak!

And then it came to me. Simon. The T stood for Tinder. We'd met for afternoon drinks in London, one Saturday last summer. He wasn't really my type, and I'm pretty sure I wasn't his, but nonetheless we'd had a fantastic afternoon. It progressed into the evening, and, emboldened by wine, laughter, and heavy flirtation, we ended up in his bedroom. I don't often do one-night stands, but we all lapse, occasionally. It was light-hearted, no-nonsense, and great fun. By the time I made the late-night walk of shame back from the train station, I was sure that I'd never see him again, but also that we'd both enjoyed ourselves immensely. Around eight months had passed, but suddenly here he was. I don't normally believe in fate, but I was prepared to be open-minded.

Anna: Hi Simon. It's been ages. How are things?
    Simon T: All good. Have you missed me?
    Anna: Yes, my aim is rubbish, haha. What are you up to?
    Simon T: Just the usual. Sorry I've not been in contact.
    Anna: Don't worry, I'm just as bad. Life is hectic.
    Simon T: I didn't know if you'd still remember me.
    Anna: How could I forget? :-)
    Simon T: That sounds promising... Anyway, very short notice and all of that, but what are you doing tomorrow tonight?
    Anna: Tomorrow? Why?

Simon T: I'm up your way for a conference and then staying over at a hotel in the evening. I was wondering if you fancied meeting for a drink?

Anna: Sadly I've moved. Sorry about that.

Simon T: That's a shame. Just a thought. I can take a hint, haha.

Anna: I genuinely have moved. That's not a fib to get rid of you! Not far though. Did you actually mean a drink?

Simon T: Yes. I'm not assuming it'll end up like the last time.

Anna: That's a shame.

Simon T: Well if you're offering...

Anna: I'm a lady. I don't make a habit of that kind of thing.

Simon T: Me neither.

Anna: Glad to hear it. And yet you just invited me to your hotel...

Simon T: Guilty. Oops.

I checked the message to Stef. It had blue ticks. He'd read it but hadn't bothered to reply. I hated myself for falling in love with him, and at that moment, I hated him just as much for making me do it.

Anna: What time?

Simon T: Is that a yes? Exciting! Half seven?

Anna: Don't get your hopes up. But a drink would be nice.

Simon T: Wonderful. I didn't for one moment think you'd say yes.

Anna: Let's just say you caught me at an opportune time.

He texted me the address of the hotel. It was about a fifteen-minute drive away. We signed off, and I spent the rest of the evening questioning my own motivations. They weren't particularly complex. I imagined Stef would be getting ready for the airport, if he wasn't already in the air. But there were still no messages. Mark's words were ever louder in my head. Painful though it was to admit, it was time to draw a line under it all. It would hurt, but I had to maintain the final shreds of my self-respect, even if that meant parking self-respect outside the door of a hotel room belonging to a travelling salesman.

Chapter 22

Friday, March 8th - Sunday, March 10th, 2019

KNOWING that Stef was due back in England helped in one sense, although he hadn't sent me his flight number so I couldn't be sure what time he'd land. So much for Flight Radar. But at least I no longer had to factor in the time zone while working out the full extent of my disappointment. I didn't bother sending a good morning message. It felt strange, after having done it first thing every day, for the last four months, but the first step of the healing process would be to stop fooling myself. They were welcome to each other. I lay in bed, trying to summon the energy to get up, but feeling incredibly low.

Eventually I made a cup of tea, then took it with me to snuggle under my duvet with my phone. I didn't look at WhatsApp, but instead checked Facebook for activity in some of the groups I follow, then my emails, and the state of our company PayPal account. Sales had been slow but it was a strange time of the year.

Some time in the early afternoon, when I was settled at my desk, the phone played its familiar popcorn noise. I didn't even look at it. I concentrated on clearing my inbox, updating my company mailing list and looking through PDF catalogues of new autumn-winter products. But knowing there was a message was playing havoc with my concentration. Was it an apology? Unlikely. Eventually, though, I succumbed.

Stef: Hi Ms Gorgeous. How are you? xxx

For heaven's sake. I didn't know whether to be most irritated by the familiarity or the triple x. It was as though nothing had changed. Everything had changed. He'd been unforgivably rude and uncaring. Every last part of me wanted to point that out. At least, that's what I thought until I started to reply. And then I managed to irritate myself to the point of distraction by giving the bastard the benefit of the doubt again.

Anna: Buongiorno. Are you safely back? I've missed you. x

How much did I hate myself for writing that? He replied almost immediately.

Stef: Sorry about the lack of messages. It's been very difficult.
    Anna: That's okay. I was just worried about you.

· · ·

It was far from okay. Why was I deluding myself? But I was so conflicted. I wanted to forget about him, but I didn't want it to be over. I wanted to tell him how much he'd upset me, but I wanted to forgive him and not mention it in case he felt bad. I wanted to believe that I was merely overreacting, and that this was what polyamory was all about. That it was my own naivety and inexperience that was causing my turmoil. Yes, we'd have to have a discussion about it, but that could wait for another day. And in the meantime I didn't want to come across as needy.

Stef: I know this must have been hard for you.

Anna: It's not been easy. When are you back at your own home?

Stef: Sunday night.

Anna: And how is Molly? If I dare ask.

Stef: Not good. I think once this weekend is done and the decorating is finished we'll be having a break. She's a different person at the moment. She's like a psycho. It's the jealousy that pisses me off. I wish I was there with you but I promised to help and I can't get out of it. We're in separate rooms though.

Anna: Are you sure you don't need my help?

Stef: Definitely not a good idea, sorry x

Anna: That's okay. I wasn't being serious.

Stef: Can I come to see you on Sunday night? I'll try to wash the paint off.

Anna: Of course, if you'd like to.

Stef: Definitely. It may not be until around nine and I won't be able to stay long but I'm desperate to see you. How's the writing going?

Anna: Not well. I've not really been in the right frame of mind. I'm going to crack on with it this weekend though.

Stef: That's good. I can't wait to read it.

Anna: I'll do my best. Anyway, it's good to know you're safely back home. Good luck with the painting. xx

Stef: xxx

I couldn't continue the chat. My emotions were back on the rollercoaster. I hated the thought of losing him, but hated my weakness at being so easily prepared to give him the benefit of the doubt. I sent a quick message to Mark. He replied straightaway.

Anna: Stef's back. He's apologised. It's been horrible with Molly. He's coming round on Sunday.

    Mark: Christ. Seriously. You can do so much better.

    Anna: It's all a learning curve.

    Mark: Sorry but it's so depressing. It'd be bad enough thinking of you with someone else if it was someone decent. But the fact that it's a twat who treats you like that is unbearable.

    Anna: Sorry. I don't know what to say. I never wanted to hurt you.

    Mark: It's not you, is it? It's him. I just don't like the bloke.

    Anna: I'm sure you'd think differently if you met him.

    Mark: If I met him I'd punch his lights out.

    Anna: Charming.

    Mark: Seriously. Somebody needs to.

    Anna: Okay. I'm going now if you're getting like that. Have a lovely evening. xx

He didn't wish me the same. I spent most of Friday trying - unsuccessfully - to concentrate on the day job, and then thought about cancelling Simon so I could have the evening free to write. But I didn't have the heart, and I was sure I wouldn't get much done anyway. And despite the forgiving tone of my messages to Stef, it was clear that I shouldn't put my life on hold for his benefit. No, Simon was going to be the beneficiary of my newly-rediscovered independence, and to hell with the consequences.

———

I arrived on time, wearing a simple dark grey dress, black hold-ups and shoes that I wouldn't want to walk too far in. Simon and I had a glass of wine, and it was just like the first time. Instant chemistry, lots of laughter, and no expectations of lifelong commitment. He suggested another and I swapped to Diet Coke. When that was finished, and we'd been chatting for over an hour and a half, he asked if I'd like to see his room. I gave him a quizzical look of mock protest, but then nodded nonetheless. He led me by the hand to the lift.

"You said 'I'm not assuming it'll end up like the last time'," I whispered as he embraced me, once the lift doors had closed.

"I can't help it if you're a floozy." He laughed.

"Me? I'm an angel. Just easily led astray by travelling salesmen."

"I'm not even a salesman."

"Marketing, whatever."

Once inside the room, he removed his jacket. I looked out the window and saw my car, five stories below, then turned back towards him.

"It's a lovely room," I said.

"I'm glad you think so."

I nodded.

"Come here." I beckoned him towards me. His simple enthusiasm was so refreshing. There were no games. I knew what he wanted, and I wanted it too.

Except I didn't. Because the closer the moment came, the more my mind couldn't shake thoughts that this was wrong. That despite knowing Stef was quite possibly simultaneously in bed with another woman, and everything between us was almost certainly over, I didn't want meaningless sex with a stranger. There was no balance to redress. And no matter how loud I could hear Chrissy's words of encouragement in my head, I just wanted to go home. But I felt for Simon. I knew he'd be frustrated if I walked away now, and he hadn't done anything wrong. I didn't want to punish him, or feel guilty for leading him on.

I think he noticed the conflict in my eyes.

"Are you okay," he asked in a soft voice, as he pulled me closer to him. I took a deep breath, then nodded.

"Are you sure?" He ran a finger down my cheek then lifted my chin towards him.

I didn't know what to say. I couldn't shake the image of Stef, and an overwhelming feeling of sadness.

Simon took my hand and led me to the bed, then sat down next to me before speaking again.

"You know, I don't know if I should say this or not," he started. "But I really like you. I think you're funny, and sexy, and I'm flattered that you're here and unbelievably excited that you're in my room." He paused, lifting my hand towards him, then interlocking fingers. "But I don't think we should do this."

I frowned, but he could sense my relief.

"Really?"

"It's been lovely to see you again, and I'd love to do it again some time. But I get the feeling today isn't the right day. There's something going on up here" - he rested a forefinger on my temple - "that makes me think this would be a mistake."

"You're very perceptive. I admire that."

"Do you want to talk about it?"

"Oh, Simon, I wouldn't know where to begin."

He tightened his grip on my hand. I leaned in towards him and he hugged me. I rested my head against his shoulder.

"Let me walk you down to your car."

He kissed me on the cheek when we parted.

"Thank you," I said. "Don't leave it so long next time."

I drove home, pleased with my resolve, grateful to Simon, and terribly confused about my state of mind.

Chapter 23

I SPENT the rest of Friday evening writing, aware of the ever-more-daunting deadline, and my ever-increasing daily word count target. Writing is immensely cathartic. It takes my mind off the stresses of daily life, but I find it hard to be inspired unless I can disappear into a zen-like state of relaxation. And I was feeling far from relaxed.

I gave up in the early hours, then tried again for most of Saturday. Finally the words began to flow. Coincidentally I was writing about a time in my life from over twenty years ago during which I also suffered heartbreak. Readers will hopefully be impressed by the authentic description of the hollow, empty feeling of loss, without ever knowing how much it was influenced by current events. As Aldous Huxley said in Antic Hay: "Perhaps it's good for one to suffer. Can an artist do anything if he's happy? What is art, after all, but a protest against the horrible inclemency of life?"

I continued through the whole of Sunday until the early evening - aside from a trip to Waitrose to buy a special bottle of wine, falafels, and some other things that I thought Stef might appreciate, in case he ended up staying longer than the promised flying visit. Talk about conflicted. I tidied the flat, showered, and made myself presentable with half an hour to spare. Just past nine, he texted to say he was walking from the car park. I went down to meet him.

Suddenly he was beside me, and it was like nothing had changed at all. He smiled, perhaps sheepishly, but still managed to convey the look of a rock star. We hugged and he handed me a rectangular package, slightly larger than an A3 sheet of paper.

"I've got you a present," he said.

"That's very kind. I wasn't expecting a present."

I led him up to my flat.

"Glass of wine? Snacks?" I asked.

"Just a small glass, but nothing to eat," he said. "I can't stay long but we can meet again for coffee tomorrow if you like."

"Wow, twice in two days. I'm honoured." If it sounded sharp, I wasn't going to apologise. I poured the drinks then led the way to the front room.

"Are you going to open the present?"

There was a note written on the wrapping paper. *I secretly hope you don't like this so I can keep it.* I peeled away a corner of the paper, and then ripped it all off, revealing a beautiful framed Andy Warhol print.

"Sorry," I said with a smile, "I think it's staying."

"That's a shame."

I reached across and gave him a kiss on the cheek, then sat back on the sofa. There were things I had to say. We both took a sip of the wine. He still looked guilty, and with good reason. He waited for me to speak.

"This is difficult," I began. He nodded. "But I've had a horrible week."

"I know, and I'm sorry." I put my hand up to stop him.

"Let me just say what I have to say and then feel free to add anything you like, and hopefully we can move on, okay?"

"Okay."

I took a deep breath and then sighed, trying to find the words to explain all of the thoughts that had been running through my head.

"You specifically told me to message you as normal," I started. "So I tried to do that, but you didn't reply."

"It was hard."

"I imagine it was. But imagine how much worse it was for me, knowing you're spending all day with someone who hates me. How long does it take to tell me you're okay?"

"I don't think she hates you."

"Oh, I can read the signs. And I was so worried about you. But you didn't tell me how you were. I kept asking. You kept not replying. What was I supposed to think? So yeah, I get that it was hard, but believe me, it was harder here. You're over there with someone who is actively trying to destroy things for me, and for all I know, she's succeeded, because suddenly there's a change in everything, and a change in you, and it was like you didn't want to know me."

He reached out to hold my hand, but I hadn't finished.

"Is this what it's going to be like? Because if it is, that's fine, as long as I know, and I can hopefully learn to live with it. But when it goes against everything you told me, it's hard to understand. And I don't ever want to put pressure on you, so I'm not asking you for anything other than to be honest with me. But I would like to know where I stand, because you mean a lot to me and I still have no idea, really, what I mean to you."

I paused. His grip intensified.

"Can I speak now?" he asked. I nodded. "Well, first of all, I'm so sorry. I really did have battery trouble, and it was very awkward to find time, but yes, I understand. I could have done more, and I am genuinely extremely sorry. But just so you know, I think things have ended with Molly now."

"You think?"

"We've been together a long time, and we had some wonderful times, but the last few weeks have been difficult. I don't know what the future holds, but as far as I'm concerned, I've seen a different side and I didn't like it."

"And is she okay with that?"

"Honestly? No." He shrugged. "She's very upset at the moment, and blaming me and blaming you, and making all sorts of threats..."

"She's so bloody hypocritical."

"Exactly."

"What sort of threats?"

"Oh, nothing to worry about. But just lashing out, you know? It's kind of understandable, I suppose, when a relationship breaks down, but that's life, sadly."

"And are you okay with that?"

He tilted his head and looked at me.

"I think it's a shame, if I'm honest, because the good times were very good. But to answer your earlier question, you also mean a huge amount to me, and I think this has all been very unfair on you, and I'd like to think you still want to see me." He paused. "If you do?"

I didn't answer immediately. I wanted to give him a moment to think about what he was saying, and to understand a tiny percentage of the anguish I'd been through over the last few days. But I'm not a cruel person, and my resolve didn't last long.

"Of course I do," I said, then finally placed my free hand over his, and returned the squeeze. Then we both leaned in for a kiss, and it was even more like he'd never been away.

"So what's the plan?" I asked eventually, when I came up for air.

"Well, I must go home in a moment," he said. "I'm so

ridiculously tired and I need to sort out some admin. Tomorrow's a busy day but if you have time I'd love to meet you for coffee."

"Definitely. Any time."

"And then it's New York Tuesday, back on Thursday, then ten days off, with the theatre to look forward to and I'd love to take you to dinner again because we've not done that for ages. Does that sound okay?"

"That all sounds lovely."

"Perfect."

A few minutes later, we stood up. It was time for him to leave, but his eye caught something on my bookcase.

"You've got an Amazon Echo," he said.

I looked at it. It was still in its box.

"It came free from BT when I had the broadband installed. I've got no idea what to do with it."

"You should set it up and then you could ask it to call me and we could have conversations."

"Can you do that?"

"Yes, just put me in the contacts."

"And the children won't mind if my voice suddenly appears?"

He smiled.

"No, that'd be all right."

He picked up his jacket and then I walked him to his car. I returned home feeling much happier about everything, my heart restored. I still didn't understand the appeal of the Amazon Echo. If I wanted to have a voice conversation I could do that on the phone, but the fact that he was encouraging me to make regular, spontaneous contact over and above WhatsApp messages was hugely encouraging. I hated myself for being so easily pleased.

I hung the Warhol picture on the kitchen wall, so I'd see it every morning when I made the first cup of tea. I felt too tired to do any writing. My mind was full of thoughts of the exciting times ahead, only tarnished by a slight lingering negativity caused by the number of times I'd called him a bastard over the last few days. But if he was true to his word, and Molly was off the scene, then just maybe, this could be the start of something altogether more akin to a normal relationship. The relief was intoxicating.

There were messages from Chrissy, Mark and Ben on my phone, but I was too tired to answer any of them. They could wait. There was one from Simon, too, but he could wait as well. I tried to read before falling asleep but I'm not sure I even managed a page.

Chapter 24

Monday, March 11th - Wednesday, March 13th, 2019

EVERYTHING was back to normal by Monday. I woke up to a *buongiorno* and three kisses. I replied with much the same. Then I had a text explaining he had to sort out some school uniform issues for the children, but suggesting meeting at four in Starbucks, which was about a minute and a half from my front door.

I sent replies to Ben, Mark, Chrissy and Simon. Chrissy immediately came back, asking for the latest, but I didn't have time to go into the details. There was lots of work to do if I was going to sneak out for an hour.

I expected the afternoon to drag, but in truth the time flew by. I left the flat at five to four, and then saw Stef walking towards me, across the Market Place. It was like seeing him for the first time. I almost had to pinch myself that he was there to see me. He was wearing the same white leather biker jacket that he'd worn on our second date, and looked just as sexy as ever.

It felt strange to kiss him in a public place in the middle of the day, and even stranger to then hold his hand as we crossed to

Starbucks, but it was lovely and filled me with optimism. I offered to get the drinks but he insisted. We found a table, and he told me about everything he'd achieved during the day. It's probably one of the least considered aspects of the flight attendant lifestyle, but daily household admin needs doing, whether it's paying bills or tackling the ironing. If you're away most of the time, little things can soon mount up to a significant to-do list.

"I'm going to miss you this week," he said.

"And very much likewise."

"Exciting times ahead though."

Towards the end, he put his head on my shoulder and I put my arm around him, feeling a welling of excitement and closeness. The dark times of doubt were behind us. It really felt like the start of something wonderful. One more trip and then ten days of freedom, never more than a mile apart, with plans already in the diary, Molly off the scene, and finally the opportunity to really spend time with each other. Summer was coming. I don't normally like summer, but the thought of glasses of wine on the balcony was intoxicating.

Sadly, it was over all too quickly, but we parted with a hug. He suggested dinner on Friday. I wished him a safe trip, then watched him walk away, back to his car, feeling a warm glow of infinite possibilities.

I texted Chrissy when I got home.

Anna: Sorry about earlier. Mad busy morning. I hope all is well with you x

Chrissy: Yes all good. Men are tossers though, but I know I'm preaching to the converted there.

Anna: Well actually, that's where I may have to disagree.

Chrissy: Oh, don't tell me it's all back on with Mr Gorgeous.

Anna: Haha. Better than ever. His girlfriend has gone. I couldn't be happier.

Chrissy: Wow, kudos to you. Top marks for scheming. Although if you get withdrawal symptoms and decide you miss the old sharing days...

Anna: You're all right. Anyway, I better go. I have three weeks to finish a book and about half of it still to write so I'm going to be busy.

Chrissy: All the more reason to share, IMO.

Anna: In your dreams ;-) x

Chrissy: Take care xx

Stef texted from the airport on Tuesday. It felt so much less worrying knowing that he was flying alone. Of course I'd still miss him, but I could crack on with work without distractions. But then I got another message just before he was due to board the plane.

Stef: So sorry, but I can't make the theatre on Monday!

Anna: Oh no! What's happened?

Stef: I've messed up on childcare. I got my dates wrong. I thought they were coming back on Wednesday, but they're not, they're back on Monday. :-(

Anna: Oh, that's a shame. But I understand. Children must come first. They see so little of you already.

Stef: I'm sorry. I'll make it up to you. Better dash now though xx

Anna: Safe travels xx

I could have screamed. I'd been so looking forward to it. Never mind how much money I'd spent on the tickets. The biggest frustration, though, was that the disappointment was taking the edge off my general sense of euphoria. I wanted to be happy and revel in it. There would be other times, and it was an understandable excuse, but nevertheless it was still deeply annoying.

And even more than that, I didn't like to think of him on a trip, worrying that he'd let me down or upset me. I wanted everything to be good, forever more. So late that night, I sent a message, knowing he would be somewhere over the Atlantic, but that it would be there on his arrival if he didn't have Wi-Fi on the plane.

Anna: I expect by the time you land it'll be the middle of the night over here. I'll probably still be awake, but just in case, I thought I'd send you a message now. You'll probably be exhausted when you arrive after a super hectic week. I am, as ever, in awe of your ability to cope with such a busy workload. Please don't worry about the theatre. I just want you to know that whatever life throws our way, I think you are a wonderful, very special person and I feel privileged to know you. xx

I woke up on Wednesday to his reply. To say the least, it wasn't what I expected.

Stef: That annoys me. I don't want to think about the future and "whatever life throws our way". It appears that we see things very differently so I am finishing this here. I hope you find happiness with someone.

I blinked, sure I'd misread it in my half-asleep state. But suddenly I was wide awake. I read it again. The words hadn't changed. It made no sense at all. I didn't recognise the person behind them.

Was it a joke? No, it looked deadly serious. There were no laughing emojis. No kisses.

What had happened to the person who'd put his head on my shoulder just two days before? The one who'd come to see me with a present the day before that? The one who had sent me thousands of loving text messages, who told me to call him on the Amazon Echo, who said how much he was looking forward to spending time with me? Who suggested dinner on Friday, told me he was looking forward to seeing me once he was back from New York, and then frequently over the ten days that followed? Where was he?

Had this message arrived the week before, I could have understood it, half expected it even. But not now. Not now he was finally free from Molly. A fresh wave of nausea overcame me as I tried to get out of bed. I lay down, but as I closed my eyes, all I could see was his smile, his eyes, the way he looked at me when he was talking to me, the feeling of his arms and the touch of his skin, the weight of his head on my shoulder.

And now, just like that, with no warning, and against everything that I thought was true about our relationship, after we'd been through so much over two years, and especially the last four months, it was over. It defied logic. Something wasn't right.

I lay back on my pillows with the phone in my hand, reading and rereading the message. But it didn't make any difference. For so many years I'd shied away from relationships, scared of making myself vulnerable. But finally I'd let somebody get under my skin, and now this. I put the phone on the duvet and the tears began to flow.

I didn't know it then, but before long the tears would be the least of my concerns.

Part 2

Crash Landing

Chapter 25

Wednesday, March 13th, 2019

I SUMMONED the energy to get out of bed and made my way to the kitchen. Any crisis required a clear course of action, and the first thing on the agenda was to make a mug of Twinings Strong English Breakfast tea. But as I waited for the kettle to boil, I couldn't take my eyes off the Andy Warhol print that he'd given me just three days before. It taunted me. It was a symbol of everything that had been good and exciting. A thoughtful, romantic gesture that spoke of warm feelings in both directions, given freely and lovingly. I could never have foreseen how quickly things could change, nor understand why.

Had I done something wrong? I couldn't think of anything. Surely my final message hadn't been to blame.

"I just want you to know that whatever life throws our way, I think you are a wonderful, very special person and I feel privileged to know you."

What was offensive in that? To me, it was a lovely thing to say: don't worry, these things happen, I don't blame you, we'll have another opportunity.

I looked at his most recent messages to me. Was cancelling the theatre a sign? I supposed it must have been, and yet his explanation had sounded believable and understandable. I read my immediate reply. Had I said something to annoy him? I couldn't see it. I'd told him not to worry and that children should always come first. He'd said he'd make it up to me. But if not that, then what? I was bereft of anything even approaching an explanation.

I took the tea back to bed, then lay down considering how to respond. Should I even respond? My golden rule of relationship avoidance has always been to bail out at the first sign of trouble. I came close the previous week, but I'd held on, and been rewarded. But this? There could be no going back.

His message was brutal, cold and impersonal. I thought of Mark's warning: *"You've fallen in love with the person you think they are. But that person doesn't exist. He's just an illusion, created by some narcissistic bastard, fuelled by a desire to control and manipulate."*

It was probably best to write the minimum possible. It would still be the middle of the night in New York. I wanted to think he'd be lying awake, tortured at the thought of losing me, but I knew that would never be true.

Anna: Wow. Where did that come from?

It got a single tick. He was fast asleep, the uncaring bastard. I texted Ben. He'd always been my rock. He replied almost immediately.

Anna: All over with the hostie. You were right. Nutjob.

151

Ben: Oh, sorry to hear that. What happened?

Anna: Not sure. Two days ago everything was perfect. He'd ditched Molly. We were planning on spending loads of time together. Then this morning it was ended by a text message. How pathetic is that? Didn't even have the guts to tell me in person.

Ben: I can't say I didn't warn you. I'm so sorry to hear that, though. Are you okay?

Anna: Me? I'm fine. Obviously my world just fell apart and my heart has been not so much broken as shattered into a billion pieces and then jumped up and down on. But aside from that, top form.

Ben: Oh, Anna. :-(

Anna: I don't get it.

Ben: But what happened?

I gave him a recap of the last couple of days. He couldn't understand it either.

Ben: Look, this sounds serious. I've got a couple of days off. Let me come and see you.

Anna: I'm really not up to seeing anyone at the moment. Thank you though.

Ben: Nonsense.

Anna: But you live miles away.

Ben: Two hours, tops. Three allowing for traffic.

Anna: Precisely my point.

Ben: I owe you an Indian anyway.

Anna: Do you?

Ben: Yes, in exchange for the guided tour of your new flat. What's the time now? Half ten. Give me the address and I'll be there at six.

Anna: You're mad.

Ben: Desperate times call for it.

Anna: You're serious aren't you?

Ben: Deadly. I'm keen to see the flat. I haven't seen you in ages. And I know you're going to spend the whole evening feeling very low, so it's the very least I can do.

Anna: Okay. If you're sure. That would be lovely. x

Ben: Perfect. We'll get him out of your system.

Anna: Oh God, not you as well.

Ben: What?

Anna: I've got two friends who have been telling me for ages that I should, to use the phrase, "shag him out of my system."

Ben: Haha. Well I can't help you there. I'm a happily married man.

Anna: Glad to hear it.

Ben: Just to clarify, I meant you can tell me all about him and we can decide what to do next. Okay?

Anna: There's nothing we can do, but okay. It'll be fantastic to see you. And thank you. x

He was right - it would be good to have something to take my mind off things - but that didn't stop me looking at my phone every few minutes, begging it to burst into life, with a message from Stef full of apology, telling me he'd intended the message for Molly and it was all a big mistake. But no message arrived. By lunchtime the grey tick had turned into a blue pair, but he didn't respond, and I knew that it was pointless to retain any last semblance of hope.

At six o'clock I was standing outdoors, waiting for Ben. He was a few minutes late, but I didn't mind. The cold air was bracing, and being outside meant I was at least no longer lying on my bed, crying into my pillow. A swish-looking black Porsche swept into the car park and then glided into a space in front of me.

"Nice car," I said when he got out. He looked very dashing in a tailored black funnel coat that accentuated his athletic frame, although his hair had receded in the couple of years since we'd last met in person.

"Thank you," he said, with a smile, then extended his arms and I had a very welcome hug.

"Clearly I should have been a pilot."

"Fast cars, fast women, what can I tell you? Comes with the territory." I think he was joking, but either way, his honesty and unquestioning friendship were a welcome relief. We linked arms and started walking.

"And is Caryn happy with the fast women?" I asked as we descended the steps and crossed the little river that ran through the centre of the town. "Restaurant first or flat first?"

"Up to you. How hungry are you?"

"I've hardly eaten anything for the last week so I should be starving, but I've not had much appetite." I thought about it for a moment. "Let's do the restaurant first then we can go back to mine for coffee after."

"Excellent plan."

We caught up on small talk as the drinks and poppadoms arrived, and I found out how he was adjusting to married life.

"Can I take a selfie for old times' sake?" he asked at one point.

"A *what*?"

"You know what a selfie is."

"I know what a self-portrait is, but I don't use made-up words like selfie any more than I use made-up words like Brexit."

"What's wrong with Brexit?"

I looked at him as though he was mad.

"Do you mean the concept in general or specifically the word?"

He grinned.

"I'm aware of the madness of the concept. But the word itself. Educate me."

"Where do I start? Aside from it being the worst kind of portmanteau, and don't even start me on those linguistic atrocities, it's fundamentally wrong. It's not even the British Exit. It's the United Kingdom of Great Britain and Northern Ireland, which - correct me if I'm wrong - is at the root of the entire problem with the negotiations, in terms of the backstop and the like. And I don't think you can blame the Northern Irish for that when they don't even get a mention in the godawful affront-to-the-language name of the thing."

"That's a fair point. So you'd prefer Ukexit?"

"No! I'd prefer to forget the whole shambles, but given a choice I'd at the very least give it a proper name, made of actual words rather than some lowest common denominator tabloid-speak nonsense." I paused for breath, wondering how far to take this. "What has happened to this country? Charlotte looks at me as though I'm mad when I shudder at her saying 'uni' rather than university. Imagine if the great statesmen of history were alive today. David Lloyd George would be called DavLo and sound like the kind of second-rate comedian you get on ITV. It's bad enough that everyone has tattoos to show how rebellious they are, despite the fact that conforming to populism is the very antithesis of rebellion."

Ben was chuckling now.

"So is that a 'no' to a picture then?"

"No. It's a yes to a picture, as long as we recognise the fact that it's a picture and use the proper term. Self-portrait would do. But if you then look at the end result and describe it as awesome, I'll steal your phone and quite possibly throw it in the river."

"I'll do my best not to."

"*And* if, at any point, you ask the waiter for a craft lager or an

155

artisanal nan bread, I'm going home, no matter how far you've travelled. You've been warned."

He reached out his arm, holding his iPhone aloft. I snuggled in close and did my best to smile as he pressed the red button. Then he did a couple more, from other angles. He texted them to me. I didn't look my most seductive, but at least it served as a distraction from the unasked question that hung heavily in the space between us.

But we couldn't ignore it forever.

"So," said Ben at last, as the main courses arrived. "Stef."

"Yes."

"Do you want to talk about him?"

"I think it's probably unavoidable."

"Can we at least agree that I was right and he was a nutjob?"

I laughed for the first time all day.

"I think we can, although I could think of a few other words, most of which would be less polite."

"Twat?"

"Yes, that's definitely one of them, although there are still ruder alternatives. He was lovely in many ways, which is what I really don't understand, and believe me, I've given him the benefit of every possible doubt. But you know me, I don't really swear."

"Right. Or tell fibs?"

"Maybe the occasional white one. But I don't actually bear him any ill will at all. I don't hate him for what he's done. I just don't understand how we got to this when two days ago we were making spectacular progress."

"So talk me through it. What's actually happened?"

It took all of the main course, and then the walk home to bring him up to speed on the basics. I only stopped when I put the key in the door, and decided it was time for the guided tour.

But once that was over, and I was coaxing the Nespresso machine into life, I saw Ben looking at the picture on the wall.

"Is this the one he bought you?" he asked.

"It is. But you know what? He even wrote on the wrapping paper that he hoped I didn't like it so he could keep it. It's a lovely print, but..." I paused.

"But what?"

"I've got a good mind to give it back to him, because this is all very, very painful for me, and seeing that there every morning is going to taunt me."

"You should. Knock on his door, say, 'Here's your picture back, you mental bastard, and while I'm here can you tell me what it is I've done wrong?'"

"If only it was that easy."

"I'll come with you now if you like."

"We've got two problems there. One, he's still in New York as far as I know. And two, I don't actually know where he lives."

"What? You've never been round there? You must know."

"Nope."

"How bizarre."

"I know, but that was one of the things that didn't add up. I never got invited. I offered to pick him up but he always either drove or got a taxi."

Ben sighed.

"'I'm sorry but it does sound like he's been playing you," he said after a momentary pause.

"I know," I said, finishing up with the coffee machine and handing him a cup. "And I'd absolutely agree with you and everyone else who has pointed that out, but trust me, it didn't seem like that when we were together. I suppose I wanted to believe. I wanted to make excuses for him. I know his street, I think, but short of going there and knocking on doors, I'm not sure which is his house."

"But you'd recognise his car?"

"Of course, if it was there. But I know that area vaguely, and there's a lot of on-street parking, so it still wouldn't necessarily help."

Ben was thinking.

"Okay," he said. "Show me your computer. We can fix this."

Chapter 26

I PULLED a second chair up to my desk and handed Ben control of the mouse and keyboard.

"What are we actually doing?" I asked.

"First of all, we're going to find out what he's been up to, and then see where he lives."

"Isn't that a bit stalkerish?"

He frowned.

"The bloke's dicked you about for two years. Aren't you curious to know what he's really like?"

"Kind of, but I'm still not a stalker. I only want to understand exactly what happened."

"Precisely. So we'll see if it's the sort of thing he does often, or if he's just gone mad. He could be married for all you know. You know his surname?"

"Bianchi." I wasn't entirely comfortable, but I was curious.

Ben typed Stef's name into the Google search bar, followed by our town. A page of results appeared.

"Have you looked for him on Facebook and Twitter? Instagram?" he asked.

"I did once, but I didn't find anything."

"And Molly?"

"I didn't even think about looking for her."

"Okay."

He looked at his watch. The frown was back.

"Are you okay for time?" I asked, sensing that maybe he wasn't.

"It's a long drive back, but let's see what we can do in an hour."

He pointed to a result and hovered the mouse over it.

"That could be him," I said. The link took us to Stef's Facebook page. There was a photograph of an aeroplane at the top, and a rather dashing profile picture, the bastard. But either he didn't use Facebook often, or his privacy settings were tight. There were no other pictures, no posts, no friends list.

Ben went back to Google and added "Twitter" to the search query. This time Stef was top of the list. We clicked through.

"He hasn't tweeted for a while," I said. The last post was from 2017. Ben clicked on the heading for *Likes*. He'd responded to a few tweets last year, but nothing recent. It was the same under *Tweets and Replies*. The *Media* heading had some old photographs. It felt weird to see pictures that were new to me, albeit in some cases several years old. Then Ben clicked on *Followers*. There were over three hundred. He started to scroll through the list.

"If you see Molly, stop me," he said.

"That's her," I said, once he was about two thirds of the way down. Ben's expression conveyed distaste.

"Are you sure?"

"Yup."

"She's, er, I'm not sure how to put this..."

"A mad-haired hippy," I said. "I know. I could never picture it either."

Ben clicked through to Molly's account. Again there was nothing particularly recent, but some of her older postings gave clues to her personality. There was a lot of pseudo-political comment, plus other messages denigrating pornography, ridiculing religion, and very little evidence of a sense of humour. I was pretty sure we wouldn't have got on, even if we had met, although that wouldn't happen now, anyway.

"Do you think he really has finished with her?" asked Ben.

"I doubt it. He was obviously full of shit. For all I know, he may never have gone to New York and he could be with her now."

"But you don't know where she lives either?"

"No, just that it's an old farmhouse somewhere."

"Okay." Ben opened a new browser window alongside the Twitter page. "Let's see what we can find out about her."

I was even less sure about this, but I couldn't deny that it was fascinating, despite feeling so wrong.

"That's her web site, I think," said Ben, pointing to a page belonging to a web design company. That rang a bell.

"How did you work that out?"

"It's at the top of her Twitter profile."

I sighed, feeling stupid as well as uncomfortable. Ben clicked on the "About us" page.

"There you go. Molly Hargreaves, managing director." There was a short profile and a headshot. She looked slightly better, but still a bit unkempt. I'm not one to judge, normally, but I'm a big fan of appropriate amounts of make-up, having used it to excess in my goth-influenced younger days. It didn't look like Molly owned any eyeliner, never mind a lipstick.

Ben opened another window and called up the Companies House web site.

"What are you doing now?" I asked, increasingly horrified.

"Checking out her business." There was no stopping him. A couple of minutes later he had her company accounts open.

"This is bad," I said.

"It's not. It's all in the public domain."

He clicked on Filing History and then opened another PDF.

"There you go," he said, adopting a tone of triumph. "There's her registered address. It's a farmhouse. So at least you now know where he disappears off to." He clicked print, and a moment later, my LaserJet burst into life. He was enjoying himself. He copied the address into another new window, clicked on the resulting map, and then accessed Google Street View.

"Does that look as he described it?"

It did indeed. It was a ramshackle old place, but probably worth a fortune given its location close to the M25 and therefore within easy commuting distance of London.

"So at the risk of repeating myself, what exactly are we doing here?" I asked.

"We're having fun," said Ben. "Now let's find Stef."

He opened the BT web site and navigated to the online phone book before typing in Stef's name along with our town. But there were no results.

"That's annoying," said Ben. "But I suppose it makes sense to go ex-directory if he makes a habit of this."

Next was 192.com.

"What's this one?"

"It's more of a people finder. I think it uses the electoral roll. It's bigger than just the phone book, anyway. What was the name of his street?"

I told him to the best of my knowledge. But again there was no result, nor when he widened the search to the whole of the town.

"That's odd," he said.

"Why, what does that mean?"

"It means he's not listed. Has he lived there long?"

"A couple of years at least, I think."

"Maybe he just hasn't registered to vote then. I was hoping to get his address so you could leave the picture outside, but that makes it tricky."

"Unless he doesn't live there at all, or that's not his real name, and the whole thing has been a fabrication." My mind was going into overdrive.

"I didn't want to be the one to suggest that," said Ben, "but it's possible."

"Wow."

It took a moment to sink in.

"But why?" I said, more to myself than anyone.

"To be kind to him, maybe he's a commitment-phobe. But who knows? Maybe he was a scam artist from the start, and he was going to stitch you up for your life savings, but then bottled out when he found he liked you. Maybe the whole airline thing is made up as well."

"But this sounds ridiculous."

"Stranger things have happened."

"I know, but even so."

Ben looked at his watch again. An hour and a half had passed in a heartbeat. He regarded me with genuine sadness.

"I'm going to have to go," he said.

"It's a shame you can't stay over the night."

He raised an eyebrow.

"In the spare room, for heaven's sake. I'm not some sort of floozy." I'd made myself blush. He smiled.

"I'd love to, but another time. I've got a busy day tomorrow." He stood up, and I followed suit.

"I'll walk you back to your car," I said.

"But then I'll have to walk you back here to make sure you get home okay."

"I'm a big girl."

"You're many things, but big is definitely not one of them."

"Okay, but you don't know where you're going."

"It's directly across the Market Place then over the little bridge."

"Fair enough. At least let me show you to the door downstairs then."

I passed him his jacket. A couple of minutes later he was outside, and giving me a farewell hug.

"I'm sorry I couldn't help more," he said.

"What *are* you talking about?"

"Finding his address."

"God. Please don't worry about that. I just really appreciate you coming to see me. It's been a lovely evening, despite everything. You probably think I'm some lonely, old obsessive."

"Not in the slightest. You're suffering with a broken heart. We've all been there, but it hurts like hell. It was lovely to see you. We mustn't leave it as long next time."

"Text me when you get home."

"I will, but you'll be fast asleep."

"Ha. I pretty much guarantee I won't."

I did try to go to bed, but my mind was far too active to let me do anything more productive than lie there restlessly, occasionally looking at my phone, feeling lost, hurt, and close to tears.

Ben texted to say he was safely home, so I sent a quick reply. Stef didn't send anything. I didn't expect him to. But there were so many things I still wanted to say to him, all leading to the same question: why? I was fairly sure it was pointless to think of writing to him. His words and actions had made his position clear. But there were so many things that didn't make sense.

Not messaging, and not hearing from him, and the thought that I'd never hear from him ever again after all of the closeness and intimate moments we'd shared, all combined to leave me with a terrible hollowness. It was like my mind had turned into a vacuum that was now being filled with ever darker thoughts, questioning everything I ever thought I knew about him.

I wanted to hear the popcorn noise one last time. Even if it was just a final goodbye, telling me why he'd made his decision. But it wasn't going to come on its own. So, against every ounce of instinct, I started to type one final WhatsApp message.

Chapter 27

Thursday, March 14th, 2019

IN the early hours of the morning, I pressed send.

Anna: "I'm going to miss you. Exciting times ahead." That's what you said on Monday. We met for coffee in Starbucks, and you put your head on my shoulder, and it felt wonderful just to be there with you. Two days later, during which we've hardly spoken, it's: "I don't want to think about the future ... I am finishing this here." Perhaps you can see why I'm confused?

I'm not sure whether you'll even read this, but I feel I have to say it. It's strange at the moment. I am so used to thinking about you, listening out for messages from you, thinking of nice things I could do for you, and looking forward to seeing you, it is hard to adjust to a giant void.

I imagine you never want to see me again, or even hear from me again. And yet I still don't understand how we got to that. I wanted to be an oasis of calm and caring for you. I thought we enjoyed time together, with no expectations and no agendas. I thought we were both equally looking forward to seeing each other again.

I am not sure what has changed, but I respect your decision. Of course I do. Maybe you have seen me for who I am: just a normal person in an increasingly abnormal world. I shall miss talking to you, and miss hearing the special noise when you send me a message. But most of all I will treasure every moment we spent together.

I've spent the last four months writing a book, motivated by your feedback, trying to write something for you, that you would enjoy, and that would be dedicated to you. And yet now I don't even know if you will ever read it. And all for what? That is a symptom of things at the moment that I just can't understand.

So, of course, I will miss you, but I've got broad shoulders and life goes on. My only regret of the last few months is whatever I did, and whatever misunderstanding I caused, that upset you so much, so suddenly, and so catastrophically when I thought we were in such a happy place. x

It got two grey ticks almost immediately. I had no idea if he was still in New York, on the way home, or already back. That was the thing that hurt the most. Being so cruelly and abruptly cut off. I don't believe you can switch off caring for someone, and yet I would never know where he was, what he was doing, and how he was feeling, and I wanted to know all of those things, even if we were no longer in a relationship.

I tried to sleep, but it was pointless. I tried to read, but couldn't concentrate on the words, and each page that passed barely registered. I kept looking at my phone. The ticks turned blue. Surely he owed me a reply, just to explain his actions, and put my mind at rest. But no reply came, and with every passing moment, my frustration and resentment grew. Who the hell did he think he was?

At just past 4am, I sent a message to Chrissy:

. . .

Anna: Hopefully this won't wake you up, but just so you know, it's all over with Stef. I'm not sure why or how, but he sent me a message and that was that. It's a bit hurtful that he couldn't say these things to my face, but how much do we ever really know someone?

I hope this doesn't come across as bitter, but I don't know what to think any more. As my friend Mark pointed out, what I've lost is not the person I knew, but the person I thought they were. But the truth is that that person didn't exist. And it's such a waste because he did *exist, in my mind, for a moment in time. For four months. And yet all the time there was a secret agenda. All the time this was always going to end in tears.*

Was I a fool to be taken in? Of course I was, but we live and learn. My only crime was to find that I cared for somebody. That I thought about somebody. That I wanted to know how they were and, yeah, that maybe occasionally they were thinking of me. And it appeared to be mutual - but that is where I was wrong.

I suppose it's time to stop giving him the benefit of the doubt. It appears, now, that it was all an illusion, fuelled by a selfish desire to be admired until the rotten core emerged from within. Whether deliberately callous or just insensitive, the real person had no regard for my feelings. He was just using me to get back at someone else, and once they'd split up, I'd served my purpose.

That is the cruel reality of the situation. And if I've been a fool, it was only to believe that he was different, that there was a connection when all along he was only ever playing a game. So, I'm back on the scrapheap, and an emotional wreck, but if this has taught me anything, it's the value of true friendships with real people. And for that I thank you. It's going to hurt for a while, but when the tears dry, I will be wiser and stronger, and I won't ever let it happen again.

I hope you're well and having better luck than I am. x

. . .

Then, for the sake of completion, I sent one to Mark.

Anna: Good morning and I hope all is well. Sadly it looks like you were right about Stef. Grade A tosspot, which I still find hard to believe, but either way it's all over and there's no going back. Best wishes for a fantastic Thursday. x

I drifted off at some point, but woke up just before eight. My first instinct was to check my phone. There were sympathetic replies from Mark and Chrissy, but nothing from Stef. It was so frustrating.

I tried to revive myself with a cup of tea before heading for the shower. Again, the picture taunted me. The tears came as I waited for the kettle to boil. I took the tea back to my bed and then lay there, thinking, wondering if I'd ever care for anyone in quite the same way ever again.

But something was bothering me.

I'd assumed Stef wasn't messaging me because he was a thoughtless bastard. But what if he couldn't? What if someone else had sent that "ending it" message from his phone? What had he said to me about Molly? *"She's a different person at the moment. She's like a psycho. She's very upset at the moment, and blaming me and blaming you, and making all sorts of threats."*

And then the feelings of heartache began to subside, replaced by a chilling sense of dread.

Chapter 28

I WAS aware that the business was suffering, and as the managing director, I only had myself to blame. The last few months had disrupted everything. My focus had drifted, and sales were plummeting. I checked my emails, but there was the usual combination of spam and suppliers chasing payment. I sent my standard post-GDPR reply to the spammers, giving them thirty days to supply all the information they held about me, and then left the invoices till later. There wasn't much else I could do with them.

In my mind I could see Stef, locked in a basement, being tortured, or perhaps his lifeless body lying cold in a shallow grave. I told myself I was being ridiculous, but I knew something had happened. However horrific the thought, it was the only rational explanation.

Toast made me gag. I made another cup of tea, but couldn't drink it. I went back into my bedroom, lay on the bed and stared at the walls, knowing that I should be heading to the warehouse for another supplier meeting, for more grief about payments, and more products to evaluate with limited enthusiasm. But also knowing that I was going to be late.

I apologised when I arrived, and got a quizzical look from our buyer, Lucy. I don't like to discuss personal issues at work. I tried to put on a brave and cheerful face, but it was as fake as the promises on the side of a bus about £350 million extra going to the NHS.

Lucy nudged me a couple of times as the meeting progressed, trying to get my attention. I felt awful, knowing I was being far from professional, but I hardly noticed the products laid out in front of me. And then I heard the popcorn noise, and suddenly I was on red alert, my mind racing. I grabbed at my phone. But my eagerness was replaced by confusion. The screen was blank.

"Sorry about that," said the supplier's agent from the other side of the conference table, swiping the screen of her iPad. "I should have switched it to silent."

It took a moment for my heart rate to recover, but I grabbed the chance to quickly check my WhatsApp anyway, just in case I'd missed a notification while driving. There was still nothing new from Stef. And worse still, his profile picture had disappeared along with his "last seen" time. The bastard had blocked me. It was one thing ending our relationship, but blocking me was simply rude and deeply insulting. Another part of my soul died. I'm forty-bloody-nine. I'm far too old and worldly-wise to put up with that kind of immaturity. Unless, of course, he was actually dead.

———

"Are you okay?" asked Lucy, once the meeting had finished.

"I'm okay," I lied. "Just tired with the move, and working long hours."

"Is there anything you want to talk about?"

Her earnest expression could have broken my heart if it wasn't already in a thousand pieces. I trusted Lucy. We'd been together for over a decade, and had enjoyed countless trips together. She knew me as well as anyone. I shook my head. She sighed.

"Can I say something then?" she asked.

She led me out to the car park, out of earshot of the rest of the staff.

"Look, maybe this isn't my place," she started, "and I probably shouldn't say anything, but I'm worried."

"Okay. About me? I'm fine, I told you."

"Yes about you, and you're far from fine. But about the business too. Sales are struggling and I'm getting hassled every day about invoices."

"I know, but it's a difficult time. Retail is bloody hard at the moment."

"It is. I get that. But this seems worse. And the girls are worried. They see the orders every day and they know how quiet it is. And it's coming into the summer, and if suppliers put us on hold, it's only going to get worse. They're worried for their jobs."

"I know, but it'll be fine, honestly."

"But's never been as quiet as this in March. Not as long as I've been here."

I took a deep breath, rubbed my face with both hands, then sighed deeply.

"I appreciate you passing it on," I said.

"Is everything okay, though?" she asked again. "With you? I don't want to ask personal questions but you don't look very well and I'm worried about you. You look very tired."

"I've not been sleeping brilliantly."

"And you look like you're losing weight."

"Are you saying I was fat?" I attempted a smile, but it wasn't successful. Lucy reached out and placed a hand on my upper arm.

"I'm not saying anything. And no, you weren't fat. But you're looking thinner than normal."

"I've not really been eating much either. It's all been a bit manic. I haven't really got sorted in the new kitchen yet."

"Oh, come on, you've got to eat."

"I know. And I will. I haven't had much appetite."

"Because of the worry?"

"The worry?"

"About the business."

"The business. Yes. But it'll be fine, I promise. We've been doing this a long time and we've been through challenges before. I'll come up with a plan."

"Like winning the lottery?"

"That would help."

"Is that why you keep checking your phone? To see if they've emailed you about the Euromillions?"

Nothing escaped her.

"Do I?"

"You know you do."

I felt awful. She deserved an explanation. But where would I even begin? How ridiculous would it sound? I fell in love with some Italian lothario who already had another girlfriend, and then he ended it, and now I think I'm going mad because the only rational explanation is that he's been murdered? Lucy, of all people, would find that absurd. She knew I was relationship-averse, despite occasionally watching me attempt to chat up the waiters when we'd been out for a meal together. And what evidence did I have that anyone had killed him? A couple of texts about a psycho girlfriend who also happened to be a mad-haired hippy cat-woman?

I made a decision.

"There are a few things going on that I need to sort out," I said. "Nothing for anyone to worry about. Just personal domestic stuff."

"Is Charlotte okay?"

173

"Charlotte's fine. Having a ball, last I heard. It's been a funny start to the year but I'm going to be back to being fully focused imminently. I'll fix the sales. Come up with some ideas for big promotions and everything will be okay. All right?"

"Anything I can help with?"

"I'll let you know if there is. But thank you for asking. Please try to reassure anyone who asks. I'm positive everything will be okay."

"Okay."

She stepped forward and we had a hug. I'm not sure where that is in the manual of modern management, and whether it's even still legal, but I held her tightly and I didn't want to let go.

When I got home, the flat was desperately quiet. The bedroom was calling to me, but I knew if I lay down I'd not get anything done, and problems would only escalate. And yet equally I didn't know where to start.

The default in such situations is a nice cup of tea. I went through to the kitchen. But the picture was still there, taunting me. And finally my patience snapped.

"Right, you fucker," I said aloud. "You wanted to keep it? You can have the bastard."

I dropped it into a Waitrose carrier bag, and set off to my car in the underground car park. Okay, I didn't know his address, but I thought I knew the street. And I'd recognise his car. So even if it was parked on the street, I'd know I was in the right vicinity, and if necessary I could knock on random doors and ask if anyone knew where the mad bastard Italian flight attendant lived. I didn't want to see him. I didn't want the conflict. I just wanted to leave it propped against his front door so I'd never have to see either of them ever again.

Within five minutes, the satnav was closing in on his street. And yes, there was lots of on-street parking, but a few of the houses had drives as well. I edged my car past the turning to his road, looking left to see if I could spot his Golf, but it didn't appear to be there. The only option was to double back, drive along the actual road, risk looking like a stalker, knowing that one of these houses was possibly his, unless he'd made the whole thing up. My heart was pounding, but I'd come this far. I did a three-point turn, and went for it.

But again there was no sign of his car. At the end of his street, I turned round and drove back for a second look. There were only about twenty houses to choose from. Some had cars outside, so I could probably rule out those. But suddenly the thought of knocking on the doors of random strangers lost any appeal it may have had previously. I pulled into the side of the road, my engine idling, not wanting to go home and accept defeat, but equally knowing I was precisely no further forward.

But then, about four houses away, a front door opened, and an elderly man emerged, with a small dog on a lead. He turned and started to walk towards me. I switched off the engine and got out of the car. He nodded in greeting as he approached, and yet again I had a fleeting realisation that I no longer lived in cold, impersonal London.

"Sorry to bother you," I said, as he got closer, "but I've got to drop off a package for a friend who lives on this street, and I'm not sure which house it is. Would you be able to help me?"

"I can try, love," he said, pausing, much to the dog's dismay.

"He's an Italian chap. Stef. Do you know him?"

"No, sorry. I know a few but I've not come across him."

I tried to wrack my brain for any further prompts.

"I think he moved in a couple of years ago, maybe has a couple of children to stay occasionally. Does that help?"

"I'm sorry." He shook his head. The dog was looking

impatient but then found something worth sniffing on a lamppost.

"Okay, sorry to bother you, but thanks for trying," I said. "The only other thing is his car. A silver VW Golf. Quite old. You haven't seen one of those parked along here, have you?"

"I notice cars," he said, and my spirits lifted. "A silver Golf?"

"Yes."

"I've seen one round here. Not for a while, though."

"You don't know which house it belonged to?"

"Sorry, not sure. I'm not being much help, am I?"

"Oh, don't worry. It doesn't matter. Thank you for trying anyway."

He started to walk away, and then turned back.

"I'll tell you what you could do," he said, "if you're not in any rush."

"Go on."

"Pop back tomorrow, about 11.30. The postman will be doing his rounds. He knows where everyone lives."

"Oh, thank you, but I don't think I could ask him. That's probably some sort of data protection breach."

"I wouldn't worry about that. He's a good old boy. Lovely lady like you, he'd be only too happy to tell you if he knows."

I laughed.

"Thank you," I said. "I'll do that then. Enjoy your walk."

"Good afternoon to you."

If he'd had a hat, I'm sure he'd have touched the brim.

I got back into my car, grateful to be out of the cold. It was a ridiculous plan, but at least that was better than no plan at all. And in any case, by the morning, maybe his car would be there. It was worth a second attempt, anyway.

I headed home via Waitrose, keeping an eye out for Stef in every aisle. I bought food and wine and tried to persuade myself that I'd manage to consume some of it. I was most confident about the wine. But then when I got home I fired up something quickly in the microwave, and managed to get through most of it. I poured a glass of wine and looked at my phone, sent quick replies to Mark and Chrissy, and then tried to lose myself in an episode from the backlog of TV dramas I'd stored up on my Sky TV planner.

I was in bed by midnight. Asleep by maybe four. And when I woke up without an alarm less than five hours later, I knew what I had to do.

Chapter 29

Friday, March 15th, 2019

SHORTLY after 11am I was back on Stef's street. There was still no sign of a silver Golf. I tried to remember what he'd told me about his schedule. He was in New York on Tuesday, but did that mean he should be home by Thursday? Maybe it was another double-header and he'd be home today or tomorrow. I missed discussing his adventures, terribly.

But at least that could explain why there was no car, and it was infinitely preferable to the thought of him lying dead or being tortured. It was weird. In the daylight, out and about, that was easy to dismiss as a ludicrous possibility. It was only at night or when I was at home alone that my mind went into overdrive. Presumably the car was therefore in a staff car park at Heathrow. Maybe I should try to wangle my way into that? I dismissed that idea as soon as I'd had it. It was a stupid thing to think. I had to try to remain rational.

I waited in my car, watching fine drizzle cloud my windscreen. Every so often, I turned on the engine and flicked the wipers.

Then, as if on cue, the postman entered the street, with a red bag over his shoulder. I got out of the car.

"Hi, sorry to bother you," I said. I already felt guilty. He was getting wet, and I was surprised he could even see me through the raindrops that had gathered on his glasses. "I'm trying to find a friend."

"I'll be your friend," he said with a smile, and it made me laugh. The ice was broken.

"Cheeky. I was chatting to a man with a dog." I nodded in the direction of his house.

"Geoff?"

"Possibly. Not sure. He said you'd know. I'm trying to drop a picture off, but I'm not sure which house it is. It's Stefano Bianchi. Does that ring a bell?"

"It does." He looked me up and down, but I appeared to pass his assessment, whatever it was. "Up there on the left, see the white front door?"

"Yes."

"That's the one."

"Oh, thank you ever so much."

"Do you want me to take it for you?"

"No, don't worry. I'm going to leave it outside. It's too big for the letterbox, but I'll pop back when it's not raining."

"Not really the weather for it today."

"No, just what I was thinking."

His expression changed, the cheerful face replaced by a frown.

"Has he recently moved?" he asked.

"A couple of years ago, I think."

"No, I mean out rather than in."

That floored me.

"Not as far as I know."

"I've not had anything the last couple of days. The last thing I had looked like one of those confirmation of redirection letters."

179

"Oh." I didn't know what to make of that. "When was this?"

"Tuesday, I think. May not have been but I remember thinking that's another one gone. You get to spot these things. And I've not had anything since."

"Wow, well, he may have done. I know he's away a lot, but I wasn't aware of that."

"Might be worth checking before you leave anything for him."

"Quite. It was supposed to be a surprise present. But yes, I'll give him a ring."

"Worth doing."

"You don't know where things are being redirected to, do you?"

"Sorry, my darling. I don't get to see that. Once they stop they get re-routed at the delivery office."

He started to walk on.

"Thanks for your help," I said.

"No problem. But if he has moved out, and you still need a friend, the offer's open." He gave me a wave as he headed towards the next front door.

I went back to my car and waited until I saw him leave the street, my mind buzzing. Had Stef really moved? He'd never mentioned anything about moving to me, but how well did I really know him? Then the dark thoughts came back with a vengeance. If Molly had done away with him, would she redirect his post? Wouldn't that lead the police straight to her door? Maybe she'd send it to an anonymous mailbox. Was that all too premeditated? I didn't know what to think.

I started to type a message to Ben, but then stopped, not knowing what I could say anyway. And on the off-chance he was on the ground and replied immediately, he'd only try to talk me out of what I was planning to do next.

I took one last look at the street, to make sure the coast was clear, and then made my move.

Stef lived (with possible emphasis on the past tense) in a semi-detached house. It had a small driveway at the front that would just about fit a Golf, so assuming he parked there, I'd know where to look in future. Not that I ever intended coming back.

There was a small front garden with a tiny lawn, leading to a passageway that ran down the side of the house, presumably to the back garden.

I felt like a burglar as I approached, not that I know what a burglar feels like, and actually thinking about it, probably not like a burglar at all, given that they'd know what they were doing, and wouldn't be shit-scared in the process. As I approached the front door I tried to look in the front room window, but it was hard to see beyond the net curtains. Presumably they were there to deter people looking in, during lengthy times of absence. The only option, then, was to go round the back. I just had to hope the postman had given me the right address.

With every footstep that took me forward, I had a strong urge to abort the mission. But I had to know. If I could see in a window and see that the house was empty, or at least full of cardboard boxes, awaiting a removal van, I'd know for sure that he was leaving. But if it wasn't...

But if it wasn't, then what? I didn't know. I just had to have some degree of certainty in my life. And if I found him lying dead on the kitchen floor, with an axe sticking out of his head, I'd just have to come up with a suitable explanation for why I was there in the first place.

There was a small wooden gate at the side of the house. It wasn't locked. Just behind the gate were three wheelie bins: one for rubbish and two for recycling. I squeezed past them, and crept forward.

The back garden was small, and didn't contain much apart from a lawn that needed looking after, and a rusty swing. But as I turned the corner I could see clearly into what I decided must be the dining room. There was a table and four chairs. It looked spartan. There were no ornaments, nor any other furniture. It was inconclusive, and frustratingly, the internal door was closed so I couldn't see anything beyond.

When I moved round to the kitchen window, my heart nearly stopped.

Chapter 30

THE glass in the back door was smashed. And judging by the rain and leaves on the kitchen floor, it hadn't happened recently. I took a step back in fear. I had no idea what horrors I might find inside.

And yet, despite my logical brain screaming at me to call the police immediately, the part of me that had suffered so much anguish in the last few days felt compelled to press on. What would I tell the police? How could I explain why I was there? And if they told me not to enter I'd never know what had happened. I had to continue.

The door was unlocked, so I wrapped my hand in my sleeve and pulled it open. My every movement was tentative and near to soundless, aside from the deafening thud of my heartbeat.

It was cold inside. What had the weather been like recently? Had it been windy? Maybe that would explain the veneer of chaos, smashed crockery, and general sense of turmoil. Or maybe it was all the sign of a struggle.

Two doors led from the kitchen. One to the dining room, which I'd already seen inside, and a second which presumably led to the hallway. Both were closed. I opened the second and edged forward into the dimly-lit, musty-smelling passageway.

"Hello!" I called, not expecting an answer. If there was anyone in the house I imagined them to be hiding, ready to take me by surprise, and add me to the list of victims. Or lying in a pool of congealed blood.

I crept to the end of the hallway, by the front door, and looked up the stairs. It was decision time. Upstairs could wait. I opened the door into the living room.

There was a lingering smell of stale tobacco but just enough light through the net curtain to reveal no obvious sign of an ashtray. I remembered the cigarette on the balcony and how he'd made a point of telling me he didn't smoke.

The furniture was tired, and tatty. Was the room just untidy or were there signs of a burglary? Nothing was smashed or upturned, but equally there wasn't a computer, and the ageing flat-screen TV in the corner by the window wouldn't be worth very much.

There were dozens of books on a set of shelves in the opposite corner, including several of my own. It was weird to see them. A pile of newspapers was gathered on one of the brown leather armchairs. I flicked through them. They were from different American cities: Philadelphia, New York, Washington, Los Angeles, Dallas, and all from random dates over the last couple of years. Maybe he kept them as a souvenir of his travels.

I tried to picture Stef in this room, but the gloom clashed with his glamorous, sophisticated, jet-set image. And yet, in some ways it could have been homely if it was tidied up, better lit, with the central heating switched on. And I wasn't sure the mess was his doing. Either way, it definitely wasn't ready for the removal men.

I stayed in the front room longer than necessary, trying to build up the courage to go upstairs. But I couldn't wait forever, and every moment was a moment longer before I'd be back home. I took a last look round and headed back to the hallway, wrapping my fist around my keys, with one protruding, just in case I needed to hit somebody.

I took the stairs slowly, my heart pounding, craning all the time to get a better view. There were four doors off the landing. Three were open, but the fourth was closed.

I looked quickly into the two bedrooms and the bathroom, and was hugely relieved to see no obvious signs of bloodshed. I opened the remaining door. It was only an airing cupboard, with a hot water tank and piles of towels and bedlinen.

I went back to the first bedroom, which overlooked the front garden. This, presumably, was where the children stayed. There were two single beds and a small desk, a built-in wardrobe and a bookcase. I looked in the wardrobe. There were a few clothes, a pile of games and some art materials. I felt a horrible sensation of prying.

The bathroom was cleanish but tired. There were a few toiletries, but everything was dry. It was a while since anyone had been there.

That only left Stef's bedroom, which overlooked the back garden. As I stood at the doorway, my overwhelming feeling was sadness. If things had worked out differently, who knows what sort of mischief we could have got up to in here. But now it looked alien. I couldn't picture us there together at all.

The bed was made, with a dark blue blanket covering most of the duvet, but that, in turn, was covered in piles of clothes. An ironing board stood propped against one wall. It didn't feel right to go through the chests of drawers, but I gave them a cursory glance anyway, looking for anything that could give a clue to who he was, and what might have happened to him. Likewise the wardrobe. But aside from a few clothes on hangers, there was nothing at all that looked even vaguely personal. And then it struck me. There were no photographs, up here or downstairs, as far as I'd noticed. Nothing to say that this was actually his house at all. I might have broken into the house of a complete stranger, albeit one with exceptional taste in contemporary literature.

My heart nearly stopped when I thought I saw movement in the garden, out of the corner of my eye. I stood still, terrified, holding my breath. I edged closer to the window, using a curtain for protection. But there was nobody out there. Just trees blowing in the breeze. I wanted to get out of the house as quickly as I could.

I couldn't see a suitcase, but that made sense if he was away. And there were no signs of an airline uniform either. I picked up some of the clothes, trying to see if I recognised any. One of the jackets looked vaguely familiar, but there was no sign of the white leather one. I wasn't very much further forward.

I wasn't sure what to do next. Go home, stop worrying? Write it off to experience? At least I hadn't stumbled over a body. Ben was right. Stef was a nutjob. He'd ditched me of his own accord, having played me for whatever reason. God alone knows what he'd think if he knew I'd been in his house. He'd probably try to get me arrested and impose some sort of restraining order. It was time to forget about him. Move on. Accept that not everything goes according to plan, and that time, eventually, heals even the most painful of broken hearts.

I turned back to the door, then stopped, frozen in horror. The bang from downstairs reverberated in my head. Along with the terrifying realisation that there was somebody else in the house.

Chapter 31

IF I was on edge before, I was now on the brink of panic. What could I do? Hide? Make a run for it? Was it Stef? Molly? Burglars? How the hell would I explain what I was doing when I didn't even really know myself. How stupid was I for ever thinking this was a good idea?

Then the bang came again. Then a third time. And slowly my breathing returned as I understood where it was coming from. I'd left the back door open and it was blowing in the breeze, banging closed periodically.

But it was enough of a warning. I had to get out.

I ran back downstairs, through the hallway, and back to the kitchen. But just as I was leaving, something caught my eye. There was a pile of post on top of the microwave. I had to look, even if just to confirm his name and address.

There must have been about a dozen envelopes in all. They were all junk mail apart from one, which looked like some kind of utility bill. But at least the name and address matched. I was in the right house. And he'd given me his real name.

Emboldened, I explored the kitchen further, looking for signs of recent habitation. I opened the fridge. There were bottles of sauce, a few cans of drink, and a bottle of milk that was over a week past its use-by date. There was half a loaf in the bread bin, but it was edged in mould. I touched it before I realised, and thought I was going to gag.

I closed the bread bin, then moved to the sink to wash my hand, stepping over broken crockery. The sink was empty apart from a few leaves that had blown in through the open door, and a bottle of washing-up liquid that had fallen in from the side. I turned the tap. And that was when I saw the blood, on the back of the tap, coming into view as it rotated towards me. Suddenly, all my darkest fears returned.

Chapter 32

IN a state of near-hysteria, I texted Ben from the car while I waited for the police to arrive. He replied straight away.

Anna: I'm worried about Stef. I think something has happened to him.

   Ben: How do you mean?

   Anna: It doesn't make sense. We got on so well. He would never have ended it like that. I think Molly has done away with him.

   Ben: What are you talking about?

   Anna: I think she's murdered him, and then sent that message from his phone. He's completely disappeared.

   Ben: Have you been drinking? It's not even 1pm.

   Anna: Stop it. I'm being serious.

   Ben: What do you mean disappeared?

   Anna: I mean he hasn't replied to my message. I've been blocked on his phone. He's not at home.

   Ben: He's probably abroad.

   Anna: Or lying in a ditch somewhere. There was blood on his tap.

   Ben: What? What blood on what tap?

Anna: In his kitchen.

Ben: When were you in his kitchen? I thought you didn't know where he lived.

Anna: I didn't but I asked the postman.

Ben: You do know you sound like a stalker?

Anna: I'm not! I was just worried. The postman thought he'd moved away so I had a look in the window.

Ben: And you saw blood on the kitchen tap? That's impressive vision at your age.

Anna: I went round the back and the window in the door was smashed. It was unlocked so I went in.

Ben: Oh, Jesus. Are you completely mad?

I was beginning to think I was.

Anna: I thought you'd say that. Anyway, the point is, I did, and there was blood.

Ben: How much blood?

Anna: Not a lot. Just a bit on the back of the tap as I turned it.

Ben: And this makes you think he'd been murdered because?

Anna: Because he's gone missing. I just bloody told you.

Ben: Okay. And you don't think it could have been from someone cutting their finger, or washing a piece of red meat or something?

Anna: It's from someone cleaning up blood after they've murdered him. But they left a bit.

Ben: And was there any evidence anywhere else? Like a big red stain on the floor?

Anna: No, thankfully.

Ben: I don't want to antagonise you, but that doesn't sound like the most brutal of murders.

Anna: So where is he then?

Ben: God knows. Where's he supposed to be?

Anna: He was supposed to be in New York a couple of days ago. Now he could be anywhere. America probably.

Ben: So maybe that's where he is, then, and maybe there's a simple explanation for the blood.

Anna: I'm telling you, that doesn't make sense. I've called the police. They're on their way.

Ben: To report a murder?

Anna: To report the smashed window so they can board it up. I'll tell them about the blood, though. I expect they'll want to investigate.

Ben: I hope so, for your sake. But equally I hope you don't get arrested for breaking and entering.

Anna: I think they'll forget about that once they realise what's happened.

Ben: Good luck. I'm going to have to shoot. Keep me posted. x

The police turned up eventually. Two uniformed officers in a Battenburg-liveried Astra. They took my name and address, and I led them round to the back of the house. I explained how I was looking to leave a picture somewhere safe, out of the rain, which was kind of true, albeit only in the vaguest sense, and then discovered the broken window and unlocked door.

"And you say the occupant is a friend of yours?" asked the older of the two, who'd introduced himself as Sergeant Jonathan Bebbington-Douthwaite. I wondered if he'd ever thought of changing his name, for the purposes of time saving, if nothing else.

"Kind of a friend, yes," I said. "He works as a flight attendant."

"Kind of a friend?"

"I suppose you could say former boyfriend."

"I see." He glanced at his colleague, a woman he'd introduced as Constable Manning, or Mainwaring or something along those lines. I wasn't really listening, still trying to process the Jonathan Bebbington-Douthwaite.

"And where's the picture now?" she asked.

"It's in my car."

"You could have left it in the house, given that the door was unlocked."

I tried to maintain my composure.

"I could have done, yes, but the picture isn't the issue here. Look." I took them across to the kitchen sink. "There's blood on the back of the tap."

"Hmmm," said the sergeant, taking a look.

"See? Blood," I said, maybe stating the obvious. "I'm worried something's happened to him. I think he may have been murdered."

Again, he cast a glance at his colleague.

"And why do you think that?"

"Because he's not here, somebody's broken in, and there's blood which someone hasn't done a brilliant job of cleaning up."

"Okay." He moved away so the constable could take a look. "Is there any other reason you think he's been murdered? Are you aware of any specific threats?"

"His girlfriend threatened him."

"I thought you were his girlfriend."

"It's complicated. He had two."

"Well that would complicate things."

"Not in the way you think. It's a long story. But can you investigate? Start a missing persons enquiry at the very least?"

"I'll tell you what we'll do Mrs, er.."

"Burgin," said his colleague.

"Yes, Burgin."

"It's not Mrs."

"Sorry, *Miss* Burgin. We'll arrange to have the back boarded up and made secure. We'll make a note of what you said, and try to contact the owner. We'll have a look around in the meantime, and see if there's any obvious sign of an intruder."

"I think the smashed window is a fairly obvious sign of an intruder."

"Possibly. But we'll look around anyway. And we'll be in touch if we need to speak to you again. Does that sound fair enough?"

"I think you're missing the point."

"No, I think I very much see the point. And I'm sure Mr, er…"

"Bianchi," said his colleague.

"Mr Bianchi will be grateful to you for calling it in."

"Unless he's been murdered," I said.

"Quite. But there's not really very much evidence of that, if I'm being honest with you."

"In which case you are definitely missing the point."

"I take your concerns on board. And like I say, we'll be in touch if we need to speak to you. But for now this is a potential crime scene, so really we should be careful not to contaminate it. Let me take you back to your car."

I sighed and shook my head.

"Fine," I said. "Just don't blame me when you find his body."

"Let's hope it doesn't come to that, eh?"

I drove home, more worried than ever. If the police weren't taking me seriously, what hope did I have? There was no point texting Ben. He'd just say "I told you so". Why could nobody else see what I could see?

I texted Chrissy. She'd be on my side.

Anna: Hi. Are you around?

Chrissy: Hey darling! How are you? So sorry to hear about the Italian bastard.

Anna: Things have moved on.

Chrissy: Don't say you're back together are you? I can't keep up. Sort yourself out, will you?

Anna: Not funny. This is serious. I think bad things have happened to him.

Chrissy: It sounds like they deserved to, from what you said.

Anna: Not like this. I'm worried about him.

I gave her the summary, told her my theory, about the blood, and the police lack of interest.

Chrissy: Wow. That sounds bad. Do you want me to come round? I could bring wine. I haven't seen your new place yet.

Anna: That'd be lovely but I think I need to keep my wits about me. Ben thinks I'm going mad.

Chrissy: Who's Ben?

Anna: You know Ben. My old friend from school.

Chrissy: That rings a bell. I lose track of all your men.

Anna: It's not hard. Most of them are idiots. It's only the names that are different. Ben's all right though.

Chrissy: How many are there for heaven's sake?

Anna: Not too many. There's Mark, who you know.

Chrissy: Do I?

Anna: Yes, if you've been paying attention. He's not an idiot either, but lives too far away and thinks Stef is a narcissistic fraud and offered to sort him out for me.

Chrissy: Maybe he murdered him?

Anna: He possibly would have done if I'd asked him to. But no, I don't think so.

Chrissy: Sounds like a psycho. And the others?

Anna: Recently? This really isn't the time.

Chrissy: It's always the time. It's nice to know somebody's getting some.

Anna: Heaven's sake. The others who aren't idiots are Simon who's more of a friend with benefits kind of a thing. I went to see him last week for a drink. Craig was the week before. He was lovely and got all my Soft Cell jokes. But that's your lot.

Chrissy: Soft Cell jokes?

Anna: Long story. Probably not funny in isolation.

Chrissy: Good going. Any others?

Anna: No. Can we change the subject?

Chrissy: It was just getting interesting.

She was relentless.

Anna: I assure you it isn't. There are a few I chat to on Tinder and Bumble and some I hear from once in a while on WhatsApp.

Chrissy: I'm impressed, keeping all those on the go while you've had Stef coming round.

Anna: Quite. You know how it is. Got to keep your options open.

Chrissy: Playing the bastard at his own game. I'm proud of you.

I hoped she realised I was being ironic, but it didn't sound like it. Context was everything, and nobody but me could understand the emotional rollercoaster of the last few months. She said she had to go. I said I'd be in touch with any news.

At the very least, I needed to know if Stef should be home, or if he was supposed to be on a flight abroad somewhere. Why had he ceased communication just when it was the most critical for me to know where he was? Maybe it wasn't a coincidence. I searched on Google for the number of his airline.

Fifteen minutes of frustration later, I was no further forward. I managed to speak to the HR department, eventually, after doing battle with an automated switchboard twice, but they wouldn't even confirm that he worked for them, never mind give me his itinerary.

I was back to the idea of finding the staff car park at Heathrow Airport. But how big would that be? There could be thousands of cars. Maybe the airline even had their own. And even if I slogged my way round the M25 to get there, how would I get in? It was pointless. Especially as every instinct was telling me his car wouldn't be there.

Chapter 33

I TEXTED Mark.

Anna: Hi Mark and I hope all is well. Just checking something. This might sound a bit weird but you haven't by any chance murdered Stef have you? I don't expect you have but I am a bit concerned somebody may have done. Let me know when you can. x

I just had time to make a cup of tea before he replied.

Mark: What do you mean murdered?
   Anna: Is that a no?
   Mark: I can't say I haven't been tempted, but I've not murdered anyone for ages. What's happened?

.   .   .

I gave him the summary.

Mark: Well, I wouldn't worry if I were you.

Anna: Of course I'm worried.

Mark: You shouldn't be. A: You deserve much better than a twat like that; and B: I very much doubt he's been murdered, sadly.

Anna: Jesus. What is it with everyone? Even if you don't like him I'm not sure that deserves a death sentence.

Mark: I never met the bloke so I don't know if I like him or not. I doubt it though, in all honesty. And I don't think he's been murdered because it's highly unlikely. You met him on the internet. Ghosting is a thing. If everyone who suddenly stopped communication with someone they met on a dating app got murdered, the mortuaries would be full.

Anna: But it wasn't like that!

Mark: Listen, I know you're hurting. But it really does sound like you're in denial.

Anna: Fine.

I left him to it. I looked down my WhatsApp chat list to see who else I could message who might be slightly more empathetic. Charlotte? Was this the kind of thing I wanted to discuss with my daughter? Obviously not. Simon? Craig? *"Not sure I mentioned it but I've been seeing someone else and he's left me and I'm feeling a bit fed up. Oh, you didn't kill him did you?"*

Lucy? For a moment I was seriously tempted. But the policy of keeping work and personal matters separate has served me well, and I'd mess with it at my peril.

There were maybe twenty other names on the list, plus a few more on Facebook Messenger and even more on the Messages app on my iPhone, but all were kind of distant acquaintances or family members that I only messaged around Christmas or New

Year, and even then they usually beat me to it, so I ended up looking like the unthoughtful one.

No, I was very much going to be dealing with this on my own.

I put the phone on its charger, then collapsed onto the sofa, wishing I'd left the tea within reach so I didn't have to get up again.

I got up, fetched the tea, and put it on the wooden floor beside me, and collapsed onto the sofa again. But then realised I'd quite like to have a biscuit with the tea, so had to get up yet again. And then, finally, I sat down. But after all of those shenanigans, and the time I'd spent on a fruitless search for someone to talk to, the tea was too cold to drink anyway, which was supremely frustrating. I grabbed a cushion and hugged it fiercely.

I closed my eyes, lost in thought, trying to decide if I was going mad, or the only sane one left. And as my mind cleared, and I reassessed, and thought about everything everyone had told me, I was beginning to think it was the former. Until I was jolted back into reality by an unfamiliar, insistent buzzing sound. It took me a moment to realise it was the intercom for the front door. Who was visiting? I wasn't just going to buzz them up. So instead I opened my balcony door and looked down to ground level, where a smartly-dressed man and woman were standing by the control panel. I didn't recognise either of them.

"Hello, can I help you?" I called down.

"Are you Anna Burgin?" asked the man, looking up.

"I am."

"This is the police. Can you let us in please? We need to talk to you."

Detective Sergeant Neil Ashcroft and Detective Constable

Corinne Wilson sat next to each other on the long bit of my L-shaped sofa. I was on the short bit. They refused my offer of tea, which was annoying, as I still fancied a cup.

"We'd like to talk to you about Stefano Bianchi," said the constable, once they'd showed me ID and the formal introductions were out of the way. She was younger than her more senior colleague, and had a slightly friendlier face than his granite stare. I imagined them playing the classic good cop, bad cop to perfection, should they ever be in front of a suspect. Close up, their suits looked more tired than they had from above.

"Thank God for that," I said. "I was beginning to think I was going mad."

"Interesting choice of phrase," said the sergeant.

"You know how it is, when everyone else is telling you you're being stupid. You begin to question yourself."

"Quite." I didn't like his expression at all. It was almost accusatory.

"Anyway, is he all right?" I continued. "Have you been to the house? What would you like to know? Have you started to look for him yet?"

"Yes we've been to the house," he said. "But first I'd like to know a bit about you. You write books, I gather."

"Yes, amongst other things."

"We found some on Mr Bianchi's bookshelf."

"He liked them. He bought some. I gave him copies of the others."

"So you fancy yourself as a bit of a detective then?" He said it with something approaching a sneer.

"Me? No, not really. I had a few adventures, a few years ago. I had some interesting friends. They're kind of the story of those."

"Yes, I've looked into them. You don't seem to be a fan of the police?"

"No, I'm a big fan. There were a couple of dodgy ones but in general I think you do a great job in difficult circumstances. I've got nothing but respect."

"But you were a close friend of Clare Woodbrook?"

"You can't be interested in Clare. Surely?"

"She was a legendary figure. I remember reading about her."

"I'll give you copies of the books if you like. You might enjoy them."

"I'm not sure that would be appropriate."

DC Wilson was making notes, occasionally looking directly at me, and occasionally allowing her gaze to drift around the room.

"Tell me about your relationship with Mr Bianchi," said DS Ashcroft. I refocused my attention on him.

"I'm not sure you'd define it as a normal relationship. We met online a couple of years ago but didn't meet in person until January this year. We got on well, started to see each other, but it was always hard."

"And why was it hard?"

"Partly because of his job, and partly because of his domestic situation."

"His domestic situation?"

I didn't have any option but to explain. I assumed they'd heard far worse.

"He had another girlfriend. But it was kind of polyamorous, if you know what I mean."

"I do."

His face was fixed. I couldn't tell if he disapproved, but still had the feeling he was judging me.

"So he was with her a lot, but she was seeing other men, so it should have been okay for us to meet too. We were all grown-ups. I wasn't looking for a boyfriend, really. But we got on, and when I moved here, it meant we'd be closer. We'd planned to start spending more time together."

"You say 'we'd planned', past tense."

"Yeah. We were supposed to be going to the theatre next week. He was going to be having extended leave. He'd split up with Molly, his other girlfriend, so yeah, we were making plans."

"And then what?"

"Well, then he finished it, which was weird. And not even in person. It was a text message while he was abroad with work."

"I see." If anything, his expression hardened. "And how did that make you feel?"

"Honestly? I was very upset. I couldn't understand it. It was completely out of the blue. So out of character. And I had all sorts of dark thoughts and called him lots of names, but then, the more I thought about it, the more I started to worry about him. Worry that something had happened to him."

"And you say he'd split up with this other girlfriend?"

"Yes. And that was the thing. She hadn't been at all happy that he was seeing me. Not that we'd even actually - you know - in the bedroom. But she started to threaten him. He said she'd become psychotic. Which was what started me thinking, wondering if she had something to do with his disappearance."

"We've spoken to his airline," said DC Wilson. "He was rostered to fly to New York this week. Out on Tuesday, back on Thursday."

"Exactly. And he sent me the message on Wednesday, from New York."

"Can you show us the message?"

"Of course, if it'll help."

I stood up, and fetched my phone from its charging pad on my desk. Then opened WhatsApp and scrolled up to his final message. I passed her my phone. She took her own phone out of her pocket and photographed my screen, before handing me mine back.

DS Ashcroft cleared his throat.

"He never made the flight to New York," he said. "The airline confirmed him as a no show. He didn't phone in sick. He just didn't turn up."

"Wow." I didn't know what to make of that. But suddenly I knew my instincts had been right all along. Something bad had happened to him.

"Explain why you were at his house this morning," he continued.

"He'd given me a picture as a present. I was trying to return it."

"And you just happened to be in his back garden?"

"The postman told me he thought he'd moved out. I was trying to check. I couldn't tell from the front, so I went down the side of the house."

"Which was when you discovered the broken window?"

"Exactly."

"And that's when you called us?"

"I, er." I paused, and blushed. I wasn't proud of what I'd done next, but there was no point in lying about it. Presumably they'd need my fingerprints for elimination, even if I'd been careful to hardly touch anything. "No, not immediately. I went inside first."

"You went inside?"

"Yes, to look around. I don't know why really. I was worried. Worried he'd been attacked. But obviously he wasn't there, and then I saw the blood on the kitchen tap and that's when I phoned it in. Have you had it analysed? Are you actually out there looking for him?"

"That's why we're here." His eyes narrowed yet further. "We hoping you might be able to tell us where to find him."

That shocked me.

"Me? I'm the one who's looking for him. I'm just about the only one who thought he'd disappeared till you two turned up. I've got no idea where he is. That's the point."

"Hmmm. You see, I don't think you're telling us the truth there."

"*What?*" The pitch of my voice was rising.

"Okay. I'll put it another way. I'm not sure I believe a word you've said since we arrived."

I was finding this very hard to compute.

"What on earth do you mean?" I immediately felt nauseous. My head was spinning. DC Wilson stared at me, dispassionately.

"We found some correspondence," she said. "In his house. He'd printed hard copies of emails. And they didn't make for pleasant reading."

"Right." Nothing was making sense. "What sort of emails?"

"Emails from you."

"I've never sent him an email. I don't even know his email address."

"But you are Anna Burgin?"

"Of course I am."

"Well unless there are two Anna Burgins, they were definitely from you."

"That's madness. What did they say?"

"They were fairly graphic. Fairly serious threats about what you were going to do to him unless he met your demands."

"What? No, no, no. Somebody's forged those. That'll be Molly."

"Molly?"

"The other girlfriend."

"Ah yes."

DC Ashcroft took over.

"We tried to track down this Molly, to speak to her. But she wasn't at home. Do you know anything about that?"

"No, I've never met the woman."

"And yet some of the threats about what you were going to do with her were very specific."

"What threats?"

"In the emails."

"I haven't sent any bloody emails. Why would I do that?"

"That's what we were hoping you would tell us. We're going to need to take your computer away for analysis." His eyes shifted to the iMac screen on the desk behind me.

"You can't take the computer away. I'm trying to run a business."

He took a piece of paper from his inside pocket, and held it up.

"I'm afraid this says we can."

"No, but... sorry. I don't know what's going on here. Molly was the one making threats. I'm the one who's desperate to find him."

"For your sake, let's hope we do."

They both stood up. DC Wilson unplugged my computer, picked it up and put it under her arm.

"Where are you going with that?"

"You'll get it back in due course, unless we need to keep it as evidence," said the DS.

I swore under my breath. The world had finally spun off its axis.

"We'll see ourselves out." He handed me a card. "If you think of anything else that may help, you can contact me here. In the meantime, we know where to find you."

Chapter 34

I STOOD in the hallway, watching the door close behind them, wondering if I was, in fact, asleep.

Of course I'd never sent Stef an email. How could I? I had his phone number, but he'd never given me his address: home, email or any other. He wasn't a Facebook friend. We didn't follow each other on Twitter. Either I'd just been visited by two impressively creative burglars who had stolen my iMac, or somebody was trying to set me up.

So, first things first: why would Stef have printouts of non-existent emails? Who printed out emails anyway? And if I'd really sent them, why would he have been so lovely with me? Why had he not run a mile as soon as he started to receive them?

So, evidently the emails were fake, and that told me two things. Someone had forged them, to try to cause trouble for me. And she - I was fairly convinced it was a she - had been to Stef's house recently, and left them in a place where she knew they'd be found. Was it the day or night she attacked him? Did that explain the blood? Or had she been back later, since she'd done something sinister to make him disappear? And if he'd never made it to New York, there was zero doubt in my mind that she'd

206

done something. The mad-haired, cat-loving, mental, hypocritical psycho bitch.

But that then told me another thing. If she was capable of that, presumably in a fit of insane jealousy, then I was also at risk. If she was capable of attacking Stef, would she also try to take her revenge on me?

I'd had enough experience of the police over the years that I didn't feel intimidated by the Ashcroft and Wilson double act. In fact, it almost made me feel nostalgic. And yes, losing my iMac was a massive inconvenience, especially as it was my main work computer, but it wasn't like they'd turned up all guns blazing and cleared the entire flat. They hadn't taken my laptop, which was strange, and gave credence to the burglar theory. I suspected they were trying to put me on edge, rather than really suspecting me of anything untoward. Surely they understood how ridiculous it all sounded?

My laptop was in the bedroom, and frankly I needed a lie down. But I also, finally, needed a proper cup of tea, so I made one of those on the way. Then I propped myself up on all four pillows, lying on top of my deliciously soft faux rabbit fur throw, and lifted the screen.

First things first. I opened the Sent and Trash folders on Outlook just to double-check nobody had used either of my computers behind my back. The emails were synchronised on both of them. I didn't see how anyone could have done, short of breaking into my flat.

That was a point. I still hadn't got round to changing the locks since moving in. That needed to be a priority, and possibly fitting a few extra bolts and padlocks, along with some kind of CCTV, while I was at it. The benefit of being on the second floor was that it was unlikely anyone would break in through a window, but I made a mental note to make sure all of those were kept locked too.

The email search proved fruitless. Which meant one of two things: either someone had broken in, sent the emails, deleted them and then permanently deleted them again from the Trash folder. Or they'd never been sent in the first place. I knew which I thought was most likely. Which was the only one that made even a vague form of sense.

It all came down to Molly. It always had, right from the start. I'd never intended to upset her. I was never in competition. She was the queen of polyamory. I was a mere novice, not really sure if it was my kind of thing at all, but willing to learn in order to spend time getting to know someone who fascinated me. But she'd done her best to ruin it. And now she was out to get me. Fine. But I wasn't going to sit around, waiting for her to strike first.

I edged my Mercedes A Class into the flow of late evening traffic, grateful for Ben's foresight in printing out the address of the farmhouse. The postcode was now in my satnav. It would take about forty minutes to get there.

Of course, I didn't have a plan for what to do when I arrived. Knock on the door and say, *"Hi I think you've murdered our mutual friend, so if you wouldn't mind awfully, could you please fuck off"*? I wasn't sure that would do the trick. I suppose, in an ideal world, I'd see the pair of them through the window, laughing and drinking wine. At least then I'd know he was still alive.

There was no chance of that.

The post-rush-hour traffic was light. The headlights of oncoming cars glistened on the wet, unfamiliar roads. I wondered how many times Stef had done this journey. And whether the final time had been in the boot of her car.

With three miles to go, I turned off the main road, and

suddenly it seemed like an even more ridiculous idea. There were fields left and right, then lines of trees. Everything to either side of me was black. I slowed my pace, not wanting to miss a turning. The rain was getting heavier, obscuring my view further.

With less than a mile remaining, the satnav lady directed me onto a single-track road. It twisted and turned. There were no other cars. If I met something coming in the opposite direction, we'd both be in trouble. The idea was now morphing from "ridiculous" into "terrifying". I started to get a bad feeling. Half a mile. The chequered flag on the screen was getting larger. Then it filled the screen.

"You have reached your destination," she said.

I slowed down. I had no idea where I was. I stopped the car, but left the engine running, my right foot poised over the accelerator. There were buildings, but they all looked dark and lifeless. I had no idea which was the farmhouse. There were several to choose from. There were no lights and no signs to guide me.

The idea went from "terrifying" to "get out of here as quickly as you can". I was spooked. I pressed the accelerator and started moving again, slowly at first, so as not to attract attention. I was partly annoyed with myself for another futile waste of time when I should have been at home, writing, and partly pleased that at least I was doing *something*.

The road continued twisting away into the darkness. I called up the recent destinations on my satnav and selected home. And around forty minutes later I was back in my underground carpark, none the wiser for my excursion, but at least she hadn't murdered me too. I feared it would only be a matter of time before she tried.

Chapter 35

RELENTLESS buzzing woke me up.

I was out of bed and heading to the intercom before I even thought to check the time.

"Hello," I said, pressing the grey button, and pulling my bathrobe around me.

"Can you open up please, it's the police," came a voice.

"One moment."

What on earth was the time?

The watch on top of my chest of drawers said just past 8am. I hadn't slept that well in ages, but it was scant consolation.

Giving myself a moment to come to, I crossed through to the living room and opened the balcony door. Two men were standing by the front entrance. Different to Ashcroft and Wilson, but neither was Molly and neither was carrying an axe.

"Sorry about that," I called down. "Buzz again and I'll let you in."

In a surreal facsimile of the night before, the two detectives arranged themselves on the sofa. This time it was Detective

Sergeant Arjun Khatri and his sidekick Detective Constable Adam Brierley. DS Khatri was quite suave with his dark skin and close-cropped beard. His colleague looked barely old enough to take A Levels.

"Cup of tea?" I asked. For a change, they both accepted. That was a start. I hastily got dressed while waiting for the kettle to boil, although I looked scary with bed hair and a complete lack of make-up.

"How can I help?" I asked as I passed them each a mug. "You haven't brought my computer back by any chance? Is there any news on Stef?"

"Stef?" asked the sergeant. "And I don't know anything about a computer."

The creative burglar concept was gaining traction.

"Stef Bianchi," I said.

They looked at each other. DC Brierley shrugged.

"We've come to ask about your movements on Friday 8th March," said DS Khatri.

"Gosh, that's a while ago." I paused for a moment. One of the perils of working from home and running your own business is that days can all merge into one. Then I remembered. "I was here all day, then went out in the evening to meet a friend for a drink at the Novotel."

"The name of the friend?"

"Simon, er..." I realised I had no idea of his surname. I couldn't just say T.

"Dowson?"

"Possibly. To be honest, I never actually found out his surname."

He passed me a picture.

"Is this him?"

I nodded.

"Can you talk me through the events of the evening?"

This was all very strange. I took a deep breath, then exhaled.

"I got there about half past seven. We had a couple of drinks. Chatted for a bit. Then we went back to his room - not for what you think." I could feel myself blushing. "Chatted a bit more, and then he walked me back to my car."

"Which was at what time?"

"I don't know. About ten-ish maybe? Why, has something happened?"

"And have you spoken to him since?" asked DC Brierley.

"No. I got back and did some work till the early hours. He's not someone I know very well. We chat every few months or so. I only went to meet him because he was in the area."

"Okay. And did he say where he was going?"

Again, I was struggling to remember.

"He had a conference, but I think that was on the Friday, so presumably on Saturday he was going home. We didn't discuss that."

"And you've not spoken to him since? No phone call? Text messages?"

"No, nothing. Why? What's happened?"

The sergeant took over.

"He's gone missing," he said. "He didn't check out of the hotel on Saturday morning. He's not been seen since."

"Wow. That's a worry." The dark sense of foreboding was back.

"We found his car in the hotel car park." He shrugged. "We were hoping you might be able to enlighten us."

"Why me?" I hardly needed to ask.

"Because you're the last person who we know to have seen him alive."

"Christ."

I took a sip of my tea. It tasted strange. It was still too hot.

"Is this anything to do with Stef?" I asked.

"Who's Stef?" asked DS Khatri.

And so I explained, giving him as much information as I could muster. Of course he didn't know about Stef. They were from a different town, working on different cases. I gave him DS Ashcroft's contact details and he said he'd get in touch. I thought I was being helpful.

"How did you track me down?" I asked, once I'd finished.

"We found his phone in his car."

"That's a worry in itself."

The DS nodded.

"And how did he seem when you were with him?"

"He was fine. On good form. Sorry, this is a lot to take in."

"He wasn't, how should I put this, 'hesitant'?"

"Hesitant? About what?"

"You tell us."

I shook my head, trying to think back.

"I've got no idea why he'd be hesitant. It was the first time we'd seen each other in ages. In fact it was only the second time we'd ever met. I didn't really know him all that well."

"He didn't give you the impression he was nervous of you?"

"*What?*"

"That he was on edge?"

"Not in the slightest. We had a great time. Good chat, lots of laughs."

"Okay." He turned to his colleague, who took a piece of paper from the back of his notebook.

"I'm showing you this," said DC Brierley. "It's a copy of the last text message sent from his phone on Friday evening, shortly after 10pm. It was to a pay-as-you-go mobile."

I read the words.

Thank fuck she's gone. What an evening! That was fucking scary, mate.

Anna's only little, but by God she can put the wind up you. She tried to screw me right over. Jesus. Seriously, she's fucking mental. I'm locking my door and putting the chain on.

I read it twice, then handed it back, feeling a deep sadness more than anything.

"Your thoughts?" said the DS.

"Inexplicable," I said. "I don't believe he sent that message."

"But you think it's about you?"

"Given that my name is Anna, I'm not exactly very tall, and he'd just spent the evening with me, I very much expect it was supposed to point you in my direction. But at no point was I anything even remotely close to 'scary'."

"According to you."

"According to whoever you want to ask. I don't do scary." I remembered my bed hair and lack of make-up, and decided to change tack. "Look at the way it's written. It's pathetic. Does that look genuine to you?"

"It was on his phone."

"I'm not arguing with that. But if someone's abducted him, is it not also possible that they sent it?"

"It's interesting that you think he's been abducted."

"I don't know what I think, but I assume that's got to be your line of enquiry. So if I was you I'd be checking the phone for fingerprints and tracing the number the message was sent to, because frankly, that's complete crap."

"And yet it seems to point the finger at you."

"Clearly." I didn't know if I was about to make things far worse for myself, but I had to say it anyway. "Ask DS Ashcroft about that. He's got fake emails that incriminate me as well."

Before leaving, they took my fingerprints and a swab of saliva for my DNA. Christ alone knows what that would match, if Molly was on the rampage. Could she have attacked Simon as another way of getting at me? They'd been in Washington. But no, they got back on Thursday, or the early hours of Friday. Simon and I didn't meet till Friday night. Shit.

The police said they'd be in touch. I was told not to go too far in case they needed to speak to me again. I had no intention of going anywhere, apart from quite possibly to the locksmith.

I showed them out, then rested my head on the front door, trying to make sense of it all.

The day was about to get far worse.

Chapter 36

I COULD see where this was going, so it was time to start compiling evidence of my own. After a quick shower to wake myself up properly, I lay on the bed, propped up on my pillows, with my laptop on top of a cushion over my legs. I needed a list of all the significant events of the last few months.

I started by exporting my WhatsApp chat history with Stef, then cleaned up the file to remove extraneous characters, and ran an elaborate "find and replace" routine to separate the postings. The result, when exported into Excel, was a spreadsheet with all of my messages in one column and all of Stef's in another, arranged in chronological order.

It was tear-jerking stuff, looking back over everything we'd ever sent to each other, at how the relationship had developed over two years. There were so many happy memories buried within. So much fun, innocent excitement, learning, exploring, making plans. It was surprisingly even: 3,353 messages from me and 3,351 from Stef, with a total of over 84,000 words. At a time when I was desperately behind schedule on a book deadline, the irony that we had an entire novel's worth of WhatsApp chat wasn't lost.

I scrolled at random, looking at some of the lovely things he'd sent to me. Our first meeting, his trips, the first time he visited me, stolen moments where we'd met for coffee, how Molly appeared to accept things, right at the start, but how that had soon deteriorated. The stressful conversations between them. But despite that, it was such a happy story, of a person who'd come along out of nowhere, stolen my heart, and made me so excited to be moving so close to him, so we could visit each other on a whim, when the mood struck, when we both felt the urge.

The biggest thing that came across was the connection, and understanding between two people who'd met through a billion to one chance. Two strangers from different countries who ended up living in the same town, looking at the same dating app at the same time. Who swiped on each other and matched, when one change in an infinite number of tiny variables over the previous forty-nine years would have meant we'd have been eternally oblivious to each other's existence.

And then, it ended, in the cruellest, most futile, most heartbreaking way. I put the laptop down. The tears came, and I was powerless to stop them.

The chime of an incoming email refocused my attention.

Hi,

Are you still in business? I want to place an order but I can't find the web site. Can you send me a link?

Many thanks!

Beccy

I was immediately filled with dread. I opened Safari and was mightily relieved to find the web site still there. Panic averted. But the email was still odd. I read it again. *"I can't find the web site."*

I'd often seen people type a web address into a Google search field rather than the location bar of their browser.

I went to Google and searched for my company name. Historically, I've been good at search engine optimisation. But although I'd typed the exact name of my company, we were no longer on the first page. We should have been at the top. We weren't on the second page either. In fact, the more I looked, and the more search terms I typed, the more it became terrifyingly apparent that we'd disappeared from Google altogether. No wonder sales had been suffering. No wonder the warehouse was so quiet. This was a major crisis.

I wasn't sure what to do. It didn't make sense. I couldn't just phone Google, so I called our hosting company with a rising sense of panic. Though it was Saturday, the support department was open. I spoke to a helpful man called Leigh who said he'd investigate at his end, and call me back.

Around three hours later, my mobile sprang to life.

"We've discovered the problem," said Leigh.

"Fantastic news. What is it?"

"It's a strange one. Your IP number's been blacklisted."

"What? By who?"

"Google."

"How did that happen?"

"It looks like someone has been onto the server, changed the security and opened it up as a spam relay."

I was familiar with the terms, but what the hell?

"Who's done that?" I asked.

"I don't know. Someone with access to your user name and password."

"Do you know when it happened?" I had visions of my iMac in a police forensics department somewhere, out of my control, and somebody causing havoc.

"Looking at the logs, there was a huge spike in traffic about ten days ago, and it's been consistently high ever since, so best guess would be then."

Not the police then.

"Why would somebody do that?" I asked, but I already knew the answer.

"Could be lots of reasons. Because they want to send spam. Or because they're trying to close you down."

"Is there anything we can do?"

"There is. We can shut it down, move you to a new server, give you a new log-in. It'll cause a bit of downtime, though. Possibly up to twenty-four hours for the DNS to propagate."

"Jesus."

"It's the best solution, though, because it'd take a lot longer than that to get off a blacklist, even assuming you could."

"And the search results will come back?"

"Eventually. Maybe not right away, but hopefully before too long."

"And you can't see who's done it?"

"No. I looked at the logs. There are lots of logins but they're from all over. You're never going to trace them."

"Because they're coming in from masked IPs?"

"Essentially. I'm sorry."

He promised to start working on it straight away, so I ended the call to avoid wasting another minute.

Who would do this to me? There was only one obvious candidate. She lived in a farmhouse, had mad hair, and ran a web development company. It was like something out of Fatal Attraction. But how could I ever prove it? I was beyond angry. Fine, take it out on me, but don't threaten the livelihoods of the people who work for me. I wasn't sure what to do next, but I knew that I was in a fight for my life.

Chapter 37

IN a fit of fury, I texted Ben, to bring him up to speed, but the message got a single grey tick. He was presumably up in the air somewhere. I tried Mark instead. He replied almost immediately. I gave him the summary of the police visits, the disappearance of Simon, and now the attack on my business.

Anna: So you still think he's ghosting me?

Mark: Christ. I don't know what to think. Have you told the police about the web server?

Anna: Not yet. Is there any point? I can't prove anything.

Mark: I still think you should.

Anna: Probably. I'll call them in a minute. But isn't spamming illegal? If they add that to my list of charges, they'll throw away the key.

Mark: It's not going to come to that. I'm getting worried about you.

Anna: I'm worried too. I keep thinking she's going to turn up with an axe, or I'll find a rabbit on top of the cooker or something.

Mark: Can you get away?

Anna: And go where? I'm skint. And it's no bloody wonder given the lack of orders.

Mark: You can come and stay here.

Anna: I appreciate that, but I can't. I've got to be close to work. I've got two sets of police telling me not to go anywhere. I'm frankly fucked.

Mark: I'm sure they'll get to the bottom of it.

Anna: You've got more faith than I have.

Mark: So who's this Simon?

God. How did I explain that? Mark was jealous enough of Stef.

Anna: Just a friend.

Mark: Who you met on an app?

Anna: Originally.

Mark: And you went to his hotel?

Anna: Yes, but I didn't go to bed with him, before you ask.

Mark: Right.

Anna: Oh, don't you start.

Mark: I'm not starting. I'm just a bit upset that you keep going off with other men when I'd have given anything for you to feel like that about me.

Anna: I can't go through all this again. You know the reasons for that.

Mark: Yeah. I get it. Time and location. Although I'd have been happy to visit you, and you seem to find plenty of time for others.

Anna: It's not like that. I wasn't looking for that kind of relationship.

Mark: Just casual sex then?

Anna: No! Not that either.

Mark: What then? Any others you want to tell me about?

Anna: I've got lots of men friends. I'm not sleeping with any of them, all right?

Mark: And again, I believe you.

Anna: Don't take this the wrong way, but I'm having a shit time, and the last thing I need is you going weird on me, okay?

Mark: I'm not going weird. I'm just a bit jealous, that's all.

Anna: Well, I've got enough trouble with one jealous psycho at the moment, and I don't really need another. I've got to go. I'll let you know if she murders me. x

Mark: Be careful x

I texted Chrissy instead, copying and pasting the update from the conversation with Mark so I didn't have to type it all again. She didn't reply. I added the bit about Mark being a pain in the arse, then left her to it. She'd get them eventually.

Early in the evening, my phone rang again. I didn't recognise the number, but there was no mistaking the seething anger on the other end of the line.

"Who the fuck do you think you are?" It was Caryn, Ben's wife. I'd never met her, but she didn't sound very happy with me. "How long has this been going on?"

"How long has what been going on?"

"You and Ben."

I had no idea what she was talking about. I pointed that out, but she was having none of it.

"Don't lie to me, you bitch."

"I'm not lying to anyone."

I opened my kitchen cupboard, trying to find a box of ibuprofen. My head was starting to kill me.

"Was it Wednesday? Or has it been going on for a long time? Do you think I'm stupid?"

"Seriously, what do you think has happened?"

"You know what's happened."

"I really don't. Ben's one of my oldest friends. We went for an

Indian, had a catch up, but that was that. What do you think we were doing?"

"Oh, I know very well what you were doing."

"Well, please feel free to enlighten me, because I think I'm missing something."

"I've seen the pictures."

The pictures? And then I remembered Ben, in the restaurant, and the conversation about selfies.

"Those? That was nothing."

"What do mean, 'nothing'?" Her voice was getting louder and higher-pitched in equal increments.

"Ben asked for a selfie." I hated using the word, but now wasn't the time for a philosophical discussion. "I think he took two, three? It was a nice thing to do. To show how we're changing. Capture a moment in time. I'm sorry if that upset you, but trust me, there's nothing sinister about it."

"I don't mean those pictures."

"Which pictures, then?"

"I'll send you them. Check your phone."

I put her on speaker so I could look at the incoming messages. The phone pinged half a dozen times.

"And you're going to deny he kissed you?"

"What kiss?" He'd given me a peck on the cheek as he left, but there wouldn't have been a picture of that. Unless someone was out there in the darkness, watching us, photographing us. My blood ran cold.

I opened the first picture, and every fear came true. There we were. Embracing. I knew it was innocent, but I could understand how it could be misconstrued. But more to the point, who the hell had taken it?

The other pictures were far worse. The one of the two of us on the balcony was understandable, if deeply disconcerting. But the others showed us in bed together. Me naked, astride him, taken through a window.

We'd never been to bed together. It looked like my bed and my furniture, but somebody would need a bloody long ladder to see through my bedroom window on the second floor.

"These are fake," I said, my voice catching in my throat.

"Bollocks."

"I know how it looks, but honestly, they're not real. They're Photoshopped."

"Bullshit."

"Where did you get them?"

"Does it matter?"

"Of course it bloody matters. Somebody's sending out fake pictures of me. I'd like to know who it is."

"Well I'm not going to tell you. Because I don't believe a word you're saying and if you're think I'm just going to sit here and accept it you can piss off with my bastard husband forever, for all I'm concerned."

"Caryn, Caryn..."

"Is he there now, is he?"

"No of course he's not here."

"Because he's not here either, and he should be."

"What do you mean, he's not there?" The unease intensified.

But she didn't reply. She slammed down the phone, and when I tried to call back she didn't answer.

I sent another message to Ben.

Anna: Where are you? I'm worried. Call me, please. It's urgent. I've just had Caryn on the phone, accusing me of all sorts, and she doesn't know where you are, either. Tell me you're safe. I need to talk to you!

. . .

But the message got another single grey tick. Wherever he was, his phone was switched off. I rushed to the bathroom, and only just made it in time before being violently sick.

Chapter 38

Sunday, March 17th, 2019

I WAS still awake in the early hours, my phone lying beside me on the bed, plugged into its charger.

Who did I know who was an expert with Photoshop? I knew Mark was a keen photographer, but I dismissed that out of hand. It came back to Molly yet again. She ran a web design company. If she didn't use Photoshop herself, she'd know plenty of people who did.

This was getting way beyond petty jealousy. First thing in the morning I'd call the police. Tell them everything. Get some kind of restraining order, if that was a real thing, and not just one of those made-up terms that you hear about on TV.

What would she do next? As it transpired, I didn't have to wait long to find out.

I picked up my phone, and checked my emails to see if there was anything from the hosting company. There was. Finally, some good news. They'd moved everything to a new server. The site would be back online some time during the next twenty-four hours. Topping the search results again would take longer, but at least it was all in hand.

But without a web site, there would be no orders. And with no orders, we'd have no money coming in. Next week was going to be a struggle. As ever, there were too many bills to pay, and my company bank account was always pushed close to its overdraft limit.

I opened the PayPal app. I try to let PayPal balances accrue for emergencies. It's always a useful backup, and has often come to my rescue when there are wages to pay, or an unexpected bill that needs to be sorted urgently. In all the chaos of the last week, I hadn't checked PayPal of late. I was hoping there'd be at least a couple of thousand pounds, and perhaps more, once the euro and US dollar balances were converted.

The app opened and I stared at the screen in disbelief. The balances were zero. That had to be wrong. I quickly reached for my laptop, and accessed the PayPal web site. But again I found the same. The transaction history showed sales coming in, but equally the credit balances being transferred away. I hovered the mouse over the screen, not sure what to do next. PayPal support was generally good, but I doubted they'd be there in the early hours of Sunday morning. It took all of my resolve not to slam the laptop shut and throw it at the wall.

And then the phone started ringing again.

I didn't recognise the number, but I was getting used to that.

"Hello," I said, tentatively. Who was ringing me in the middle of the night?

"Anna Burgin?" asked a voice.

"Speaking."

"This is the APG control room. We've got a confirmed alarm activation at your premises in the Waterside Business Park."

Not this, surely? I was immediately wide awake, already half out of bed, as she continued.

"The police are on their way, but we have you listed as the keyholder. Are you able to attend?"

"Yeah. I'm on my way."

For heaven's sake.

I was in the car within seven minutes, blasting through deserted streets. Within a further fifteen, the warehouse came into view. A strobe light was flashing under the alarm box, the siren piercing the still night air.

There was no sign of a police car. No sign of anyone. I was alone, on a deserted industrial estate, in the middle of the night, with a psychotic enemy who was trying to destroy me. Where was she?

I drove slowly past the warehouse. There was no obvious sign of damage to the fire escape doors. I turned the corner, past the main entrance. The roller shutter was still down. Round the second corner I could see the loading bay. That looked intact too, but the security light flicked on as it detected the motion of my car. It was strangely reassuring, until I realised it put me in the spotlight. Was she hiding in the shadows, watching me? Taking aim?

A spider crawling across a sensor could trigger an alarm. But the police would only get called if a second sensor was activated too. I discovered the source of one of them. A smashed window, at ground level, in the far corner. Behind it, the security grille appeared to have held firm. So where was the second sensor? Was somebody moving around inside?

No matter how protective I felt towards the warehouse, I wasn't getting out of the car until the police arrived. I turned around, then pulled in to the side of the road, keeping the smashed window in view. I'd see anyone who tried to get in or out. The security lights would come on if anyone got close to the loading bay.

I kept my engine running, checking my mirrors, but then got spooked just waiting there in full view. A sitting target. I started driving again, looping round and round. The siren stopped, restoring calm. And then went off again.

After maybe twenty minutes, flashing blue lights came into view, getting closer. I edged forward as the police car approached, then got out of the car as two uniformed officers did the same.

"Are you the keyholder?" asked one of them. I was too tired and too wired to catch either of their names. I didn't recognise them, despite the plethora of their colleagues I'd met in recent days. They asked me to open up and disable the alarm, then escorted me inside. We searched the building, but there were no obvious signs of intruders. And then we got to the broken window.

There were shards of smashed glass on the floor, although the security grille meant some of it had fallen back outside. But the glass was the least of the chaos. Somebody had pushed over one of the shelving racks. Stock was strewn across the floor.

"How've they managed that?" I asked, talking mainly to myself.

"Some kind of a large stick pushed through the grille, like a broom handle, maybe," said one of the policemen. The racks were small, each with six chrome wire shelves. I supposed it was possible.

"Would that have set off a second sensor?"

"Possibly."

They radioed the details back to base, and arranged for a 24-hour security company to come out to board up the window, stressing that I was a single woman, on my own. I made mugs of tea while we waited. Their radios were busy, but they ignored most of the messages, only responding when it was directly related to me.

"It's kids, probably," said the policeman at one point. "We've had a lot of this kind of thing. If it's any consolation, they'll be long gone by now."

I wasn't so sure. And it wasn't much consolation.

Within the hour, the window was boarded up, the alarm reset, and I was on my way back home. The police said they'd keep an eye on it overnight, driving past occasionally. I couldn't thank them enough.

I was back in bed by half past five, exhausted, but living off adrenaline. There was a message on my phone from Chrissy but I was too tired to read it. I closed my eyes and tried to will myself to sleep. It took a while, but I managed it eventually. But I wasn't asleep for long. By 8am I was standing by the intercom, pressing the grey button to silence the buzzing. And shortly after that, I was arrested.

Chapter 39

THIS time it was different. DS Arjun Khatri and his pal DC Adam Brierley gave me just long enough to get dressed before I was escorted to their car and driven to a police station. The lack of handcuffs was both a relief and slightly insulting, as though they didn't think me capable of making a run for it. They confiscated my phone, cutting off yet one more connection to the outside world, and then left me alone in an interview room, to ponder my fate.

Thankfully, it wasn't a long wait.

"So, we did what you said," began the DS, once he was seated opposite with the recorder running, having informed me that this was a voluntary and informal chat and I was free to leave at any point. All of which sounded implausible. "We spoke to DS Ashcroft. It appears you're making a bit of a habit of threatening people."

"I'm making a habit of getting accused of it," I said. "And equally someone is making a habit of faking evidence."

"So you claim."

"Because it's true. No sign of Simon, then?"

"Not yet."

"Shouldn't you be out there looking for him?"

"Not if we think we're talking to someone who can tell us where he is."

I looked around the room.

"I can't see anybody," I said.

"Very funny. You seem remarkably relaxed."

"Believe me, I'm anything but. I've had an hour and a half in bed. I'm knackered. I've got someone with an insane vendetta against me. And so, if I come across as anything less than utterly terrified, I assure you it's just the delirium kicking in."

He paused, staring at me, waiting for me to hang myself. My eyes focused back on his.

"We've been through Simon's phone," he said, first to crack. "We've found lots of messages from you. You told us you'd never slept with him."

"No. I just said I didn't last Friday. We'd met once before."

"And is this something you do normally? Picking up strangers and going to bed with them?"

"Oh, spare me the moral judgement. For your information, no. But that was an exception. We got on well. It was one of those things."

He paused again. This time I didn't wait.

"Is that why I'm here? Because you think I'm some kind of floozy? And even if I was, is that a crime now?"

DC Brierley had been silent up till now, but passed me a piece of A4 paper.

"I'd like you to take a look at this," he said. "Do you recognise the words?"

I scanned them. The sentence that stood out was *"if you don't want to end up like Simon, you know what you have to do"*.

"Never seen them before," I said.

"Really?"

"Yes really. Let me guess, this was supposedly in an email I allegedly sent to Stef?"

"Yes."

"Well, there you go then. There's your link."

"Precisely."

"Not with me!" I almost shouted at him, then took a moment to regain my composure. "I'll tell you what I told the other two. You should be speaking to Stef's ex-girlfriend."

"We are." He outstretched his hand in my direction.

I shook my head, exasperated.

"Not me! Molly whatever her surname is. Hargreaves. Do I really need to go through all of that again? Look at the wording. It's like the text message. It's clumsy. It doesn't sound natural. It's evidently somebody manufacturing evidence. Seriously, you want to be speaking to her. She's faked pictures of me sleeping with one of my very best friends and sent them to his wife. She's hacked my web server and emptied my PayPal account. I've had an hour and a half's sleep because last night she smashed the window at my warehouse. You should be offering me protection, not making out like I know anything about rubbish like this." I pushed the paper back.

DS Khatri took over.

"And do you have any evidence for all of this?"

"What evidence do you need? Do you want to see the fake pictures? I could show you those if you hadn't already confiscated my phone."

He nodded, eyes narrowing.

"We're downloading all the data as we speak."

"Do you not need a warrant for that?"

"No."

"Are you sure?"

"We're entitled to access data when there are reasonable

grounds to believe there could be evidence in relation to an offence."

"And what about if there are reasonable grounds to believe the owner of the phone has an insane stalker?"

"We have all of the reasonable grounds we need." He paused, then changed the subject. "We've been looking into you. You appear to have financial problems."

"Me?"

"Yes you."

"Not really." I shrugged. "There are a few cashflow issues at work, because someone hacked the web server so we've hardly had any orders. And then stole the PayPal."

"Did you ask Simon for money?"

"No, of course I didn't ask Simon for money."

"And yet we go back to his final text message. *'She tried to screw me right over.'* That implies you tried to blackmail him."

"And as I've already told you, I don't believe he sent that message."

DC Brierley passed me another sheet of paper from the pile of emails taken from Stef's house. I read it.

Do you want me to tell the airline about your coke habit? Do you think you'd be allowed into the USA if they knew you'd lied on your ESTA? Five grand, but it's going up.

I passed it back.

"I've got nothing more to say about these that I haven't already."

"Where were you last night?" asked DS Khatri.

"Which bit of last night?"

"Yesterday evening."

"I was at home. Presumably if you've got my phone data you can see its location."

"It says where the phone was. Not where you were."

"Well, I was at home, with the phone. And if you look at the history you'll see I had a call from a woman called Caryn Maguire who was furious because she thought I was sleeping with her husband, and she then sent me the fake pictures. And I stayed at home until I had to go to the warehouse in the middle of the night because the alarm was going off, and if you don't believe that you can check with your colleagues because two of them were there with me."

"Do you know Chrissy McCulloch?"

That caught me off guard.

"Yes of course, she's my friend."

"When did you last hear from her?"

"There was a message this morning but I didn't get a chance to read it."

They looked at each other. There was a knock at the door. A uniformed officer entered.

DS Khatri stopped the recording, then both detectives stood up and walked towards the door.

"Am I still free to leave at any point?" I called after them.

"Stay exactly where you are," he said, without turning back towards me.

What did they mean, when had I last spoken to Chrissy? I leaned forward and rested my head on the table, closing my eyes, feeling desperately tired. I'd have done anything for a nice hot shower and a cup of tea and eight hours of uninterrupted happy dreams about romping through meadows, or at the very least not this kind of nightmare.

A few minutes later they returned. DS Khatri restarted the recorder.

"Why are you asking about Chrissy?" I asked, before he had the chance to take the initiative. "Do you think I've been sending threatening messages to her as well?"

"No."

"Thank God for that. Any chance of a cup of tea, by the way?"

"No."

"Cheers."

"Tell me about your relationship with Chrissy McCulloch."

I threw my head back, then rubbed my eyes before continuing.

"Chrissy's a friend. One of the mums I've known since my daughter started reception class. We chat via WhatsApp, and that's about it, these days. Why? What's any of this got to do with her?"

"When did you last see her?"

"In person? Ages ago. We have like a long-running thing where we keep nearly meeting for a drink or coffee but never actually get round to it."

"So you didn't see her yesterday?"

"No, of course not. I told you, she sent me a message this morning if you don't believe me."

His voice lowered.

"I'm very sorry to tell you that the message this morning was not from Chrissy."

"Oh brilliant. So you believe someone's hacked her phone then, but just not mine?"

"It was from her daughter, Scarlett, using her account. She's been involved in a serious car accident."

"*What?*"

He handed me my phone. I read the message. Scarlett sounded very upset, understandably. Chrissy was in hospital. Details were absent. I could have cried.

"Interview suspended at 11.03," said DS Khatri. "You're free to leave."

———————

I didn't have Scarlett's number, but I tried to call Chrissy's mobile in case Scarlett had it with her. There was no answer. It was ridiculous. I was standing in an unfamiliar street, with no idea how to get home, nor even any money for a bus fare, three friends missing, one quite possibly in a coma, and my world falling apart around me.

I went back into the police station and asked to speak to DS Khatri.

"Come to make a confession?" he asked when he arrived.

"No. I've come for your help. I need to know where she is. Chrissy. Which hospital? I can't get in touch with her daughter."

"Come through."

He led me into a different room this time. Much less formal, with no recording equipment, and much more comfortable chairs. He disappeared, but returned a few minutes later, with a handwritten note that he passed to me.

"That's the details of the hospital, but I'd call them first. I'm not sure she's up to visitors." His voice was softer than normal. More sympathetic.

"Can you tell me how she is? Is she going to be okay?"

"I don't know the details. I'm sorry."

"But was it definitely an accident? It seems like someone is going round killing my friends. Am I at risk?" I knew the answer to that before I said it.

"There's a lot we don't know at the moment. But I would caution you to be vigilant."

It wasn't just my friends. She was trying to kill my company too, and doing a very good job of it, by all accounts. But that was just bricks and mortar, and my livelihood. These were real people. She had to be stopped.

"Any chance of a lift home?"

He nodded.

"Wait there, and I'll arrange someone to take you."

I called the hospital as soon as I got home. The news was vague because I wasn't a family member, but they told me that Chrissy was in intensive care, and they were doing everything they could.

I texted Ben again, but my earlier messages still had single grey ticks. It was pointless. I tried to call him, but it went straight to voicemail. Where was he?

Enough was enough. It was time to go to see Molly. Properly this time, and in the daylight.

Chapter 40

I PARKED by a gate on the verge of the single-track road, and made my final approach on foot, recognising the name of the farmhouse on a tiny sign at the entrance to a long driveway. It hadn't been visible at night. So this was it. This was where she lived. I was unarmed, obviously, but I kept my phone close at hand, with the police emergency number programmed into my contacts so I could call it in an instant, if needed. Where was Ben when I needed him? Or even Mark. Something in the back of my mind told me there was more to Mark than met the eye. Maybe I was better off alone. Isn't that always the way?

The driveway was long and tree-lined. The new-season leaves obscured my view, but equally gave me an element of cover. An element of surprise. I kept close to the edge of the path, all senses alert, ready to run at the first sign of danger.

Slowly, I started to approach the house. I held back, watching it, looking for movement, then took a few more paces forward before stopping and looking again.

And then I saw Stef's car. The number plate was unmistakeable. I edged closer. It was covered in a layer of dust and bird debris, as though it hadn't been moved for a while. One mystery was solved, but others deepened.

There were no other cars. If Molly had one, it wasn't here, unless it was parked inside one of the outbuildings. There were two of those. One large barn, and a smaller one that looked like an external storeroom.

The windows of the house were dark, but the curtains were open. It looked cold and impersonal, like the setting from a horror film. The irony wasn't lost on me. Keeping under cover of the trees as far as I could, I walked in an arc around the house, looking for any signs of life. There were none.

I didn't know whether to be relieved or frustrated. I settled on terrified.

But I couldn't stop there. I was here to fix things, so, with my heart beating fast, I approached the front door and, overcoming one last moment of hesitation, pressed the bell. A loud, old-fashioned chime came from within, but no sign of movement. I tried again. Still nothing. The door was locked, but I'd learned my lesson about entering houses uninvited, anyway.

I moved to the window to look inside. The glass was filthy. The paint on the frame was tired and peeling. The house would be cold in winter. There was a large inglenook fireplace, two old leather sofas, and a Persian rug on the wooden floor. It was far from tidy. Shabby, rather than a rustic idyll. It didn't look freshly painted. Maybe they'd been decorating the bedrooms. I didn't want to think of the two of them there.

Encouraged by the lack of response to the doorbell, I made my way round the side of the house. Another, smaller window gave a view of a staircase. Further round again, a wooden gate-style door led to the kitchen, but again it was locked. Again there was no sign of life. The kitchen was a mess, with crockery piled up by the sink, and tins, appliances and general clutter on all of the available work surfaces. Like the others, the window could have done with a good blast of Windolene.

A sudden noise stopped me in my tracks. It sounded like a twig breaking. Then two birds flew up in the air, their calls breaking the eerie sense of calm. What had disturbed them? I shrank back, against the wall. If there was anyone out here, I was in trouble.

But nobody came, and the silence returned. I continued round the back of the house, and then came to a room that looked like an office. Was this where she worked? I got as close to the glass as I could. An old desk was positioned in front of the window. There was a similar look of chaos, but a large flat-screen monitor stood next to an HP LaserJet printer. And then my blood ran colder still.

Between the two stood a pile of paper. The picture printed on the top sheet was immediately recognisable. Caryn had texted me a copy only the night before. It was irrefutable proof. I nearly yelled in anger, but managed to stop myself just as I heard the sound of a car, getting louder. I quickly left the window and hurried to complete my circuit of the house, hiding among the trees. I wanted the element of surprise.

But then the engine noise faded. Whoever it was had driven straight past along the road, without stopping. I waited for a moment, to make sure. The silence returned.

I crept across to the smaller of the two outbuildings.

It didn't have any windows, and the door was padlocked. Whatever was in there would remain a mystery, for now. The other building was larger, and made of overlapping wooden panels. It had a giant wooden door, but with two heavy-duty padlocks preventing entry. Ominously, on the ground, there were parallel grooves in the mud a few inches apart, as though something - or somebody - had been dragged inside.

There were small gaps between some of the panels where the

241

wood had warped. I tried to see through them, but it was too dark to make anything out. Even the torch on my phone didn't help. There didn't appear to be a car inside, but I couldn't vouch for anything else. There was, however, a horrible aroma of decay. Of something rotting within.

My instinct was to run, but I had to know what was beyond the door. The padlocks were far too robust to break through. There had to be another way.

I moved away from the front, down the side of the barn, with the store room on my left. Perhaps there'd be another door. Perhaps it would be open. There wasn't. But I did find another, larger gap between two of the wooden panels at just below knee height. I got down to the ground, on the damp, wild grass, and tried to peer in. It was too low to see anything. Time to think.

Lying on the ground between the two buildings was a large branch that had fallen off a nearby tree. A rat scurried away as I bent down to pick it up, causing me to flinch.

I inserted one end into the gap and tried to use it to lever the panels apart, but the branch was rotten, and snapped as soon as I applied pressure. There had to be something else. Another smaller branch lay further along. I tested it for resilience. It was fresher than the first. I put it into the gap and leaned on it with all my weight. There was a creaking, wrenching noise as the wall panel bowed and then finally snapped, creating a hole that was large enough to look through.

I wished I hadn't.

It was dark, at first, with no natural light. But the faint beam of my iPhone torch was enough to make me gag and retch in horror. A body hung by the neck, suspended on a rope attached to a beam. Stef. His face beaten, blood running from the gash on his temple, and down over his stubble, and onto the white leather biker jacket. I recoiled, scratching my hand on the sharp edge of the panel as I leapt back. But the broken skin was the least of my worries.

I had to get out of there. Call the police. Put an end to this now. But I was momentarily paralysed with shock. I almost looked back through, just to make sure, but I never wanted to see that again. I got to my feet, reaching out to the wall for support, taking deep breaths, trying to stop the shaking. Trying to get rid of the smell. I half ran, half staggered back towards the driveway, trying to steady my hand enough to unlock my phone and press the button to call the police. It was only the sound of another car engine that stopped me in my tracks.

Chapter 41

THE noise was getting louder. But this time the car didn't drive past. As it got close, the pitch stabilised, as though it was slowing down, and then the accompanying tyre noise stopped. The engine remained, idling, out there somewhere, not far away. I listened acutely for the sound of a door opening, or slamming shut, but it was just an engine, ticking over. A four-pot diesel thrum. I edged back along the driveway, seeking cover among the trees, trying to catch a glimpse of the car, or who was driving it, but my efforts were in vain without risking being seen. I couldn't call the police now. I had to remain silent.

I shrank back further into the trees and crouched down on the ground, scared for my life. She was clearly insane. I couldn't let her catch me here. Not now, not now I had proof of what she'd done.

The wait was interminable. What was she doing? Was it even Molly? It could be anyone. But why stop there, so close to the driveway? Maybe she was blocking the entrance. Did she have some sort of remote security camera, streaming to her phone? It wouldn't surprise me. She was technologically advanced. Maybe she'd been watching me all along. Maybe she knew exactly what I'd discovered. She'd be waiting for me, calculating her options. Deciding exactly when to pounce. Or maybe she was as scared as I was - terrified of being caught and stopped in her tracks. It didn't sound likely.

But then, from nowhere, the engine note increased and I heard the car pull away, accelerating quickly as though it couldn't wait to get out of there. Had she dropped someone off? I had to risk it. I ran to the end of the driveway, but I was too late to see the car before it disappeared around a bend in the road. My Mercedes was still there though. Advertising my presence. I had a sinking feeling that I'd just sealed my fate.

I ran to my car and floored the throttle, trying to put as much distance between myself and the farmhouse as possible, heading in the opposite direction to whoever had just been there. But I wanted to call the police, report what I'd found, so they could see for themselves, arrest her, and this nightmare could end.

I stopped the car as soon as I hit the nearest village, comforted by the thought of other people being close. But before I made the call, I hesitated. They'd want to know why I was there. They might think I had something to do with it. I wanted to get home, lock my doors, and get my life back on track. It was too late to save Stef, and it broke my heart. But the tears could come later. For now this was all about survival.

The weirdest of all thoughts went through my head. What if it wasn't Molly? What if it was Mark, in a fit of jealousy? What if it was Ben? Why was he so keen to come to see me? Why was he so insistent about taking a picture? Why was he so determined to find the address of the farmhouse and print it out for me? Had he manufactured everything to lead me here?

No, that was all ridiculous paranoia. It was Molly. It had to be. How else would she have a picture of Ben and me on her desk? But how did she hack the server? Had she posed as a customer, then sent me an email, containing a virus, and taken control of my iMac? I thought Macs were supposed to be less susceptible to viruses, but clearly they're not immune. I wanted to grieve, for Stef, for our future together. Cut down in his prime, and for what? Because his polyamorous girlfriend couldn't cope with the thought of sharing him with me?

She had to be stopped. For her own sake. Before I found her and took my own personal form of retribution.

I thought about calling the police anonymously, but that would only make things worse. What if they found my DNA on the broken wall panel where I'd scratched my hand? They'd certainly go looking for it.

I dialled 999. I gave them the details and told them to contact DS Neil Ashcroft or DC Corinne Wilson. But just because I'd reported the crime, didn't mean I had to wait around for them to investigate it. Yes, there would be questions to answer, but all in good time. I wanted to get as far away as possible.

My thoughts were stopped by the sound of an incoming WhatsApp message. It was Ben. Thank God at least he was alive.

Chapter 42

LTHOUGH I was desperate to read the message, I checked my mirrors to first make sure nobody was creeping up on me. Was my relief misplaced? I'd had what seemed to be a message from Stef even after he'd been killed. What if Molly had Ben's phone too? No, that was too far-fetched. Why should she?

I opened the message.

Ben: Jesus, Anna, what's going on? I've had Caryn apoplectic. Is this something to do with the mad cat woman?

I sent an immediate reply.

Anna: Ben! Thank God. I've been so worried about you. Where are you? I thought you'd disappeared. So much has happened. I've found Stef!

Ben: Well done. How is he? I've been in Timişoara.

Anna: He's dead.

Ben: What?

Anna: I just found his body at the farmhouse. The police are on the way.

Ben: Jesus, fuck. Are you okay?

Anna: No, not really. It's all got a million times worse. I'm so sorry about the pictures.

Ben: Don't worry about the pictures. I'm much more worried about you. How did you find him? What happened?

Anna: It's been everything you can imagine and worse. You disappeared. My friend Simon disappeared. Chrissy's in hospital. She's been planting evidence against me. Hacked our web server. Stolen all the cash from PayPal. I decided to go and confront her.

Ben: The mad cat woman?

Anna: Who else? She wasn't in but there was one of the pictures of us on her desk. I saw it through the window. Then there was a barn. There was such an awful smell. I'll never, ever forget it. Then I saw him, hanging there.

Ben: You don't think it was suicide?

Anna: No. He'd been beaten up. There was blood all over.

Ben: Jesus, Anna. Where are you now?

Anna: I've got no idea. Some village just down the road. I've just called the police so they can sort it out. I just want to get home, get away from all of this. I've had less than two hours' sleep.

Ben: You must be knackered. Is going home wise? She knows where you live.

Anna: I know. God, what a mess.

Ben: Look, do me a favour, will you? Go and book into a hotel for a night. Anywhere. I'm back tonight. I'll come and see you first thing tomorrow, and help you sort this.

Anna: That's a lovely thought, but shouldn't you be at home? Sorting things with Caryn? I told her the pictures were fake and she slammed down the phone on me. She thought you were with me.

Ben: She loses track of my schedule. To tell the truth, we've had a few *issues recently and not been talking, but I didn't want to bother you with all of that. You've got enough on your plate. I'll speak to her. Explain what's happened. And I'll text you tonight and make a plan for tomorrow. I'll be there as soon as I can, okay?*

Anna: Okay. Perfect. And thank you.

Ben: It's the least I can do. Take care xx

Anna: You too xx

I ended the chat and put the phone in the door pocket. I didn't want to go home. What if Molly was waiting for me? If she knew I'd discovered the body she'd be playing her end game and I would be next. But I didn't want to go back to the farmhouse either. Two police cars went screaming past me, lights flashing and sirens blazing. Then, a minute or so later, an ambulance. It was far too late for that.

For the first time, I noticed the pain from where I'd cut my hand. It wasn't deep, and had stopped bleeding, but I wanted to clean it up. I wanted to clean up everything. Have a shower in boiling water to wash away the smell. The sights. The memory.

My hand could wait. I reached for my phone and searched for the address of Chrissy's hospital, then entered the postcode into my satnav. I'd go there first. It was time to care about the living, and it would give me a chance to think.

───────

The hospital car park was full, but I found a space eventually, by watching a couple walking across the tarmac, and then waiting patiently while they got into their car and pulled away. The receptionist told me where to find the intensive care unit, but then called after me, telling me to wait while she phoned them, to make sure it was okay to visit. I ignored her and set off through the maze of corridors on my own.

Eventually I found the right department, but the double doors were locked. I pressed the buzzer on an intercom to gain admittance. The doors didn't open, but a minute or two later, a nurse appeared, walking towards me. She opened the door and stepped aside, waiting for it to close behind her before starting to talk to me.

"Can I help you?" she said.

"I think my friend is here. Chrissy McCulloch. I wondered if it was possible to see her?"

"Come with me."

But instead of leading me through the doors and onto the ward, she took me across to a bench that stood against the wall, just round a corner. We sat down.

"I'm afraid we can't allow visitors at the moment," she said, a serious expression on her tired-looking face. It was the kind of face that I imagined would light up when she was smiling, but there probably wasn't much to smile about in her line of work. She had my immediate admiration.

"Can you tell me how she is?"

"Are you a member of the family?"

"No, just a good friend."

She nodded.

"We're only allowed to give updates to family members, I'm afraid."

"I understand that. I don't want the full medical history. I'm just worried for her, that's all."

The serious expression softened.

"I understand that." She hesitated. "Look, she's in a bad way. We're doing everything we can."

"But she'll be okay?" My heart couldn't take much more of

this. What if it was Molly who had run her off the road? I felt like I was hallucinating.

"We hope so. It's early days." She reached out to squeeze my hand, but then recoiled as I winced.

"Sorry, I injured myself," I said, by way of apology.

"So I see." She lifted my hand for a closer look. "Would you like me to dress that for you?"

I smiled, grateful for the small kindness.

"I'm sure you've got much more important things to worry about."

"Come on, it'll only take a minute."

She led the way to a small office, just off the corridor, then told me to sit and wait. She was back a moment later with some antiseptic, cotton wool, and an assortment of dressings.

"Have you had a recent tetanus jab?" she asked, as she reached for my hand.

"About five years ago, from memory."

"It's worth checking. If it's not within the last ten, speak to your GP's surgery, okay?"

"I will. I'll check."

She asked me to wash my hands in a sink in the corner. The pain was acute as she then dabbed the antiseptic, but after everything I'd been through, I had no right to complain.

A few minutes later she was finished, and my hand looked impressive, with a professionally applied bandage.

"Try to keep it dry for now," she said. "If you can keep it on for a couple of days, so much the better. But if there's any sign of swelling, or the pain gets worse or you start feeling like you've got a fever, seek medical attention immediately, okay?"

"Shall do. And thank you."

The nurse promised to pass on my good wishes to Chrissy as soon as she was able to, and I thanked her again. I wish I'd taken more notice of her name badge. I'd have loved to have written to the hospital, with a proper letter of thanks. But knowing the modern world, she'd have probably got into trouble for going out of her way to help me.

I set off for the car park, stopping on the way for a cup of tea and a KitKat in the canteen.

"You look like you've been in the wars," said an elderly gentleman on an adjacent table.

I looked at my hand.

"You should see the other guy."

I said it without thinking, and then suddenly the image was back, pounding though my skull. Of Stef's lifeless body hanging, from the rafters. And his beautiful white jacket covered in blood. It was less than a week since I'd hugged him in Starbucks while he was wearing it. How little I knew then about the carnage that was about to unfold. And that was when the tears came. Great wracking sobs, and an uncontrollable display of emotion. What a day. What a week. What a complete bloody nightmare.

"Are you all right, love," said the man, but I waved him away, and then felt bad because it must have looked so rude.

"I'm okay, I just need a moment," I said, through the tears. "I've had some bad news. But thank you."

He passed me some paper napkins. And again it was the small display of kindness that nearly tipped me over the edge. Why wasn't everybody in the world as thoughtful and decent as that?

I made my way back to my car, eventually, and once I felt up to it, I pulled out of my space and headed in the vague direction of home. I still wasn't sure it was safe to go there, but on the way, I came up with a plan.

Chapter 43

J UST before the entrance to my underground car park, there's a pay and display public one. Early on Sunday evening, it's usually virtually empty. I pulled in there. My flat was a two-minute walk away, but if Molly was waiting to ambush me, I expected her to be underground, out of public view.

I dialled the number for DS Ashcroft.

"It's Anna Burgin," I said, when he answered on the fourth ring.

"Anna," he said. "I think I owe you an apology."

"You heard about Stef's body at the farmhouse then?"

"I'm there now, with him."

"That's good. It's horrendous, but I had an awful feeling that something like that had happened to him." I shuddered.

"I will need a formal statement. Probably tomorrow."

"Of course. I don't know where I'll be, but I can come in if you like. Or I can call you and arrange a time. I don't suppose you've caught her yet?"

"The girlfriend? Not yet."

"But you're looking?"

"I appreciate what you've done for us, but I can't give out operational details. I'm sorry."

"But she'll be coming for me."

"I suggest you go away somewhere. But if you're worried, call me, day or night, okay?"

"Thank you."

It was weird. It was such a different type of conversation. It was good to be on the same side.

"Actually you could help us. I don't suppose you know his next of kin?" he asked.

I thought for a moment. Thought of the children. My loss, however tragic, could never compare to theirs.

"I know he's got an ex-wife somewhere. They were going through a divorce, although I'm not sure it's finalised yet. I'd imagine there'd be some paperwork at his house."

"There will be, I'm sure. I just thought it might speed things up if you knew."

"Sorry I can't be much more help."

I was beginning to have second thoughts about the pay and display car park. It was awfully dark. At least the underground one had lighting. Should I risk it?

I didn't know who had been driving the car that hovered out of sight at the farmhouse. But if it was Molly, she could be here, now, coming to get me. Then again, if it wasn't, she could be anywhere. Maybe even out of the country. It would be ironic to escape my insane, murderous stalker and then get mugged by a local hoodlum.

"I don't suppose you can give me a time of death?" I asked. "I appreciate that's probably confidential."

"It's yet to be confirmed, but the initial estimate is about two days ago."

That didn't help either way.

"I don't suppose you can tell us where you were on Friday,

just for the sake of elimination, can you?" he continued. "From after the time we left your flat."

"I, er..." And then I paused. Because I knew exactly where I'd been on Friday. I was driving down to the farmhouse. My first thought was how close I'd come to interrupting a murder. Could I have done anything to prevent it? But then I had another, more pressing concern. *"For the sake of elimination."* Despite the friendly tone, he clearly hadn't yet ruled me out as a suspect. And if he checked any Automatic Number Plate Recognition cameras in the area, he'd know that I'd been there. At which point, the cordial conversation would be replaced with something altogether more hostile.

"I was in the flat, all evening," I lied, and then realised I'd probably just made it ten times worse. Because now when he did see my car on the ANPR, he'd know I was trying to hide something. Would he ever believe I'd said it on the spur of the moment, while absolutely exhausted, and both physically and mentally drained? I had to get off the phone before I said anything else.

I ended the call and decided to risk the underground car park.

But the more I thought about Friday, the more a feeling of panic crept in. How would I explain myself? And if they didn't have ANPR, they could triangulate my mobile phone and prove it that way. Or could they? I hadn't made a call, as far as I could remember, so could they still do that? My knowledge of modern police tracking methodology came largely from watching episodes of the TV series Hunted, and judging by that, they could do anything.

But could Molly? She'd already hacked my web server, emptied my PayPal account, forged pictures and faked emails. Could she also track my phone? Or was I just getting hysterical? Maybe that's how she knew I was at the farmhouse, how she knew I'd discovered the body, how she knew to drive there, to spook me. I didn't know anything any more. All I knew was that I had to turn off my phone, immediately. Park the car, and then disappear as best I could.

I headed towards the underground car park, readying my fob to raise the entrance shutter, but as I approached, it was already open. That was unusual. I drove down into the depths, underneath the flats. Suddenly, it didn't look well-lit at all.

Chapter 44

I'D never been so pleased to see my upstairs neighbour. He was unloading carrier bags from the boot of his car, in the space next to mine. I reversed in alongside him, then got out and locked my door.

"Hello, Anna," he said. "Are you settling in okay?"

"Yes, thank you. I'm getting there, I think."

"My television doesn't disturb you, does it? You must let me know if it does." He was such a gentleman, and always seemed quite formal, but in a friendly way. I guessed he was in his mid-to-late seventies, and obviously slightly hard of hearing. He'd introduced himself when I first moved in, on the night I bought the Domino's pizza, and I'd seen him a couple of times since, but I'd forgotten his name already. I'm useless with names. Malcolm? Melville? Quite possibly something different altogether.

"Not that I've noticed," I said with a smile. "Do you need a hand with any of the bags?" He was struggling to carry everything.

"I couldn't possibly ask you to do that," he said.

"You don't need to. I'm offering."

I reached out and took a couple from him, but kept one hand

free to open the doors. I'd have carried all of them if he'd asked, out of sheer relief at not being there alone.

I led the way out of the car park, across the courtyard and into our block.

"Actually, while I've got you, could I ask your advice about the central heating controller?" I asked. There was nothing wrong with the central heating controller, but it was all I could think of at short notice. I didn't want to enter my flat alone.

We dropped the bags upstairs and then he came back down with me.

To be fair, there were so many switches and controls connected to the heating system, I hadn't worked it all out, but I'd made the water heat up every morning and the room heaters all had their own separate controls anyway. I tried to sound enthusiastic as he explained everything to me, although in reality nothing was going in. When he finished, I thanked him and he returned upstairs.

I wanted to get out of there as quickly as possible. I packed a few essentials into a toiletry bag, then stuffed a few clothes into a holdall. It was a long time since I'd had to do this kind of thing. I thought those days were over.

I took one last look around the flat, making sure I hadn't forgotten anything. Then grabbed a phone charger. That would help. I switched out the lights, then opened my door and screamed as I came face-to-face with somebody standing directly outside.

"I am so sorry, I didn't mean to startle you," said Malcolm, or possibly Melville.

I took a gasp of air to try to regain my composure.

"That's okay, I just wasn't looking where I was going," I said.

"I've brought you a small gift to say thank you for helping me, but also as a kind of a late house-warming present. I've been meaning to drop something in."

He produced a bottle of white wine from behind his back, and handed it to me.

"That's jolly kind. But honestly, you didn't need to do that."

"It is a pleasure, my dear."

I looked at the label. It looked like a good bottle.

"Well thank you very much indeed. I'm sure it will be delicious."

"I'm looking forward to having you as a neighbour." Was he flirting with me? Surely not. No, he was just being friendly. He noticed my bag. "Are you going away somewhere nice?"

I had no idea where I was going.

"Just a work trip for a day or two. Hopefully back soon, though." I was keen not to appear rude, but I didn't have time for small talk. "I'm supposed to be there already, but I've been running late all day."

I shrugged, and he took the hint.

"I shall let you get on your way. I hope it's successful."

"Thank you. And thank you again for the wine."

I put the bottle on the floor in the hallway, then left my flat and double-locked the door. My neighbour went upstairs as I went down. I was reassured that he hadn't stopped to talk to anyone else. He struck me as the kind of person who would make conversation with a stranger. That meant Molly wasn't waiting out of sight upstairs.

When I made it down to ground level, it was decision time. Where now? I didn't fancy the underground car park on my own. There was a small hotel on the Market Place, about a one-minute walk away. That would be perfect if they had a vacancy.

They did. But as I was checking in, a police car went flashing past with blue lights and sirens shattering the evening calm.

"Somebody's in trouble," said the receptionist.

I didn't point out that it was quite probably me.

The room was comfortable and functional. It looked out over the Market Place, which was perfect. I could keep an eye on things. The police car was blocking the passageway that led through to my flat. I didn't know if they were looking for me, or attending to a disturbance in one of the bars. It was unlikely to be the latter.

I put my bag on the bed, then took the toiletry bag through to the ensuite bathroom. Every time I opened a new door I expected Molly to jump out and grab me. The sleep deprivation was making it worse, and I hadn't eaten all day. If I lay on the bed I'd either fall into the deepest-ever sleep, or more likely, lie awake traumatised by flashbacks of the horror that I was sure would haunt me forever.

The police cars disappeared. I checked my phone for a message from Ben, then remembered I'd turned it off. Turning it on would give my location away. I'd have to brave the outside world, move far away from the hotel. Go out in public, just for the sake of remaining hidden. I cursed myself for not thinking to pack a hat.

Checking the coast was clear, I raised my collar and tried to make a dash for it, while simultaneously trying not to arouse suspicion by moving unusually quickly. It was a delicate balance, and being well-balanced in anything has seldom been my forte.

I left the Market Place and took a narrow street, past a selection of restaurants, a Wetherspoons, and several shops that had long since closed for the evening. The hunger pangs grew as I passed the Indian where I'd spent the evening with Ben. But now wasn't the time to book a table and enjoy delicious food in comfort. Instead I popped into a fast food takeaway and bought a bag of chips for the first time in years, and picked at them as I walked.

Taking random turns, and moving steadily further away from the town centre, I found myself climbing a gentle incline of tree-lined residential streets, full of warm lights and happy families. I'd never felt more alone.

The architecture changed, from Victorian terraces to 1970s estates. I'd never seen this part of the town, and wasn't sure I ever would again. I wasn't sure I'd ever see my own flat again.

After forty-five minutes, I decided I'd gone far enough. It wasn't without risk, but hopefully it would be minimised. I had no idea, really. For all I knew, there could be a police station around the next corner. They were probably already tracing my every movement on CCTV, laughing and joking at my simple naivety, or playing rock-paper-scissors to decide who'd have the pleasure of bringing me in.

I turned on my phone, and waited for the SIM to connect to the network. I opened WhatsApp, just in time to see a message from Ben arrive. It had been sent twenty minutes ago, just past 9pm.

Ben: Caryn still moody, but least of my worries. How are you? I'm going to leave first thing in the morning, and do whatever it takes to sort things for you. I'd come tonight if I could but I think we'd both be better for rest. That's the theory anyway. Did you get to a hotel okay? Text me when you can.

I've been thinking about tomorrow. It's probably best to meet somewhere. There's a village about 20 minutes from you, according to Google Maps, called Little Beckton, with a country pub called the White Stag on the right, just as you come into it. Should we meet there? In the car park? I can be there for 9am if that's okay. Let me know. But text me in the meantime, just to let me know you're okay.

. . .

I replied immediately.

Anna: All good, and yes I'm in a hotel. I think the police are looking for me too, so I'm keeping my phone off. White Stag sounds perfect and yes, rest would be good, though I doubt I'll sleep. Better dash. Good luck with Caryn xx

I turned off my phone, then started walking back in the direction of the centre, but taking a different route through different streets. It was good to have a plan.

The rain started. Gently at first, then getting heavier. By the time I arrived back at the hotel I was cold, wet and exhausted. But at least I was still free, and nobody had tried to kill me. I was desperate to find out the latest from Chrissy. Desperate to speak to Mark. But everything would have to wait. I had no idea what Ben could do that would actually help me, but at least it would be good to see him.

Or so I thought. How wrong I was, again.

Chapter 45

THERE were so many things that could still go wrong, but a few hours of fitful sleep, followed by a hot shower, at least made me feel slightly more human.

But if I was going to meet Ben, I still had to run the gauntlet, twice. First I had to brave the underground car park. And then I had to avoid the police and the ANPR cameras.

I had a plan for dealing with those. It was definitely illegal, but in the greater scheme of things, what could I do?

I left the hotel just after eight, after finishing a cup of substandard tea, and convincing myself that I'd be back. The car park was relatively easy. I hovered by the flats - out of view of my own front door, just in case the police were in there, watching out for me - and waited for one of my many neighbours to go downstairs. It took about ten minutes, but then a man I'd never seen before emerged from the block opposite. I followed him down, close enough to feel protected, but hopefully not so close that he thought me weird.

There was no sign of Molly. My car was still there. Yet to be impounded. I suppose that made sense. If it moved they'd be able to follow my number plates and I'd be giving myself away.

I opened the boot, lifted up the false floor and removed a toolkit. This was madness, and I felt terrible, but I'm sure Malcolm, or Melville, would understand, if he even spotted it.

Crouching down at the back of his car, out of sight of anyone passing, I undid the two screws that held his number plate in place, then did the same with mine. With a slight degree of tweaking, I managed to make the switch. The front would be higher risk.

Footsteps sounded on the metal staircase, and a moment later a couple emerged. I vaguely recognised them from the floor below mine, but ducked down again before they could see me. It was good that I'd heard them on the stairs, though. That gave me confidence that I'd at least have warning before anyone else turned up and caught me in the act.

Five minutes later, my 17-reg Mercedes A Class was sporting the number plates of a 15-reg Fiat 500. Assuming I didn't get picked up by a speed camera, and assuming I could swap them back before Malcolm (or whoever) next used his car, nobody would ever need know.

One of the benefits of working from home is that my morning commute involves just a ten-second walk from my bedroom to the living room, unless I stop off at the kitchen, or decide to go in the shower. It's bliss. But it hadn't prepared me for peak rush-hour traffic. Even just pulling out of the car park was a challenge, and I then had less than a hundred yards to change lanes, which meant waiting patiently until someone in the line of near-stationary traffic was kind enough to let me in, while causing a hold-up in the left lane in the process. Judging by the angry beeping from behind, those I was delaying weren't particularly sympathetic.

Once in the correct lane, I had a roundabout to navigate, and then another line of almost-unmoving cars. There was nothing I could do. I'd thought I was leaving in plenty of time. My satnav said I'd get there with ten minutes to spare, but that presumably assumed I'd be moving. It took the best part of five minutes to get to the next junction, and the traffic was just as bad on the far side.

By the time I'd cleared the town, my estimated time of arrival was 9.02, and I was still far from travelling at the speed limit. I wanted to call Ben, to let him know I was running late, but I couldn't risk turning on my phone.

What was I thinking? The number plate switch was madness. It made me look even more guilty. It made me drive much more cautiously than normal. I wanted to turn round immediately and swap them back. But the traffic in the other direction was worse, if anything, and I'd end up even later. I had to continue, and would deal with the consequences later.

On the radio, the 5 Live news was as depressing as ever. The funerals of victims of a terrorist attack in New Zealand. Details of the investigation into the crash of a Boeing 737 Max. Theresa May desperately trying to get the backing of the DUP for her ridiculous Brexit deal. I turned it off. I had enough to worry about already.

It was quarter past nine before I turned off the main road in the direction of Little Beckton. According to Google, the pub was about three quarters of a mile away, on the right-hand side, just before the village itself began. The satnav told me I was two minutes away. There was nobody behind me, so I slowed down, keen not to miss it. And then suddenly it came into view.

But this was far from the idyllic country pub I'd imagined. It was yet another victim of the decline in the trade. The windows were boarded up. The pub sign stood on the ground, leaning against the wall of the building. Paint was peeling from the front, and the For Sale sign looked like it had been there a long time.

The entrance to the car park was falling victim to overgrowing weeds, but there was evidence that they had recently been disturbed. And there, in the far corner, by some sort of garage, and facing into the trees, was Ben's gorgeous Porsche.

I thought he'd get out of the car to greet me, but he didn't. I pulled into one of the few parking spaces that looked least like a jungle, and then walked towards him. I could see him in the driver's seat. Maybe he was dozing. Maybe he hadn't spotted me.

I approached the car, ready to knock on the window, picturing him waking up, getting out and giving me a much-needed hug. But as I reached the car I knew something had gone horribly wrong. It wasn't Ben behind the wheel. It was Molly.

I'd never seen her in person, but I recognised the hair. But still she didn't turn to face me. She was staring straight ahead. I wanted to run. I had to get out of there. But then I noticed the blood from the gash where someone had slit her throat.

I screamed. I stepped backwards. Straight into the man who was standing behind me

"Anna," said Mark. His expression was almost inhuman.

Then, from nowhere, a bullet ripped into him and he dropped to the ground in front of me. And emerging from the trees was Stef.

Chapter 46

MY first thought was that he'd saved me. The second was that it was impossible, because he was dead.

He walked out from the trees, holding the gun, pointing it at me. My eyes were fixed on the end of the barrel. It was shaking slightly, as though he was nervous. But when I finally looked up, into his eyes, I saw a cold, hard look of hatred.

"You finally got to meet Molly," he said. "Albeit not on one of her better days."

"Stef. I don't understand. What is going on? Where's Ben?"

He laughed, and it sickened me.

"Ben? I'll take you to Ben."

On the floor beside me, Mark was twitching, his eyes pleading. He reached out a hand towards me. A second bullet stopped him dead.

"What the fuck are you doing?" My voice sounded as though it was coming from somewhere else.

"You're just like all the others."

"What are you talking about?"

"You lied to me."

"What?"

DAVID BRADWELL

"*'Oh, Stef, I love you.'* But you're still going on a first date with Craig. Meeting up with your fuckbuddy Simon. Didn't think to mention those, did you?"

"*What are you talking about?*" I was getting increasingly hysterical.

"What did you say to Chrissy? *'You know how it is. Got to keep your options open.'* I've read your messages."

"What? How?"

"Oh, you're sorry now. How is she by the way?"

"You absolute bastard!"

He laughed.

"I thought you were different at first. I know, stupid of me. But what can you do? I wanted to chase you. I love the thrill of the chase. I wanted to capture you, like a delicate little butterfly. I didn't want you to want me too. That makes it all too easy. Until I found out it was all an act."

"But of course I wanted you. You know I did."

"Bullshit!"

He was up close now, and raised his fist as though he was going to punch me. His jaw was trembling.

"Who was that in the barn?" I asked.

"Oh that? I thought you'd work that one out. What did you call him? Your 'Stef substitute'?"

"Craig?"

"That's the one. I lent him my jacket. Shame to lose it, but needs must."

"You killed Craig?"

"He brought it on himself."

"You're mad. You're actually insane."

"I don't think so."

The thoughts were flowing thick and fast. I took a step back, trying to assess my options. Could I run? Make it to my car? Call

268

the police? But there was no way out of this. Stef moved towards me, then took a step to the left, to block off my escape.

"Where's Ben? Simon?"

"I'm going to take you to them. Good old Ben, the best friend, and Simon the sleazy fuckbuddy. See if they're so keen on you now."

"What are you talking about?"

"Your queue of men. You couldn't resist, could you?"

"Whoa. First, you don't tell me who my friends are. Second, I've never slept with Ben and I didn't sleep with Simon. And third, even if I had, you're supposed to be the champion of polyfuckingamory."

"It's about trust. But in any case, I told you at the start. I'm essentially monogamous. I read the books. I found I didn't like them."

"You said it was going well. It was an exciting lifestyle choice."

"So? I lied. You were so keen I didn't want to disappoint you."

"You didn't want to disappoint me! So you killed my friends?"

"That came later."

"Jesus. I can't believe this." I was too scared, too angry to cry. "And Molly?"

"She wanted it both ways. At least, she used to." He nodded in the direction of the corpse in the driver's seat.

"What do you mean you read my messages?" I said, tasting the disgust I felt with every syllable.

"You fell asleep. I installed a little app on your phone. It's not too hard. Parents use it to keep track of their children."

"That's impossible. You'd need my password."

"I know your password. I watched you type it in when you installed Flight Radar. I stuck a little keylogger on your Mac as well. You really do need to be more careful. Not that it matters any more."

How long ago had he planned this?

"I thought you might be different," he continued. "I thought you might be the one woman who actually spoke the truth. But no, I saw the things you said, and then I knew you were just like the others. And when I saw what your so-called friends were saying, encouraging you, some of the horrible things they said about me..." He nudged Mark's body with his shoe. "I couldn't let you get away with it. Any of you."

"But why?"

"Because you got to me. I wanted you."

"But you could have had me."

He laughed, and for the very first time I saw that beneath the veneer, he was actually ugly.

"But I didn't want to share. And you were just like all the others. You tell me one thing, but you're still on the apps. Still meeting others. Still visiting them in their hotels."

"None of it was like that!"

"It's no good lying to me now. I've seen through you."

"You're mad."

"No, not mad. I just don't like being lied to. And I'm not very happy with how people talk about me when I'm not there to defend myself. What did Mark say? *'He sounds like a dick. He's just an illusion, created by some narcissistic bastard.'* Acting the big man, offering to sort me out for you? I mean, come on."

We both looked down to where Mark lay dead between us.

"And Ben. Lovely Ben. He was always your favourite, wasn't he?"

"He's one of my oldest friends."

"And what did he say? Right from the outset? Hosties are kinky and pliable but nutjobs? I didn't like that. I thought it was deeply offensive, in fact. The typically arrogant self-important shit I expect from a pilot."

"Where is Ben?"

"I told you, I'm going to take you to him. But if you try to run, I'll kill you. Then I'll kill him. It won't be painless. He deserves to see the error of his ways." His expression was vacant, as though he was alone, in his own twisted world. "But if you come, and if you do as you're told, then at least you'll be reunited."

"And then what?"

"I'll leave you. It'll look like a lovers' tiff that got out of hand. Assuming the police find you before the wild animals do. Everyone knows you're having an affair. They've seen the pictures. I'll just disappear."

"You can't just disappear."

"I think you'll find I can."

"You'll get tracked down."

"I'll take my chances."

My car was only a short sprint away. Maybe I could take my chances too.

"Don't even think about it," he said. Then he grabbed my arm and started to drag me in the direction of the garage.

Chapter 47

BEN and Simon were sitting back to back. Both were gagged and tied to their chairs. They looked filthy, and semi-conscious, as though they'd both been badly beaten and hadn't been fed for days.

"I know what you're thinking," said Stef. "Ben only texted me yesterday." He took a phone from his pocket. "Just because a WhatsApp comes from somebody's phone, it doesn't mean they've sent it personally. It's basic." He threw the phone across the room, where it smashed against the dilapidated brick wall, then he turned back to my two friends. "They've been waiting for you."

I wanted to run to them, free them both, get them out of here. Call an ambulance. Do everything I could to end this nightmare. But Stef was enjoying the moment.

"He's not quite the glamorous pilot now, is he?" he said. "And as for the other one... what sort of man texts you out of nowhere, when you haven't seen him for months, and asks you to his hotel? And what sort of woman says yes?"

"But what about your house?" I asked, desperate to change the subject, trying to give myself time to think. We were a long way from anywhere, in a deserted building in the grounds of a derelict pub. There was no point screaming. Nobody was going to come to my rescue. "What was the blood on the tap?"

He laughed again, walking around the room, to the far side of Ben and Simon. He picked up a third chair.

"I had to keep you interested. I had to make you look for me."

"So you faked all that?"

"Obviously. God, you're so gullible."

"I was worried about you! I thought something bad had happened. I thought Molly..."

"Yes, I know exactly what you thought. I read your messages, remember? Mark wanted to rescue you. I gave him his chance, but frankly the odds were stacked against him. And Chrissy. God. The woman has no morals. She was trying to encourage you."

"So you arranged an accident?"

"It wasn't hard. I met her. Told her I wanted to give you a big surprise. Swore her to secrecy. She was shocked at first, but soon came round after a couple of drinks. She liked a drink, old Chrissy. You shouldn't really drive under the influence though. Especially when you don't know quite what you've taken. A little nudge and well... Her reactions weren't the sharpest."

He placed the chair down next to Ben and Simon.

"And the web server? The PayPal? The fake pictures?"

"What about them?"

"One question: why?"

"Because you were lying to me. You deserved to be punished."

"But I didn't ever lie to you!"

"You're lying to me now. All I ever wanted was to meet someone I could trust. But you're all the same. It's all a game, isn't it? You meet someone, you get on well. But you can't leave the apps alone. You miss the thrill of the swipe. The new match."

"No!"

"You think the grass is always greener. You're scared to

commit. I didn't want you to commit. I told you, I don't have time for that kind of relationship. But what I did want was exclusivity, and more than that, to know I could trust you. Sit down."

"No."

And then he slapped me, hard enough to really hurt. I was repulsed by his touch.

"I told you to sit down."

There wasn't an option. I sat down on the chair, facing forward, and perpendicular to the others. The smell of urine and neglect was overpowering.

He threw me a roll of duct tape.

"Attach your legs to the chair, and don't piss about. I've got to drag Mark in." All the time, he was pointing the weapon at me. I didn't have an option. I wrapped the tape round my first leg a couple of times. He told me to keep going, then switch to the other leg and do the same. By the time I'd finished, I wasn't going anywhere. But my arms were still free, so I hadn't given up hope.

"Put your arms behind your back," he said. He put the gun on the floor as he wrapped huge amounts of tape around my wrists, forcing my arms together, tightly, painfully. I did give up hope then. "I'm not going to gag you because I haven't finished with you, but I'll be back in a moment."

He picked up the gun and headed out of the door. If I was hoping for some miracle recovery from Ben and Simon, I was to be sorely disappointed.

"I'm so, so sorry," I said to the pair of them. I couldn't see them, as they were behind me, but one of them grunted. I think it was Ben.

There was no time to come up with a plan, even if it had been possible to do so. Stef returned a moment later, dragging Mark's lifeless body, which he then dumped callously, up against the wall.

"Show him some respect. Jesus."

"Respect! You want me to show him respect? He was the worst of all of them."

"What *are* you on about? Nobody here has done anything to you. Their only crime has been to offer me support because I'd fallen in love with you and I was missing you."

"And that's what you think, is it?" He started to laugh. He was borderline hysterical.

"Of course it's what I bloody think."

"Oh, my God." He shook his head. "You're even more gullible than I thought. Let me tell you about your good friend Mark."

Chapter 48

STEF pulled up a fourth chair so he could sit facing me, about ten metres away. The gun was on his lap. Had this been the movies, Mark would have made a sudden, unexpected recovery, crept up behind him and disarmed him. But there was no coming back from a bullet through the heart.

"Why do you think I started having my doubts about you?" asked Stef. "Actually, let me save you the bother of thinking. Mark tracked me down."

"He did what?"

"He followed me on Twitter. Started trolling me. Told me to leave you alone. Gave me some bullshit story about how the two of you were an item, and I should leave you in peace."

"I don't believe you."

"No, I don't expect you do, and unfortunately he's in no position to corroborate. But when I came back from Washington, he told me he wanted to meet me. So I said yes. I went to see him last Monday, after I'd been with you in Starbucks."

"You're making this up."

"Oh, believe me I'm not. But it gets worse. Far, far worse." He paused and chuckled, appearing to be deciding whether to continue, or just end it all here and now.

"And then?" I said, in an attempt to break his train of thought.

"Ah yes. So we met. Neutral ground. A Tesco car park, of all places. He continued talking crap, threatening me, trying to get physical. Then, when he thought he'd made his point, he said he was going. But the more I thought about it, the more he'd pissed me off - so I followed him."

"I don't believe a word of it."

"It's all completely true, I promise you. Have you ever been to his house? I have. I can describe it for you if you want me to."

I didn't like where this was going.

"No," I said, my voice faint.

"So, he let me in. Well, I say let me in. Didn't have a lot of choice really, after I'd punched him. Then while he was out cold I had a little look around. And believe me, the man was fixated on you."

"He was a good friend. We just lived too far apart for it ever to be any more than that."

"Really? It seems like nobody told him."

"I told him."

"Seems like he didn't listen then. Where do you think I got the pictures from?"

"What pictures?"

"Of you and Ben? Obviously, I had to Photoshop Ben's face on somebody else's body, but you looked fairly realistic, don't you think? And you recognised the room? I certainly did. It was from your old flat. Your good friend Mark had been stalking you, spying on you, taking photographs through your window. He couldn't do that now you're on the second floor, but the old flat was at ground level. Little chink in the curtains while you're getting romantic, and the next thing you know, he's making his own voyeur porn."

"No!" I didn't want to listen to any more of this. "You're talking shit."

"I thought you might say that." He took his phone from his pocket, then called up the Photos app. "Let me show you these. I copied them from his hard disk."

He started flicking from picture to picture. I couldn't bear to look, but I had to. And it was true. Pictures of me out and about, at home, on dates, in my bedroom. Some dated from long before I'd ever met Stef, but all were since I'd first met Mark. I knew he was a keen photographer. He'd spoken about it often. I had no idea I'd been the unwilling subject.

"Fair enough, I took the picture of you and Ben giving each other a peck as you waved him off," Stef continued, "but who do you think gave me the idea? As for him" - he pointed a thumb in the direction of Mark's body - "I've done you a favour."

My head was at the point of imploding. I'd never felt so violated. Men. Just when you find one you think you can trust, you realise you have no idea what's going on in their perverse, perverted minds. Ben wasn't like that. I was pretty sure Simon wasn't either. But my world was falling apart around me and I didn't have the head space to begin processing all of that now. All of my energy was needed to concentrate on survival. And trying not to throw up.

Mark. The bastard. I didn't know which of the two of them was worse. And then I remembered Stef had actually killed people and was now getting ready to kill me.

"So what's your plan now," I asked, desperate to change the subject.

"My plan?" He shrugged. "I haven't really got a plan. But I told you, I have a low threshold for people lying to me. And I do rather think the hypocrisy deserves retribution, don't you?"

"I've never lied to you."

"And again, bullshit. I've read the texts."

"All of which were out of context."

"And I suppose meeting your fuckbuddy here was out of context too?" He nodded at Simon.

"We didn't do anything. We chatted. Had a drink. That was that."

"And again, bullshit. I saw you go upstairs with him."

"So what? I went to his room. We didn't do anything. And even if I had, what the hell has it got to do with you? Isn't that polyamory for you? I thought you loved all that."

"No, because even polyamory is all about honesty. You should have told me you were doing it. And in any case, I told you, I don't really think it's for me."

The realisation was sinking in. He'd been following me. Watching me. All the time I'd been looking for him, he'd been there, just outside of my field of view

"What the hell do you think you're doing, stalking me?" I said. "You're as bad as Mark. There's your hypocrisy for you." I was losing my temper, and Stef was losing his patience.

"I've heard enough now," he said, his voice unnaturally calm. "It's time to say goodbye."

"What do you mean, goodbye?"

But it was the last thing I said. He put duct tape over my mouth, wrapping it tightly, then adding a second layer. I could barely breathe, with only my nose and eyes left uncovered, and my sense of panic getting out of control. He added extra tape to my arms to hold them in place, then I watched, with terrified eyes, as he went over to a bag in the corner of the room and returned a moment later with a syringe.

He held it up, flicked it with his finger to force the air to the top, then squeezed slightly until a drop of a clear liquid emerged from the end of the needle. I had no idea what it was, but it looked deadly.

He walked towards me, his cold, compassionless eyes fixed on mine. I tried desperately to free myself, but the struggle was pointless.

"You're lucky I liked you," he said. "This is going to be painless, apart from a slight scratch from the needle. You'll just drift off in to a peaceful, dreamless sleep. The others?" He gave one last shrug, eyes flicking to Ben and Simon. "Let's just say, I hope I'm a good shot because there are only two bullets left."

And that was when I knew it was all over. My last thought was Charlotte. My beautiful daughter. I hoped one day she'd come to terms with this. Find happiness, be a success. And never know what it was like to look into the eyes of a monster.

The needle entered my upper arm. He pressed the syringe. It tingled at first. Then a growing sense of numbness started to cloud my brain. I felt my breathing slow. The temperature was falling. My last sight was Stef, standing in front of me, holding the gun, taking aim at Ben. Then the deafening sound of a gunshot as my eyes started to close. I fought so hard to keep them open, but it was a losing battle. One last look, and he was no longer there. I couldn't fight it any longer. I let them close, to blank out the horror, giving in to whatever was on the far side.

Chapter 49

S OMEBODY was putting a mask over my face. There were voices. Shouting. Blue lights. More people. Uniforms. I was aware of another needle. My head spinning. I was lying on the ground. No, not the ground. Something padded. Where was I? I wanted to sleep. Voices urging me to stay awake. Calling my name. More shouting. Sirens.

Then I was moving. Feeling terribly sick. Cold. In the back of a van. With pipes and wires and equipment. People looking at me. Strangers. Someone squeezing my hand. Telling me everything was going to be okay. How could it be okay? I was dead. Stef had killed me. Was this the afterlife? I wanted to sleep, so desperately just to sleep. They wouldn't let me. Talking more urgently, louder. The van was getting faster. Not a van. The sirens were relentless. The pain in my head was excruciating.

Malcolm? Melville? What was his name? Where had he come from? Why was he looking at me? I was dreaming. It was a weird sense of floating, but every so often my body would lurch against the straps of whatever I was attached to.

"Where's Ben?" I said. In my head it was clear and lucid. But my ears only heard the faintest murmur.

"She's coming round." Somebody was talking. More voices saying things I didn't understand, with a pace that I found hard to relate to.

And then the motion stopped and I could feel cold air and see the sky. Beautiful clouds. Then a ceiling. Strip lights. More movement, but smoother. No more sirens but lots more voices. And then I closed my eyes again, and this time there was nothing that could stop me.

I woke up with the worst hangover I'd ever known, and believe me, I've had some bad ones. I tried to sit up, but the nurse told me to lie still. The drip in my arm reminded me of the time I'd had my appendix removed, but on that occasion I didn't have DS Ashcroft standing over me.

"Take your time," he said. "Everything's going to be okay."

But it wasn't going to be okay.

"Ben? Simon?"

"They're both in safe hands."

"Stef shot them."

He reached out and squeezed my hand.

"Don't worry about that for now. Close your eyes if you need to."

I didn't need to be told twice.

He was still there when I woke up. It was dark outside, but there was subdued light in my hospital room.

I tried to sit up again. This time a nurse propped up a pillow behind me, and passed me a plastic cup of water.

"What time is it?" I asked, my voice feeble, breathless.

"Nearly midnight," said the nurse, her voice not much louder than mine. "How are you feeling?"

I had to think about that for a moment. How was I feeling? There was so much I didn't understand. My head ached, my arm felt tender, and the saline drip was still causing considerable discomfort.

"Very tired," I said at last, in little more than a whisper.

"Would you be up to a few questions?" asked DS Ashcroft. The nurse gave me a smile of encouragement. I nodded.

"Can you tell me how everyone is?" I asked "Ben. Simon. Stef?"

He came over and sat on the edge of my bed.

"Ben and Simon are..." He scrunched up his face. "Okay. They're alive. They were extremely dehydrated, so they're being closely monitored."

"And Stef?"

"He's dead."

I closed my eyes, seeing him for one final time.

"What happened?"

"That's what I was hoping to ask you." His voice was soothing. All of that would come, in due course, but I wanted to know how I wasn't dead. I'd heard the gunshot.

"But how did you find us?"

"You've got your neighbour to thank for that."

"My neighbour?"

"Maxwell."

Of course it was Maxwell. I remembered him telling me now. I'd thought it was ironic that he lived in a flat rather than a house. But despite now knowing what he was called, I still couldn't picture him as my knight in shining armour. The elderly gentleman against a fit Italian killer.

"How come?"

"We came to see you last night. New information had come to

light. But you weren't home. We spoke to Maxwell, and he said he'd let us know if he saw you. You stole his number plates."

"Oh God. Am I in trouble?"

"You should be, but I think we can overlook it."

"Thank you. But that still doesn't explain..."

"This morning he saw you going down to the car park. He's quite observant." He raised an eyebrow. I understood the unspoken inference. Busybody. "He went to the car park to find you, but by the time he got there you were just leaving. But you'd swapped the plates, so he followed you. He knew something was up."

"I still can't see him charging in. He must be, what? Seventy-something?"

"Just turned eighty."

To be fair, he looked good for it.

"Even more so then."

"He didn't. But he saw you. Saw Stef shoot someone in the car park, and called it in. He had my card. We got there as soon as we could."

That sounded much more plausible.

"Stef was about to fire when we arrived. We had no option." Again it was what he didn't say that told the story. So that was the gun shot. And that was why Stef had disappeared from view.

"I don't want to sound callous, but whoever pulled the trigger, thank him for me," I said.

"It was a *her* actually."

"Even better."

There seemed some kind of justice in that.

"He'd given you a strong barbiturate," DS Ashcroft continued. "We don't know which one yet. But it's a good thing we got there when we did, or you'd have been in good company."

"Good company?"

"Victims of barbiturate overdoses. Marilyn Monroe, Judy Garland, Jimi Hendrix. The list goes on."

"Wow."

"The paramedics gave you a blast of Megimide, and you've been on a saline drip. Your arm might be a bit sore, but you'll make a full recovery."

"Say thank you for me. To the paramedics, and Maxwell, and all of the police, obviously."

"I will."

I found myself counting the ceiling tiles, trying to take my mind off everything I'd witnessed, and off the killings of which I'd so nearly become a part. Normally I only do things like that in an argument. Eventually, I returned my focus to DS Ashcroft.

"So what was the new evidence? I assume you tracked my car?"

"Your car?"

"On the ANPR on Friday. Close to the farmhouse. But I can explain, really. I didn't actually go there. It was dark. I turned round and went home."

He smiled.

"You've been watching too many TV programmes. We might have picked you up on cameras on the main A roads if we'd been looking. But we weren't, and there's nothing anywhere near the farmhouse."

"Oh." So the whole going-on-the-run thing could have been avoided? But I'd still have gone to meet Ben. I'd still have walked into a nightmare. And if I hadn't swapped the number plates, God alone knows how it could have ended, not that I think God exists. In fact, I've never been more sure of it. "So what was the evidence?"

"Well first of all, we identified the body. Craig Almond."

Shit. So it was true then. Poor Craig. Killed simply because he knew me. I felt terrible. I doubted I'd ever forgive myself.

285

"And then," DS Ashcroft continued, "we came across something in Stef's house. A pile of newspapers."

"I saw them. On the chair."

He nodded.

"They were his trophies."

"His what?"

"His trophies. They each had stories of unsolved murders. Prostitutes. Women on dates. Always women. And when we looked into the murders, they'd all taken place in cities that Stef had visited, at times when he was there, according to his rota. The description of the killer always fitted too. But of course, by the time the bodies were found, he was always back on the plane, or back home, thousands of miles away."

"Jesus. So you're saying he was a serial killer?"

"It's how it often starts. Maybe an accident. Maybe spur of the moment. But they enjoy the power. They feel invincible. And in his case, he had the perfect getaway."

This was all too much to take in. How well do you ever really know someone? I had no idea. No indication of his darker side. But Patrick Bateman's colleagues probably thought he was just another banker, even if slightly more annoying than the rest of them. Which is a pretty high bar.

Now he'd explained the rescue, DS Ashcroft had plenty of questions of his own. He wanted to know everything about my relationship with Stef, so I took him through it, from the first message to the moment I saw him emerging from the trees. By the time I was finished, it was long after midnight and I was exhausted. He left me to rest. I couldn't imagine sleeping. Every time I closed my eyes it was like having a giant IMAX projector inside my head, displaying the images on silver screens inside my eyelids. But the painkillers took me in the end, and I slept for the longest I'd managed for months.

Chapter 50

Monday, July 22nd, 2019

I MISSED the editor's deadline for book five, *Court Me Kill Me*, but she was very good about it, in the circumstances. I was only a week or so late, and to make up, I promised I'd tell the story of Stef in book six. *Court Me Kill Me* sold more on pre-order than Cold Press managed in its first 18 months, so the pressure is on, although I'm not sure anyone is ready for something as fresh and as traumatic as this. I may have to wait a while until it all sinks in.

I finally met Chrissy for the long-promised glass of Sauvignon. She's still in physiotherapy, but the long-term prognosis is good. Simon is okay, but was hesitant about date three. He's stopped replying to my messages.

I went to Craig's funeral and met his wife. They'd been happily married for twenty years, or so she told me. Who'd have thought? I didn't explain how I knew him.

The police returned my iMac, and I immersed myself in my day job. Lucy is happy because I've paid lots of suppliers. Sales improved, not least because of the weather, which was gloriously wet and miserable in the first part of the summer. That encourages people to stay inside, online, cheering themselves up by buying things, rather than outside having ill-advised barbecues. Sadly there's a heatwave on the way, according to the weather reports. I hope it doesn't last long.

Ben patched things up with Caryn. They hadn't been having problems previously. That was all in Stef's twisted fantasy world. I took them both for a fantastic Indian and presented Caryn with a giant bouquet. It was a bit of a cliché but she appreciated the gesture, I think. There were hugs. Ben is back flying again. He clarified the nutjob comment. Apparently all hosties *are* still nutjobs, kinky and pliable, but very few turn out to be deranged narcissistic serial killers. Which is just as well, as there are loads of cabin crew on Tinder.

Talking of Tinder, I've deleted all of the dating apps. I'd say "once bitten, twice shy" but "once nearly murdered" is probably more accurate. And anyway, I'm determined never to make that mistake again. Not just the "nearly being murdered" part, but the opening my heart, making myself vulnerable, and daring to fall in love. It never ends well.

That said, I'm still not an angel. I've been seeing a man called Neil. We met in unusual circumstances but there was a definite spark. His input as a detective sergeant could definitely help the authenticity of the book, although I don't ever imagine I'll become the next Mrs Ashcroft.

We met for coffee, then drinks. Then more drinks. We went to a comedy show. He took me to a concert, and invited me to his house. We've been out for meals. In fact, we've seen each other regularly over the last few weeks. He helped celebrate when *Court Me Kill Me* came out, and even made me a cake. He's quite quirky but he makes me laugh. We've discussed all sorts of days out, from indoor ski slopes to immersive theatre. I even dared to give him his own special sound on WhatsApp.

I saw him this evening, and finally introduced him to Charlotte. She's been staying with me for the last few days, since the end of exams. Neil had been on holiday for the last ten days, so there was a lot of catching up to do. He showed me the holiday photographs, and I had a tinge of jealousy. It was a glorious evening, with a gorgeous bottle of wine, and nice chocolate. I'd do a lot for chocolate.

Just past midnight, I sent him a message:

Anna: Thank you so much for coming. It was wonderful as ever to see you. I'm heading to bed now as I feel worn out. Looking forward to the next time. xxx

He replied:

Neil: And likewise. I missed you terribly. Thank you for inviting me. Sleep well. xxx

But just now, thirty-six minutes later, I've got this:

Neil: Hi. I've enjoyed every minute of getting to know you, but I've come to the conclusion that this isn't for me. This isn't a judgement on you. You're brilliant and super-sexy but I can't take this any further. Sorry. xx

. . .

Like I said, men, in my experience, are not like normal people. And if you need any proof of that, try dating in 2019. We soldier on.

The end.

SPECIAL THANKS...

Dying To Make You Mine was huge fun to write but couldn't have been done without chatting to lots of friends about their experiences in the world of online dating. Most of whom probably won't want to be named, haha.

Special thanks as ever, though, to Carrie O'Grady for fantastic editing, great advice, and enormous encouragement - together with Carol Lewis for proof-reading duties while on an aeroplane. Thanks also to Cathy Kisbey-Green and, of course, my renowned pilot friend Tim Atkinson, for remarkable insight...

FEEL FREE TO SAY HELLO... :-)

If you enjoyed the book, have any queries, or just want to say hello, I'd love to hear from you via www.davidbradwell.com. While you're there, you can download a **FREE copy of the Anna Burgin series prequel** - In The Frame.

You can also follow me on Twitter: @dbshq - or see what Anna is up to: @AnnaBurginNW1

If you enjoyed Dying To Make You Mine, you should read the books Anna mentioned in the text. **Cold Press** is the first book in the Anna Burgin series.

London. 1993. Investigative journalist Clare Woodbrook goes missing on the brink of unveiling her biggest-ever story. Is it kidnap? Murder?

Worse still, the police investigation into her disappearance is being headed up by a corrupt DCI - himself the subject of one of Clare's current investigations.

Clare's researcher Danny Churchill sets out to find her, and enlists the help of his flatmate - feisty fashion photographer Anna Burgin. But they soon realise that nobody can be trusted. And as the search becomes ever more desperate, suddenly their own lives are very much on the line.

Packed with intrigue, twists, conspiracies, and dark humour, Cold Press is a hugely entertaining British thriller, with a sting in the tail.

Order Cold Press NOW in print or ebook format at Amazon, Kobo, Barnes & Noble, Apple and more.

After Cold Press, the story continues in **Out Of the Red** - book 2 in the Anna Burgin series.

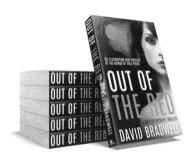

The gripping, twist-filled sequel to Cold Press.

Investigative journalist Danny Churchill is hot on the trail of Graham March - the disgraced former police DCI. The investigation takes him to Germany where he soon starts to uncover dark secrets and new depths of depravity.

Back in London, and aided by his flatmate - fashion photographer Anna Burgin - Danny's investigation intensifies, but as he gets closer to the truth, the body count starts to rise.

Help is offered from the most unlikely of sources, but if Danny accepts, is he doing a deal with the devil herself?

Order Out Of The Red NOW in print or ebook format at Amazon, Kobo, Barnes & Noble, Apple and more.

And after the interlude of In The Frame, the sequel to Out Of The Red is **Fade To Silence**.

You know you've got problems when being hunted by a Serbian hitman is the least of your worries...

Balkan gangsters, corporate spies and a fugitive killer are all on the loose in London, but when a body shows up, all of the evidence points to the victim's wife.

Journalist Danny Churchill wants to find the truth. But when reports emerge of a huge shipment of weapons heading to the UK, it soon becomes the most dangerous and action-packed investigation so far.

Packed with twists, intrigue and dark humour, Fade To Silence is book 4 in the bestselling Anna Burgin series.

Order Fade To Silence NOW in print or ebook format at Amazon, Kobo, Barnes & Noble, Apple and more.

The sequel to Fade To Silence is **Court Me Kill Me.**

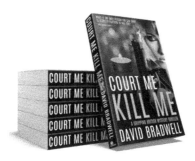

What if the only person you can trust is secretly plotting to kill you?

Fashion photographer Anna Burgin faces a career in ruins after her studio is destroyed, but when armed police burst into her home, she realises it's the least of her worries.

Murders in Seattle, Frankfurt, Venice and London all point to one common killer - and the chief suspect has just been in her house. The evidence is compelling, the body count is rising, but as news emerges of a corrupt business network that reaches into the heart of the police, nothing can be taken for granted - especially the promises of the person who offers to protect her.

Packed with twists, intrigue and dark humour, Court Me Kill Me is book 5 in the bestselling Anna Burgin series.

Order Court Me Kill Me NOW in print or ebook formats at Amazon, Kobo, Barnes & Noble, Apple and more